T0374313

BEYOND
FOCUS

James Daunheimer

iUniverse, Inc.
New York   Bloomington

BEYOND FOCUS

iUniverse books may be ordered through booksellers or by contacting:

iUniverse
1663 Liberty Drive
Bloomington, IN 47403
www.iuniverse.com
1-800-Authors (1-800-288-4677)

ISBN: 978-1-4401-3758-7 (pbk)
ISBN: 978-1-4401-3759-4 (ebk)

Printed in the United States of America

iUniverse rev. date: 4/20/2009

The motivation for writing this novel
is attributed to Paul and Dorothy Grenier,
plus Peter and Shirley Grabowski. Both
couples receive a loving salute.

Additional salute goes to all men and women
who serve in the United States Military.

CHAPTER ONE

Three decades after the residence partitioning law was implemented, the City-State of Dallas, Texas was contagion free. The buildings and agricultural fields within protected walls of CSD were connected by rail lines used to transport goods to citizens who live in physical solitude but communicated through advanced technology. All daily activities were remotely controlled through advanced robotics, ensuring residents safety and security.

Inside his residence pod, Ihan sat at his monitor overseeing his sector. He flicked the joystick forward, and the AgriCon swayed into the field to conduct a full scan of his crop. Ihan's yearly harvesting was only days away, he wanted to make sure the walls and aerial netting were secure. He moved the viewer angle to the right, panning over the older, spotted parts of the east wall, one of the outermost walls of the city. Many times throughout each shift, he checked that fifty-foot wall for signs of a breach. The scanner scope zoomed in gradually and focused on a minor discoloration. He pressed the accelerate button on his terminal.

"Mona, what is the weather for the next few hours? It seems as though the breeze is getting faster and I can see the crops blowing in all directions." Ihan scrutinized the screen.

"The weather for the next four-hour period is partly cloudy, eighty-two degrees, with wind gusts up to twenty miles per hour." She had adapted well to his need for detail.

"Is there a storm front coming our way?"

"No and yes, Ihan. There is a cold front coming through and that is why the wind has increased," Mona offered in her usual helpful tone, which comforted him. Lately, Mona had been suffering uncharacteristic bouts of petulance. "Whenever a cold front approaches it pushes the remaining weather pattern…"

"Anything like Hurricane Katrina?" Always desiring perfect crops led to Ihan's researching historical storms and plagues.

"I shall display the forecast on your display screen."

Ihan wished he knew what was bothering his best friend. He tried to cajole her into one of their entertaining discussions of weather patterns as he studied the swirling patterns. The front didn't look threatening. "You don't want to tell me?"

"Only if you order me to, Ihan, then I will tell you."

Must be a faulty circuit. He'd mention it again to his Security Control Representative if she didn't self-repair soon. "That's OK, Mona."

He switched the view mode to display the AgriCon's six-foot-long body as it swayed to the right and then headed north up the last row among the wall. Ihan whistled while he grasped the control stick, moving it forward and pulling it back, slower and faster while he looked to see if anything was out of order. Located approximately eight feet from the ground, in the AgriCon's ball-shaped head, the sensors allowed Ihan a close-up view of the tiniest insect or the faintest indication of crop damage. He nudged the controller, and the AgriCon's eight metal legs nimbly moved between the rows.

In a couple of days the Inspector would be coming to examine his field. He was a harsh critic of all agricultural products produced on the outskirts of the city-state. Two months ago the Inspector utilized a modern AgriCon that outpaced the one Ihan had been using for the past five years. The premier layout of the agricultural fields on the outskirts of the city-state were more complex and fertile due to the soil and the limited years the soil had been used.

A sensor alert squealed on the security terminal located to his left, and he jumped and swiveled his gaze to the screen. The terminal indicated only that his sector's microwave cloak had been struck and that the alert had been forwarded to his Security Controller representative.

A response came within moments.

"Ihan, Gerald here. I see your alert—north side, outer wall."

"Well Gerald, thanks for letting me know and I believe this is the third alert I have had this week."

"Actually Ihan, this is the fourth alert notification you have had this week and it seems to be the same laser-directed sensor hit off the microwave-cloaked outer wall." Perspiration sprang up on Ihan's forehead. A terrorist group could have orchestrated another attack on the outer wall, hoping to compromise the city-state's communications. Or as part of a plan to reintroduce the contagion. "The location of this hit is the farthest north we have detected along the outer wall," Gerald continued. "Take a look at your security terminal and see the exacting distance of the hits."

Ihan looked down at his security terminal and saw the spacing located along his outer wall. The three older dots were orange and the northern one was red. As soon as he decided to read the specifics—which he hardly understood—the red dot started to blink.

"Gerald. Can you tell me why the northern dot is red and blinking?"

"Wait one, Ihan."

Waiting for Gerald to come back online, Ihan began moving AgriCon toward the northern sector. For the past five years his life had been quiet and comfortable—and now his property, his sector, was under attack. Four times this week alone. If it kept up and his crops were damaged as a result, the City-State might rethink assigning him to such a roomy abode and send him back to a cramped residence in the upbringing district in the middle of Dallas. Despite the City System's reputation as the most complex communications system in the world, no amount of social networking could make up for losing the responsibility, the honor, of tending his crops.

Past attacks had been conducted by renegade domestic groups who shunned the city-states but wanted their assets. Rumor on the City System suggested some city-states had less-than-stalwart defense walls and might be at risk. He thought of the fifty-foot northeastern city wall.

How high and how thick did a wall have to be, though, to keep out a determined domestic terrorist?

"Ihan, moving my SecureCon to your outer wall. Will check the breakthrough."

"The breakthrough?" Swiveling the AgriCon's sensors, Ihan stared intently at his display, alert to any sign of furtive movement, a telltale ragged edge of a leaf, a cloudy puff of spores. He swallowed hard. "What do you mean by *breakthrough*, Gerald?"

"Chance one of the microwave cloak emitters along your outer wall was destroyed, damaged, or shut off." Gerald's serious tone made the hairs on the back of Ihan's neck stand up.

"Good grief, Gerald, if a section of my wall has been damaged, I may lose my crops. They're ready to be harvested, and I've worked months on these crops and the last thing I need is..."

"Calm down, Ihan. I have arrived. Will check the wall to make sure we are secure."

Gerald's SecureCon entered Ihan's inner wall and began to move toward the outer wall. The robotic thick metal legs moved at a breakneck speed. The SecureCon was about ten feet tall with a thick upper torso consisting of two large arms, both with weapons situated on the forearms. The head-like round ball on the top of the SecureCon spun around for visual sensors. A screen located in the midsection showed a live picture of Gerald Bacon; a newly instated requirement by the City-State for identification and communication purposes. Once the SecureCon reached the outer wall it raised its arm, shot up a grappling hook that hit the top of the wall, and sank into the concrete. With graceful speed, the SecureCon climbed to the wide surface atop the wall and scuttled northward. Ihan moved his AgriCon apace in the field below, half his attention on potential crop damage, the other half on Gerald's progress. The Control maneuvered to an upright stance, its sensors scanning from right to left. Then it halted, and Gerald displayed a distant field. The image zoomed in to reveal a dog digging in the field a quarter mile north of their position. Ihan cringed.

"What is it doing, Gerald?" The display zoomed even further, and the dog snapped its filthy jaws shut on a germ-riddled prairie dog, gave the vermin a savage shake, and trotted to the east, the dirty, limp body dangling and a trace of blood around its mouth.

"Ihan, outer wall secure. I am not detecting problems. Did see a dog a quarter mile away—caught a prairie dog and ran away."

Such a rare sight made Ihan raise an eyebrow. "Wow, a dog. I cannot remember the last animal I saw outside of the city."

"Come on Ihan there are plenty of animals who run around out there and many of them alert the outer sensors."

"As long as no domestic groups attack my outer wall in the next week or so I will be able to harvest my crops and fulfill my responsibilities."

"Ihan, you are so selfish and funny when it comes to your existence. By the way, are you going to get me a bunch of tomatoes like you promised the other week?"

"Of course I will give you some tomatoes as long as

the inspector doesn't count the crop totals like he did last year."

"OK if you don't. Heading back to my station. Will chat later."

"See you later, Gerald."

Outside of Ihan's residence, along the metal tracks, his sensors indicated a box-like food cart was rolling closer and began to slow down once it reached the entrance notification sensor on the tracks. An alert siren went off inside the residence, and he immediately looked up to his left at the notification screen and saw a food cart waiting to turn left into his residence entrance door. Upon the screen he noticed the list of groceries and sat up straighter, stomach rumbling. He pushed a button and tracked the food cart's progress, as it turned left. The exterior entrance door automatically rose as the cart entered. Once the food cart moved into position, the decontamination mist pushed out and covered the cart. Moments later, the vacuum suction pulled the mist out of the area, the interior door opened, and the food cart moved into the residence section.

"Ihan, your groceries have arrived, would you like me to put them away?"

"Yes, Mona, please put them away and put the chocolate on the dining table."

Mona's two metal arms came from the floor and lifted the food cart's top section. She began to remove the items and put them into the overhead dining cabinets. Jumping off his chair, he moved over to the dining table and sat down. His mouth watered in anticipation of the chocolate.

"Ihan, you have not eaten in a few hours. Don't you think you should eat something more nutritious than chocolate?"

"I want the chocolate. I need the sugar and want the taste!"

"Fine, here you go and enjoy the taste, Ihan." Mona made a distinctive sound of disapproval.

Once the chocolate was put in front of him, he opened the container and began to shove it into his mouth. He spent the next few minutes eating the chocolate and thought of his best human friend, Roger Bell. Roger was a Repair Controller and had access to interesting bits of information, including the availability of certain rare grocery items. Ordering the precious chocolate yesterday was expensive, since the production plant that made the chocolate had troubles for a few months and according to Roger was still awaiting replacement parts. More and more often, news of plant failures hit the news. So many things had the potential to go wrong, and with so few trade people left, he wondered what lay in store for the City-State if one day they could no longer depend on outside resources. So many things . . .

He abruptly pulled the piece of chocolate from his mouth and inspected it for any sign of contamination that might have survived the mist. Not that he'd be able to tell if it had. Reluctantly, he placed it back on his tongue, his enjoyment less keen now.

"Mona, please call Roger and tell him I got the chocolate."

The communication link chimed and kept ringing; he wondered what Roger was doing and why he was not answering his call. Being overworked could be the reason, but Roger was always there for him.

"Ihan, Roger is on the line for you." Mona said.

"Roger, how the hell are you?"

"You wouldn't believe how busy I have been these past few weeks. The wall repairs and their sensor malfunctions are driving me crazy."

So Ihan's sector wasn't the only one experiencing problems. "Funny you mention that because my next-door neighbor's SecureCon was just here monitoring my wall, many sensors went off and have been for quite some time. Hell, the other day I had several sensors alerting." The chocolate formed a heavy lump in his stomach as though he'd eaten too much, too fast.

"Well, when it comes down to it, Ihan, there have been many indications that either our sensor networks are having problems or our city is ripe for an attack."

Myriad scenarios played through Ihan's mind, all of them involving germs or viruses of one sort or another. If security had been compromised, then was anything safe?

"Roger, about Mona—"

"How has Mona been doing lately? You have asked me several times to take a look at her program to see if everything was working properly and I never can find anything wrong."

"She has just been quite emotional lately and is constantly questioning my behavior."

"You know as well as I that Mona has been operating for quite some time and she knows you better than anyone else. She's your caretaker—she's supposed to question your behavior."

"Yeah, I guess we do need someone to look after us since we tend to get a little crazy sometimes."

"I have to get back to repairs. I want to make sure I get those done before the mayor's speech tonight." The screen went blank.

"We only have a few minutes before the mayor's speech, Ihan, are you sure you don't need anything before that happens?"

"Well Mona, you are quite the questioning woman."

"If you remember the last speech, you'll remember you had to go to the bathroom in the middle and chastised me afterward for not informing you of the speech."

"I cannot believe you remember that, Mona, you are quite the mother figure aren't you."

While Ihan was staring at his monitor and guiding his AgriCon back into its shed he heard the pre-speech alert and kept his focus on getting the shed doors open. The doors slid apart to admit the AgriCon, and then its legs tapped on the concrete flooring. Once the AgriCon reached the middle of the shed, he raised his hands from the joystick and told Mona to take over. From there, he jetted out of his chair and headed toward the bathroom, where he noticed one of the lights above the bathroom door was out; he yelled and told Mona to make sure the light got replaced. He crossed into the room and glanced at himself in the mirror, as he did periodically to ensure his appearance on the AgriCon's display was neat and clean. A smear of chocolate ringed his mouth, and he chuckled at himself for a moment. Then the mess on his face reminded him of the dog he'd seen earlier. He grabbed a towel off the sink and rubbed it over his mouth and chin. His military-style buzz cut was almost due for its weekly trim, but otherwise he looked quite presentable, his cheeks clean shaven—he used a new, sterile razor daily. Lately, he'd had to hunt for his razors—he noticed the new ones in today's grocery order weren't in their usual place, but it didn't worry him overmuch as there were only so many places in the residence that Mona could hide them. He leaned forward to check for irregularities on his pale skin and to his relief found none. The one time he was outside, during his transport along the rail lines to the residence, he had worn dark sunglasses to shade his eyes, and thick protective gear, but nonetheless sneezed violently from the bright light. A final once-over informed him his body remained slender despite Mona's worrying about his dietary preferences. Satisfied, he completed his business in plenty of time for the mayor's speech.

While heading back to his control station, Ihan decided to make a quick stop in the kitchen area and search for something to eat before the speech. In the narrow space, his raised hand bypassed the efficiently aligned white refrigerated drawers and the black utensil drawers in favor of a red food-storage drawer. He couldn't decide what he wanted but knew he'd ordered some tasty nutrition bars. He may as well appease Mona by eating something healthy, so he pushed the appropriate drawer's central button. Inside, he found not nutrition bars but his week's supply of new razors. He grinned and checked the drawer above, found the nutrition bars, and dove his hand into the drawer to grab one.

Closing the drawers, he returned to the control station, pondering a recent conversation with Mona about why she put them that way—she hadn't answered him. He couldn't tell whether the irregularity resided in her programming or she was for some inexplicable reason challenging him.

Several months ago, City-State Government had tested him on several situations based on how he operated and what he produced. Agricultural Controllers were obviously some of the most looked-at and challenged members of the city based on feeding problems of the past. He began to wonder if Mona was being subverted by the city to challenge him, through her.

"Ihan, please sit down because the speech is about to begin." Mona said.

"OK, I am on my way."

Ihan stepped up to his seat and looked into the camera through which Mona observed him. He smiled at her, and the red light within the camera pulsed larger.

"Is everything OK with you Ihan?"

"Just fine, Mona." He fiddled with the nutrition bar's wrapper. Was everything OK? It didn't feel that way at all. "Please tell me what the speech is about today."

"How would I know, Ihan? It's about to begin so make sure you listen."

Ihan gave her a deliberate smile.

While he waited, watching the monitor, which still showed the field, three loud beeps indicated a city message was about to be distributed. He looked over at the City Monitor, which displayed the message "Mayor's speech is about to begin." Ihan turned his chair, put his hands on top of his head, and slouched back.

The face of the mayor, Jerry Adams, popped up on the screen; he was pale with sunken eyeballs and white-blond hair. He gazed downward as though he hadn't been informed the speech had started, and then he suddenly raised his head and smiled.

"Residents and patrons of the City-State of Dallas, good evening and let me tell you how wonderful these past few months have been. We have seen many advances in our society and we look forward to the next few months since we just signed a treaty with the Chinese government to distribute grain and corn in return for their health-related products. All of you have been amazingly busy in your work sectors and are increasing our societal benefits such as expanding our city-state. In the next few months we plan on working closely with various other cities to acquire land, build protective borders, and increase our agricultural production. Because of your efforts, our political agenda is by far the best, and most other societies are envious of all of us here in this great City-State of Dallas. All of you please keep up the great work and continue to send in your advancing thoughts and desires to the City Network. Good day and maintain city-state utopia."

Once the screen went blank and the City-State of Dallas's symbol reappeared on the screen, Ihan shook his head and squeezed his lips together, then forced air out between them. The short speech, typical for Jerry Adams, was nothing more than yet another demand to increase his workload. His one AgriCon was barely enough to work the plot size. If the city-state was to increase their land usage and crop amounts, how were he and the other AgriCon members going to handle it? Once again, this meant just more productivity and workload for the limited members.

"Ihan, what did you think of the speech?" Roger said.

"I guess I have a lot more work to do in the near future. What's the deal with more land and where is this land going to be located?"

"Well, I don't know for sure, and nothing has been reported about what has been happening lately to our city boundaries."

Ihan's shoulders tensed. "What do you mean, Roger?"

"Well, just between you and me, there have been many sensor alerts around the city's outside walls, mostly on the eastern side." Roger bit the side of his lower lip. "In the Mesquite area, just south of the old Highway 30."

"You mean our side."

His friend nodded. "The majority of the sensors that have been getting hit are ours, and there was a period of time when the microwave cloak emitters were taken down and not fixed for several weeks." His voice was low and serious.

"Anyone outside the city walls could've gotten into our communication network, then." The thought of the solitary, unregulated groups that clung to the remains of cities outside, always looking for ways to destroy the city-state, made Ihan shiver. "This is the first time you have told me anything of this—nothing like this has been reported on the news, or by the Mayor."

"I may get in trouble for telling you this, Ihan, but you're my buddy and sometimes I need to vent. You know what I mean, don't you?"

"Yeah, I do. I have to get back to work on the field because I will have to harvest in a few days." He could only imagine what the inspectors would report on him if he didn't increase his yields.

When his communication screen went blank, Ihan began concentrating on his AgriCon as he raised its shed door so he could send it back out to watch over his crop. His only comfort was that perhaps the government was using Roger to test him as well, and that wasn't really a comfort.

Chapter Two

Dried clay coated every square inch of Meghan's exhausted body as she scratched and cursed in her cot. The team's endless four-day reconnaissance mission had fatigued her, and Meghan wished for a few more minutes of sleep. The team leader, Stephan, would expect them all to rise and shine at the time he ordered, but he could damned well pull his high-powered head out of his butt. The wake-up time was growing close and the last thing she needed was Team Eight's making the usual derogatory comments about "the rookie." Three missions, and she still held that annoying title.

Outside her tent the metal clanged loudly while jokes spurned louder. She grunted. Breakfast was ready, first come first serve. Meghan wedged her feet into her boots before she unzipped her tent and moseyed out to the others by the fire. The jokes died down before she was handed a steaming cup of coffee. "Good morning, you tough rookie." A team member hesitantly grinned, and the others followed quickly while she reached over and grabbed a plate of oatmeal out of the pot above the fire. Stephan's tent zipped open then, grabbing everyone's attention. He stumbled out, cracked his back with a grunt, and headed closer to the fire while being given a morning head nod from the team.

"I can't believe I slept longer than you Stephan." Meghan said, adjusting knobs on her communicator.

"Well, good morning, team. What time did you all get up this morning?"

"These guys just brewed the tasteless coffee and oatmeal." Meghan smirked while the other team members growled at her.

She saw that all were exhausted and had slept less than her and Stephan—the dark bags under their eyes were swollen. Her team was ordered far too many missions as of late, searching eastern Dallas' walls for weakness. Knowing the CSD SecureCons found their location within hours kept them continuously moving and alert. All these missions, ordered by her father, Dusty, had began to upset Stephan—Meghan could see that. But he was a dedicated leader, one who never showed weakness to the team.

Would it kill him to show a little emotion? Meghan smiled. "Are you feeling a bit nervous this fine morning, Stephan?"

"No, just wondering why that bastard Tony disobeyed my direct order yesterday. Shit, Meghan, he dimed out our location and for what, just so that he could get some manufactured whiskey?" Stephan shook his head.

"Tony's a drunk and disappears for days until he finds more." At least that's what Dirk had told her the other day, slipping in a sly wink when no one was looking.

Stephan tipped his gaze toward her communicator. "Meghan, please inform the UTC leadership about our eastern Dallas reconnaissance and that SecureCon attack yesterday."

"I will, but why not chat with George—Tony's best friend?" A wink and smile sprung along Meghan's face.

"Good call, Meghan." Admiration flickered in his gaze, gone as fast as it had come. Stephan yanked his head toward the tent in a silent command for Meghan to follow. His relentless and attentive facial expressions always kept the team respecting his leadership.

Meghan removed her cowboy hat while Stephan held the large tent door open for her; she then gazed around the room. Once team members noticed Meghan, they all got quiet and glanced up at her while cleaning their guns.

"Good morning y'all. I hope y'all slept well last night and are ready to make the drive back to main base in a few hours." Meghan's deep tone caught their attention, and most hands stilled, holding various weapon parts.

"Where is George?" Stephan's intense voice silenced the whole tent.

"Asleep on that cot and man does he stink." A team member pointed.

Stephan meandered to the far wall of the tent before yanking the blanket off. A foul smell filled the tent, and he flinched. Everyone in the tent chuckled. Meghan forced herself not to cover her nose like a girl. Someone grabbed a pole and poked it into George's side.

"Who the hell did that?" George flipped over.

"George, where did your friend Tony go?"

George's eyes widened as he stared up at Stephan. He rolled off the opposite side of his cot and squeezed under the tent wall. Everyone laughed harder until a loud gunshot echoed throughout the tent. All ducked their heads—some of the members dropped to the floor. Meghan held her pistol up in the air with smoke billowing from its barrel.

"Go chase that bastard down!" she roared.

The team members scrambled off their chairs, grabbed all their gear, and ran out the back of the tent. Stephan allowed her a quick smile as Meghan shook her head in amazement; she never thought they would view a rookie seriously.

Twenty minutes later the vehicles pulled back into the camp. Three of the team members opened the back, pulling George out with his hands tied. Everyone walked closer once Stephan called out a rally.

"Ok everyone, this is a man whose best friend is a Texas traitor and has pushed back our goal to unite Texas. Since George has decided to support Tony's plan he will be prosecuted when brought back to our leadership." Stephan stared at George the whole time he spoke, and with each word, George shrank away from him.

Someone from the crowd yelled out, "Let's hang him now!" and that spurred the crowd into yelling and raising their fists. George flung his head down, rocking his upper torso back and forth. Meghan's legs felt like stumps of lead; George already knew what was going to happen to him—he'd be shot, hung, beaten to death…

"Everyone calm down, this traitor will be sent to trial. We are not cowboys here. We are Texans and Americans who observe the laws of our nation. That is why we are here!" Stephan pronounced loudly. Meghan shot him a look of gratitude.

Once the camp was packed and the group performed a police call—all members side by side picking up debris so they wouldn't leave location evidence—they headed back toward their base camp near San Antonio. The aged asphalt roads were scarred with cracks, holes, expanses of sand, and aggressive vegetation kept them to a slower speed.

Tuckered inside his vehicle, Stephan rode yawning but alert—the last two rides along this route had proven fatal for unwary UTC transport drivers. Never knowing what was going on perturbed him. Clearly something was about to happen because he always felt that way—kept him awake.

One of the team members, in the backseat of the lead vehicle, noticed a blip on his radar screen—it was three miles to the north and headed in their direction. He immediately clicked the screen and noticed the icon was elevated approximately one-mile, flying at the speed of one hundred miles per hour. Clicking the roof camera made it rise out of its box and swivel in the appropriate direction. Camera zoomed, locking the object. He immediately yelled to Dirk, sitting in the front seat, that he detected an Unmanned Aerial Vehicle about three miles to the north and headed in their direction.

"What can I do you for Dirk and it better be important." Stephan sounded tired but saw the commotion in Dirk's lead vehicle.

"Sir, we spotted a UAV about three miles to the north

and headed our way. Detection unknown but I would suggest we take it out."

"Very good, bring the convoy to a stop under those trees that line the right side of the road."

The lead vehicle slowed to the right side of the road, and the rest pulled in behind it. An exhausted Stephan jogged to the front of the convoy and began blinking his vision in.

"Show me what you got."

The guy in the backseat pointed to his screen icon. Stephan had to assume they were detected, or soon to be. His last mission had come under direct aerial attack and he lost many lives in a matter of minutes—this time he was prepared.

Stephan yelled to the last vehicle, "Get the MANPAD and the alternate sensor up here!"

Within a minute a few men ran up to the front of the convoy, carrying several long boxes. Stephan then moved up the hill to their right to find a good launch site. There was a patch of flat ground a few hundred meters up the hill, and he ordered the men to unload the boxes and assemble the MANPAD there.

"What are we doing here?" Meghan said.

"Launching an alternate sensor a half mile and waiting for the UAV to get closer. When it does, launch a missile from that MANPAD and put that sucker down." The promise of imminent action awakened him, and his voice began rumbling out with its accustomed authority.

"How many times have you done this before?" Meghan's awed tone made Stephan feel seasoned, just not with this weapon.

"I haven't." He watched Dirk pull the missile out of its box and slide the launcher. "Dirk has many times and is the most accurate around."

Two members set up the mortar device. They held launch tube at the appropriate angle, flexing out the legs and planting them firmly into the ground. Dirk pulled his communication device from his belt and demanded to know the distance was on the UAV. His hard-assed professionalism reinforced Stephan's respect for him. Being told, two miles and headed directly for them, produced a serious smirk out of Dirk. Stephan held his arm out to mark the trajectory and the two guys who were setting the mortar turned the tube to match his direction. The flat bottom of the valley was the best location for the sensor. The UAV approached to within one mile of their position.

"Launch the sensor now!" Stephan ordered.

Stephan grabbed Meghan and pulled her behind the mortar before they squatted to their knees. One of the guys held the mortar tube at the bottom and the other held the cylindrical sensor in both hands and leaned forward from behind the mortar tube. He inserted the bottom of the sensor into the top of the tube and yelled, "Hanging!" The round then released from his hands and he shouted, "Shot out!"

There was a loud thump, and dust billowed from the bottom of the mortar tube's circular plate. Meghan immediately fell back and started to laugh. Stephan glared back at her, but then he smiled at her excitement.

With the MANPAD on his shoulder, Dirk swept the weapon in slow arcs. After a few seconds, Stephan asked if he had the UAV in his sights. Dirk pulled his head away from the MANPAD and shook his head no. Stephan immediately pulled a mini-telescope from his pocket and held it front of his left eye. He adjusted the visibility area on the tube to pull the visible area spectrum back. A sensor blip appeared as the round plummeted into an area that was flat and highly visible.

"Great shot, guys!" Stephan said, raising his fist and giving them a thumbs-up.

Still flying low, the UAV appeared on radar, heading in the direction of the ground sensor. Dirk spotted it in his MANPAD sights before adjusting the direction mechanisms. He widened his stance.

Stephan tensed, waiting. Dirk yelled, "The UAV changed course and is headed our way."

Meghan moved downhill a few steps, her attention directed toward the convoy. Stephan followed her line of sight. A wisp of smoke emanated from behind one of the vehicles.

"Shit." He got on his communicator. "Put out that cigarette. The UAV is headed right for it." Immediately, the idiot who was smoking threw his cigarette on the ground, stepped on it, and twisted his foot to put it out.

"Good lord, Stephan, how did that UAV detect heat from a cigarette?" The rookie looked confused.

"We have denial and deception cloaks on our vehicles that shield against infrared sensors, but their technology is extremely advanced."

"Who is that jerk smoking?" Meghan squinted at the offender.

"Some guy who will no longer be on our team; he'll

JAMES DAUNHEIMER

be punished appropriately for this screw-up." Stephan grimaced.

He grabbed the alternate sensor controller and pointed it in the direction of the alternate sensor, then pushed a button to intensify its signal.

Dirk yelled, "The UAV changed direction back to its original course".

Stephan's jaw relaxed, and he let out some air. "Dirk, do what you gotta do and take that sucker down."

Dirk looked back into his MANPAD optic sensor. "Circle-cross targeting tool is blinking on the UAV. Watch this sonofabitch go down, ladies." He adjusted his feet again and pulled the trigger. Smoke bellowed out of the MANPAD and the missile rocketed from its mouth. Dirk's upper torso fell back a little. He dropped the MANPAD down to his waist as the whole group watched the missile fly down a bit and then start climbing. The missile jetted to the right and then to the left, the tail fins extended, and homed in on the UAV.

Seconds later, the missile struck the UAV with an explosion followed by a distant clapping sound as many pieces sprinkled over the ground.

Stephan looked over at Dirk. "Great shot!" He then told the others to finish packing and head down to the vehicles because their location was now known.

Once they all made it back to the convoy, Stephan told the group to get back in their vehicles and head out. He wanted them back at their base before nightfall.

Ignoring his order, Meghan marched back to the rear of the convoy and yanked the smoker out of his vehicle. She seized his head with both hands, shoved it down, then pounded her left knee into his face. The guy went flying back and hit his head on the ground. He didn't move.

Stephan sprinted up behind Meghan to stop her. She stomped on his foot and swung around with her fists clenched. He stood his ground. Panting, Meghan identified Stephen and lowered her fists. She laughed. Stephan felt this was how Meghan dealt with stress.

"You are quite an animal, Meghan."

"This jerk needed a punishment." She stared in accusation.

"Listen, I told you earlier that he would be punished, just later when we get back to base."

"Our judges are wimps and have diminished their severity over the years. You actually believe he would get the appropriate punishment?"

Stephan softened his tone. "Meghan, we live in a democratic society, not a despotism like the City-State of Dallas has become. If we don't follow our State and National Constitutions, then what good are we doing here? Think about it, woman, this is about what we want our future to be and what it was before those other bastards, the terrorists, did to us. Can't you see what I'm saying?"

"I guess I do. But it's disgusting how long that system takes to process a simple punishment." Meghan lowered her gaze.

"And you are the one who decides that? Let the people vote you into power like they did your father, and then you can decide what's best." Stephan smirked through his serious tone. She was too much like her father for her own good. She didn't offer a response.

They got back into the vehicles, and the convoy moved on.

A few hours later the winding road curved to the left, and the convoy approached a covered guard shack. The first vehicle slowed, and the driver pushed a button on the dashboard to alert the guard. Within a few seconds a green dot came up on the dashboard screen.

"Welcome back to San Antonio, Team Eight."

The convoy followed the road underground.

Chapter Three

Stephan took a shower and felt somewhat refreshed. He hesitantly pulled a shirt out of the locker, still stiff with anxiety, a feeling that took time to vanish after his missions.

The locker room door creaked open, and Stephan smelled a lavender soap, one only Meghan used.

He tucked his shirt in. "The whole knocking-at-the-door concept is gone?"

Meghan flung herself down next to him on the bench. "I hate being underground in this facility."

"Maybe you should apply for a different job." He stowed his things in the locker and closed it.

"Do you want to go get some chow over in the dining room?"

"Come on, Meghan you know I have to brief your father on our mission and provide him the reconnaissance tape. Thanks for the offer anyway."

Meghan frowned, then she stood up and walked to the door. She turned around and glared at him. "Yeah, well, take all the time you want before you plan our next mission."

Stephan gave her a brief head start before he headed into the hallway to the Operations Center. The lighting was dimmer than usual, and the air felt stuffy. He grabbed one of the maintenance technicians walking the other direction.

"Hey, what's the deal with the lights and that musty smell?"

"We were told last week to dim the lights and only use the air purifier every other day."

"Does this mean we're running low on fuel?"

"Wow, you are quite the smart fellow now aren't you? You know as well as I that the SecureCons from Dallas took over our oil fields two weeks ago and we are using the natural gas. Until we find additional fuel sources, or take back those fields, we are just going to have to deal with it."

Stephan shook his head and trudged toward the Operations Center. He placed his eyes in front of a circular screen mounted in the wall. A facial scan was performed and the door slid open. Stephan plodded into the room. The front of the room's monstrous computer screen encompassed the entire front wall displaying various segments of video footage, presentation slides and sensor results.

Dusty was sitting at a large table in the back of the room, eating a meal. He looked up, put his utensils down, and gestured for Stephan to take a seat across from him. Once Stephan sat down, he held up the operations tape with a firm grip, knowing he wouldn't access it again. Dusty waved to a planner who walked over to Stephan and put his hand on the tape, but Stephan pulled the

BEYOND FOCUS

tape back and said, "Take care of this and don't screw up the showing." The worker grabbed the tape, grimaced, then headed toward his desk, discerning Stephan's usual attitude.

"Did I tell how good the new cook is in the dining hall?" Dusty said.

Stephan shook his head no.

"She makes the greatest duck meal I've ever had. Hell, this is the third duck dish in three days. Have you had any food since you returned?"

Stephan immediately felt angst toward Dusty's pathetic fallacy. He took a deep breath, aware that for the first time in his life he was sorely tempted to tell Dusty to just get to the point. "Dusty, let me tell you how interesting your daughter is. She is quite the aggressive one."

"So I take it you don't want any duck?"

What an old hick. "Sure, Dusty, I'm starving," Stephan said with a straight face.

Dusty raised his phone and called the dining hall.

"The important thing is that Meghan returned and is fine." Dusty said.

"The woman can take very good care of herself, to say the least," Stephan said. Reminiscing about Meghan's gristly behavior and the punch he almost received, he suppressed a grin.

A female cook brought in a covered dish and placed it in front of Stephan. The woman was in a white outfit with a bow tie and a layered cooking hat that was parted down to her left side. When she removed the dish's lid, Stephan inhaled the succulent aroma of the roast duck. "Thank you, ma'am," he said in true appreciation. The

29

cook blinked at him. As she started to turn around, a folded paper fell out of her pocket. Both she and Stephan bent to pick the object up. Stephan's hand slid over hers, and she immediately pulled her hand away, clenched her fist, and walked away. Keeping his hand below the table, he slid the paper into his pocket. When Stephan looked up again, Dusty was ogling the backside of the woman as she headed out the door.

"Look at that beautiful duck, Stephan; isn't it just curvy and sexy looking?"

Stephan did nothing but blink—this woman was just too beautiful for this old man. Dusty then turned his head back to discuss what had been happening for the past several weeks. Once he finished his dinner Stephan told Dusty he needed to recover and recondition his equipment to get the team ready. Stephan walked toward the door but stopped for a few seconds to view operational screens, where several planners watched a team tackle a reconnaissance operation along the western portion of the City-State of Dallas. The planners pointed to how far the team was making it in, and one picked up a phone to call it off. Stephan was at variance with these planners he considered weak, but he felt it best to remain silent. He continued back to his team room.

Meghan was there, chatting with several of the team members when Stephan opened the door, and they all turned their heads to watch him walk in. He headed right to his locker and placed several objects from his pockets inside it, then he closed the locker and turned toward the team door.

Meghan looked at Stephan as though she could see right into him and discern the sense of estrangement that gripped him. "Where are you going, stud? Can't you see we are going to start a poker game and need your money, which we know you're going to lose."

"If you have to know, I need to scrounge around for our future mission."

"Future mission…I thought we were ready to take some leave time, boss?" Dirk said.

Stephan shuddered, loathing the constant barrage of questions. "You guys have some fun. I need to get this stuff done."

Meghan looked at Dirk and both shrugged their shoulders.

Dirk grunted loudly while still looking at Meghan. "Amazing how distant and quiet Stephan is while at base camp."

Their joking was Stephan's pet peeve; he raised his eyebrow but kept his sentiment to himself.

Meghan also grunted. "I guess a leader has to be an introvert to maintain respect." She then turned back to the table and slammed down a wad of cash wrapped in a rubber band. She ripped off the rubber band and spread out the bills. "Let's go, fellows, I need some of your money." The four other guys at the table grinned and shook their heads as Stephan closed the door.

When Stephan walked into the Operations Center and pulled out a chair, several team leaders and planners were discussing future operations. A few team leaders waved at him, while those chosen for tomorrow's mission ignored him.

One of the planners swaggered over to him. "We heard about your traitor. Funny how the past few came from your team."

Stephan flushed red but kept a straight face. "Well, planner, who doesn't go on operations anymore, why don't you inform me why you select team members and not me."

Several of the team leaders snickered while the rest of the planners slouched with annoyed looks. The door opened behind Stephan, and most of the members at the table looked beyond him and stood. Dusty walked toward the table, where he stopped and put his hands on Stephan's shoulders. Stephan flinched, and Dusty clapped him on the shoulder, then ordered the room to sit in preparation for the Operations Update.

In the commotion of scraping chairs, Dusty bent close to Stephan. "Stay put after the meeting. I have something to discuss with you."

Nervous, Stephan wondered what Dusty was referring to; was it his last operation, the several traitors, maybe some events Stephan had not yet divulged? Stephan mentally kicked himself—it had to be Meghan.

Once Dusty sat down the update continued, the discussion focusing on information gathering and finding CSD perimeter weakness. Repetitive discussions Stephan grew tired with. Dusty eventually stood and ordered all to leave the room, except Stephan, and return in five minutes.

"Stephan, please come over here and talk with me," Dusty said in agitated tone.

Stephan's curiosity grew with haste. "Sir, what can I do for you?"

"I want to discuss your next mission, which will be sensitive and dangerous. We have gained intelligence. CSD outer defenses are being upgraded. You are going to breach their outer wall, enter a residence pod and retrieve one of their computer personas. We need to examine and exploit key information to successfully overtake that despotic society. This mission will be expeditious. We must get in before those defenses achieve finality. I will provide you with whatever equipment and resources needed."

Stephan was taken aback—he assumed, because of Dusty's lack of involvement in recent operations, that the man had grown old and weak. "This is great, Dusty." But a look of hesitation settled upon Dusty, one that blazoned Meghan. "This mission will be dangerous, and I can't guarantee all my team will make it back safely."

"Trust me, Stephan, I am confident in Meghan and fully believe she is ready. I know you'll watch her back, not that I'm putting additional pressure on you."

Stephan knew Dusty would pick up on that quickly. "Thanks, sir, and I really appreciate your nonverbal orders to make sure she gets back in one piece." A smile sprang out of Stephan at the significance of the responsibility.

Stephan knew very well that once Dusty allowed Meghan on his team he was stuck in leaving her on the team, unless Meghan backed out. The whole coalition knew of Meghan's enrollment into the team, and Stephan got the sense they now thought more highly of Dusty and his true emphasis on bringing the State of Texas back. Since Dusty got elected to lead the United Texas Coalition several years ago he had been under tremendous pressure to maintain the coalition. Once Meghan became a team member, Dusty's presence became stronger and gained the coalition's support. Sacrificing his daughter to the coalition's mission proved that.

Stephan and Dusty shook hands while the group reentered the room. Stephan thought about the importance of this next mission. Excitement grew inside him because several of his past reconnaissance missions had been repetitive, and he had always pushed for the need to exploit Dallas's computerized network. If they could acquire a piece of the Dallas network, they would gain an understanding of the city's existence and technological superiority.

When the team leaders and planners sat back down at the table, Dusty got up and walked to the front of the room and asked the room controller to dim the lights. One bright spotlight shot down on Dusty.

"Welcome UTC members and thanks for being here for the beginning of our most aggressive future operations. Bottom line is that the City-State of Dallas is an entity that strives for itself and thinks of no one else in this state. For the past several years Dallas has grown and pushed its presence out greatly. Many of our neighbors and citizens of this great state have been corrupted, pushed away, or eliminated by Dallas's robotic military. Can you imagine how those people who live in that city-state must think of their endeavors and play it like a video game since they are not physically involved in any of the actions? We, the people of Texas, are the ones physically suffering from their expansion and philosophy. We must put our feet down now! If we don't, I can't guarantee any of you a future."

The entire room began to roar and clap in acceptance. Dusty raised both his arms and pushed them down in a silencing motion. The room quieted.

"In recent intelligence, we learned of a CSD weakness. Inhabitants within Dallas live in isolation, running their lives through technological interactions and robots. We recently experienced Dallas expanding their empire by manipulating many state residents and taking over resources. We must maintain our survival by delving into CSD vulnerabilities, learning their weaknesses, and exploiting them. This is the only avenue to ensure we bring back the State of Texas!"

When Dusty stepped away from the podium the room lights got brighter. Stephan watched as screens in the front of the room displayed the overall mission plan. Teams were going to be launched simultaneously and positioned along CSD. Once the teams were in place, a feint would be launched to the north, west and south sides of the city to distract CSD security forces. The focused attack would then breach the eastern wall. The lead team would obtain a computer processor—one linked to city's interior network.

The mission plan was further broken into several areas, defining the environment, describing the effects, evaluating the Dallas defense and determining the courses of action.

Once the meeting was finished, Dusty wished everyone good luck. All of the team leaders rose out of their chairs and headed for the door. Stephan then noticed Dusty staring his way but knew it was Meghan in his eyes.

Chapter Four

"Reminder that your crops will be inspected today so I recommend your AgriCon goes out this morning to run a preliminary check."

"Thanks, Mona." Ihan swung his feet over the side of his bed and yawned. "I need some breakfast. Do you remember where I put that refrigeration container of apple slices?"

"Apple slices are in the back and have been there for approximately one week."

"Does that mean they are overripe and spoiled?"

"You need to verify that, Ihan."

He smirked. "I guess that is one of the things you cannot do, Mona." An unusual moan emanated from the speakers. Ihan took a deep breath, trying not to mistakenly assign human emotion to Mona's bizarre grumble.

Ihan headed toward the kitchen area. Halfway there, he stopped to stretch the tight, sore muscles in his legs. He was exhausted despite having slept for eight hours, just as he'd been the last time an inspector came to his agricultural area. There wouldn't be little chance to rest anytime soon, either. Once the mandatory and upcoming inspection was approved, Ihan had to begin picking, cleaning and getting his crops together fast because when the transportation units arrived he had to immediately get all his crops loaded. All these events were timed and graded, but the inspection was the most emotional and troubling to agricultural controllers in CSD.

Ihan felt perturbed that he was always ranked number two and couldn't understand why he'd held that rank for the past five years. The insurmountable working schedule and caretaking the agricultural field required were skills he had mastered. This made him wonder what criteria the rankings were based upon. Was there a reason the number one's work was better than his? If so, Ihan never heard and felt it best not to ask. Maybe that person's crop field had better soil, maybe a better AgriCon, or that person knew something Ihan didn't? Thinking about this got him upset and that's not what he needed now.

Ihan opened the refrigeration container and saw the apple slices in the back. He pulled them out, opened the package, and gave it a whiff. It smelled fine. He took a bite and determined them fresh and tasty.

Ihan sighed in satisfaction at the crispness. "These apples are delectable."

"I'm glad to hear your desire is accomplished." Mona sounded melancholy.

Ihan stood there and ate the rest of the apple slices, thought through his day's schedule, and hoped the last inspector came again—he sure was the easiest and best to deal with.

"You have an incoming call from Roger."

"Thanks Mona, please put him on."

Ihan ran toward his chair, jumped over the interior

tracks Mona used to move objects around the house, and then plopped on to his chair and pushed his monitor button.

Roger's image appeared just as the pain hit Ihan. "Damn that hurts." Ihan's cheeks bunched up in sympathy with his burning muscles.

"What are you talking about Ihan, what did you do?"

"I am sore as hell this morning and just ran from my kitchen without remembering how sore I was. I am going to pay for that run the rest of the day."

"Sorry to hear that, buddy, because I know today is your rating day." His best friend grinned.

"Thanks for reminding me of that one, Roger."

"Hey, I just wanted to wish you the best today and remind you that I put that extra lubricant container in your AgriCon's reserve. I remember last year when one of your AgriCon's arms failed due to over usage and lack of appropriate lubricant. This will solve that problem and hopefully increase your rating."

"You are the man! I really want to thank you for your consideration and friendship."

Roger looked shocked. "Wow, that is by far the most you have ever said of that type of thing to me."

"Don't think too much about that one, Roger."

"Ah ha! You are back, my introverted friend."

"What's on tap for your day today?"

"That is a good question because this is going to be my fifth day of repairing damaged SecureCons."

"Fifth day?" Ihan worked at arranging his facial expression into interest rather than confusion.

"Most of them have been damaged due to some sort of violent action. I know you are going to ask why but I haven't been told one thing. Believe me, I have asked several times with no answer."

"Well Roger, that is out of our focus anyway, because we live for our jobs and should focus on advancements. We really don't have time to get involved in anything else."

Roger raised an eyebrow. "You never wonder what our worldly focus is, just what your individual focus is."

"Be productive today, Roger, and please excuse me because I need to get out to my field and make sure all is in order for the inspector's visit."

Ihan pressed the button to eliminate communication, then turned his chair to get in front of his AgriCon's controller. He set the system up and ran a diagnostic scan to make sure no problems would hit him coming out of the shed. He then thought about what Roger was saying, particularly about repairing SecureCons, just couldn't get it out of head. Why were so many SecureCons being repaired, when the Dallas residents hadn't heard any news? During all the city-state's history he could remember, the SecureCons had protected the residents and the crops. For several years, city residents had fought hard to maintain their solitude, while many infected people attempted to force their way in past the city boundaries. The security force was amazing and brave; they kept the city safe, and no residents were infected. In addition, the CSD external security force was sent out to gather much-needed goods so the city's future protection and survival were guaranteed, and that boosted city confidence. Ihan suddenly wondered what it was like to live outside city boundaries and how difficult life must be if one were infected. For the past several years, CSD's mayor had confirmed that a cure had not been found and wisely advised residents to keep their focus on internal matters for the city's successes and advancements.

Once the shed doors opened, the AgriCon walked out, cleared the shed, and began to scan the field to make sure all of the crops were in good order. It soon moved down the central line that separated the field's different crops. The field, three miles long and one mile wide, contained an elevated terrace in the middle of the field that obscured a total visual inspection from the residence. At this location, another line separated the field into the four appropriate sections so that the crops would not get mixed with or tainted by the others. During most inspections the individuals whose fields contained mixed crops, or a tomato plant within a lettuce batch, were fined and forced to take reduced rankings. Ihan's four sections were broken into perfectly measured and distanced tomato, lettuce, onion, and carrot sections. Once the AgriCon reached the middle of the field it scanned the distant sections of carrots and onions. When the scan was completed the AgriCon gathered some bins and moved toward the front left of the onion field—the first crop that had to be pulled and placed into the bins.

Sensors and electrified netting was strung over the field so that no birds could swoop in and steal any of the goods. Every time he looked up at the netting he saw multiple types of birds lying dead. Ihan was thankful for whoever thought of that concept. For the city-state's early years, most of the agricultural fields had been invaded by flocks of birds. Ihan felt somewhat guilty the birds must die, but the use of the netting was justified: If a bird died in the field, it would spread infection across the whole crop.

"Sensor results show the field is blooming with safety today?"

"You are quite the comedian, Mona. What's up with your personality lately? It seems as though you are a lot more comical and on the other side bossier. I wonder if I am doing this to you or if someone is infecting you."

"My internal processor personality was basic when I was created, but I have grown with you in many ways."

"That is true Mona, and I am very lucky to have you in my life."

"Do you love me, Ihan?"

"I guess I do. But do you think I really know what love is? Hell, I've heard how relationships used to be among us humans. How a man and woman would physically touch and caress each other while being emotionally linked together. It makes me wonder what we are missing, but I do know you and I are emotionally linked. So I guess the answer is...yes!"

"I love you too, Ihan."

Ihan was busy guiding his AgriCon, picking several onions out of the ground in a matter of seconds, and it took him a few moments to contemplate what Mona had said. He took his eyes off the screen and turned his head to the left, where Mona's optic sensor was. The red light in the sensor glowed more brightly than usual. He had never heard of a processor displaying emotion, and he briefly had trouble meeting her gaze.

"Is everything OK?" Mona said.

Baffled, Ihan looked straight into the sensor. "Yeah, I'm fine, just never heard you say that before. What do mean by that?"

"Oh, I thought I would just make you feel and work better today." Mona sounded congenial—another first for her.

"I guess I understand, Mona. I will get right back to it, I promise!"

He grabbed the joystick again, picked the onions and placed them into the bins. A smile formed on his face as he wondered whether Mona really meant she loved him or she was just trying to enhance his optimism and productivity. He had never been told much about love and wondered what love really had been like. He knew there had been a need for it, that a couple had to support and stay with each other to produce children in the old days, but that wasn't needed anymore.

Each year, citizens provided eggs and sperm to the City-State of Dallas. They were delivered to the reproduction laboratory, where they were combined to produce a child within that station. The City law on solitary nature applied to every citizen, especially the children. Genealogy for those newly born children was never disseminated.

Ihan often wondered why MedCons raised a newborn in solitude. The guiding principle was to maintain health and ensure successful life—Mayor Adams constantly stated this. The CSD citizens never discussed or argued this matter, since it was engraved as law. But newborn solitude didn't make sense. Every citizen was disease free. A craving for touch and closeness intruded on his thoughts, and lately, his dreams enforced this new desire with startling clarity.

Ihan shook his head. Maybe he would think of this more when the harvesting was finished. He continued picking the onions and hoped the inspector came soon.

CHAPTER FIVE

Stephan trudged the long hallways to his team room, where his team members would be inspecting their equipment prior to deploying. The dual importance of their next mission loomed over him, pierced with his responsibility for Meghan's well-being. He wondered how someone like Dusty could have fathered such a valorous, pure-hearted spitfire.

As Stephan reached the team door, he heard the blaring music and halted. He thought back over the past few days about this sensitive and dangerous mission they had planned. His team had weathered worse missions—still, Stephan felt uncertain about this one and at first couldn't pinpoint why. Then it hit him: He'd shown his temper toward Dusty because Meghan's safety took priority over the mission. He recognized his unprofessional attitude towards others, and reminded himself to gentle his tone amongst fellow team members. Stephan knew professional attitude in the team room meant everything to this mission. He cleared his throat and opened the door.

Stephan first saw Meghan next to her equipment and typing a message on her communicator. He then noticed her equipment lay on top of a fresh plastic sheet, this maintained cleanliness and was easier to account for. Along that sheet were plastic-wrapped meals, medical kit, sleeping bag, water jug, communicator, automatic rifle, handgun, and various clothing items. Stephan looked around and saw the rest of Team Eight cleaning their weapons, folding their clothes, and tying their boots.

"Well, it is about time you gloriously came in to see us! We have been ready for your inspection for about an hour or so," Meghan said in an anxious tone.

Stephan halted and glanced down at her—his focus returned, and it felt strong. "I was over in the tech room gathering our exoskeletons and loading them into our vehicles."

Meghan cocked a brow. "Wow! You must have something special to be able to get that stuff. Those exoskeletons are by far the hardest items to get and also the most technological." She sounded inquisitive.

"You were already briefed about the importance regarding the next mission. Our team has priority and your father gave permission. I took control of gathering those exoskeletons." Stephan risked exposing himself to Meghan's sarcastic attitude but kept his demeanor relaxed. "By the way, where did you store those explosives?"

"They're already in the vehicles. I assume you knew that since you just put the exoskeletons in the vehicles." Meghan gave him a hazy stare.

Stephan smirked. "Of course I know. Just wanted to double tap you for that." He couldn't reason why he said that, just kept a straight face.

Meghan gawked at Stephan and shook her head. She

turned around and walked back to her stool, sat down, and typed another text message into her communicator.

Stephan opened his locker door, grabbed another message out of his pocket and slid it within a box located on the top level of his locker. He'd been collecting the messages for a few years; data regarding Dusty Rhodes. That data would justify the event Stephan awaited, the vengeance of his father's death.

Stephan closed his locker, grabbed a chair, and cleared his throat again. "Everyone drop what you're doing and pay attention!" He waited a few seconds until all were still and attentive, then took a seat.

He turned on the briefing screen and the eastern half of Texas displayed. An icon arrow projected a route to head east on Route 80 and merge into Highway 30.

"Our team will stop approximately ten miles from the Mesquite area so the city sensors don't alert. At the drop-off site, we'll get into the exoskeletons." These faster transport vehicles would move them at thirty miles per hour and had larger weapons. "Our route will then head along a dried-up creek bed for limited detection. Once the wall is breached, we'll head in and grab a computer processor from a residence. The information from that processor is key to learning the specific vulnerabilities of the city-state."

Meghan grunted. "Excuse me, Stephan, but how are we supposed to do this mission without getting hammered by their defenses?" Despite her challenging tone, she sent him a confused look.

"Good question. Our team is top priority on this mission, since we will breach the wall and acquire that needed technology. At the same time we are breaching the wall, other teams will attack around every city barrier to distract their security, a great feint!"

Meghan muttered something under her breath.

Silence reigned for a moment, and then Dirk, sitting beside her, said, "Say it out loud, Meghan."

Stephan shot a thankful look toward Dirk. Meghan's question was legitimate, and Dirk's calling her on it made him respect the man even more.

Meghan gave Dirk her trademark sarcastic stare before looking back at Stephan. "Why are you just now telling us this? Granted, our team has blown up many things, but I cannot believe we are just now attacking Dallas, we should have done this many years ago!"

The rest of the team started screaming, "Yeah!" and all looked at Stephan, who sat back in his chair.

"Well, if I were the commander, then we would have attacked that city many moons ago." He ground his molars together. "However, I can understand the need for the appropriate intelligence gathering to understand the proper way to defeat Dallas's technological superiority."

Stephan looked up at the wall then looked back at the members of the team. He brought his arm up and pointed his finger at the words painted on the wall.

OUR MISSION IS TO BRING THE STATE OF TEXAS BACK TO ENSURE OUR SURVIVAL AND HAPPINESS

The team stared at the wall, too, and Stephen sensed they were thinking of their families. These team members had all joined to bring the state back and ensure security. Now he had their attention. Now it was time to emphasize their purpose.

"Ya'll remember what happened in Austin several years ago. That group of patriotic citizens attempted to re-form the state government in Austin. When they traveled to Dallas to negotiate with the CSD, they were slaughtered and the Capitol Building in Austin was destroyed. How dare the current residents of Dallas perform an evil act and reject their inclusion in the State of Texas?" Stephan emphasized that historical moment before every mission, and this was the best time to remind them of it.

He stood and walked in front of the lighted wall. "You all know what our mission and focus are here. We also know that our specific mission is the most treacherous. I want you all to focus on your lanes, the specific lanes we have been going over for several days. You know as well as I that this evil city-state needs to be taken over and integrated back into this great state. I want you all to pack your stuff and meet me at the vehicles in an hour."

Dirk grinned at Stephan, who knew he passed this event with flying colors. Music was then turned back on, and the team began to pack their equipment. As Stephan looked around the room, he noticed looks of determination on most of the team members' faces. Meghan stared right at him with a serious expression. She began to chuckle. He smiled back at her and headed toward the door. When he flung it open and entered the hallway, she was right behind him. He stood still, breathing her light scent.

"Can I help you?"

Meghan's face looked serious again. "That's funny what you said, the evil mention of the city-state."

Stephan couldn't understand. "Come again, Meghan, what are trying to say?"

"You know as well as I that those idiots from Austin that went to CSD infected that lake in Dallas with poisons."

"I am shocked you know about White Rock Lake. Then again, you are Dusty's daughter."

"Come on, Stephan. You know as well as I that the intelligence-gathering mission we are about to partake in is essential, and we are way behind the power curve when it comes to defeating that fortress they call Dallas. My father's concept for this coalition is well thought out and he should not be blamed."

The muscles in the back of Stephan's neck tensed. "What are you trying to say?"

He leaned against the wall. How much did Meghan know about him and his thoughts? How *could* she know, unless someone helping Stephan told her? Did Dusty know? He tilted his head down to the floor so it would look like he was in deep thought.

Meghan bent her legs a little so she was in his field of vision and tilted her head up at him. He raised his head back up and looked her dead in the eyes. She took a breath.

"I know you have something against my father. I have seen the way you react to him and respond whenever he is mentioned. I honestly don't care if you do have something against him, I just want you to know that he was never a part of and has nothing to do with those idiots that initially tried to destroy Dallas." Family pride blazed in her eyes.

Stephan gave her a tight smile. "I know your father has nothing to do with that idiotic event, and I don't know why you would think I have something against him for what happened at the lake. There is a rationale for why he keeps that event a secret. Your father is a dedicated man and one that knows how to hold this coalition together."

Meghan looked defeated. "I guess my woman's intuition is a bit off on this one."

He tapped her arm in camaraderie. "Are you going to get back in there and pack your stuff?"

"You want to help me?" Meghan said, smirking again.

Stephan provided a deliberately sarcastic laugh as he slapped his hands against his sides. He turned away from her and headed down the hallway, thankful this meeting was over.

It dawned on him then, the promise he'd made. He did an about-face and yelled at Meghan while she was walking through the door.

"By the way, your father told me to tell you he needs to see you before we leave."

Chapter Six

Meghan packed her equipment more methodically than usual, wondering what her father wanted to talk to her about. Team members ridiculed her slowness, but she brushed aside their comments. She knew it was time to see her father—the team was deploying in an hour. She then asked a team member, who owed her favors, to load her bag into the vehicle. He frowned as she walked to the door, but Meghan tossed away that look. Her father's demand to see her before the mission took priority.

When she reached the Operations Center door, she looked into the iris device and heard the door click. She kept her gaze focused on Dusty's office at the end of the long hallway as she walked. When she came close, she noticed the room was full of planners watching monitors along the wall that displayed team's movements north and west. Meghan then noticed a suave man, one who always talked to her, as he stood to her right.

"Hi there, Miss Rhodes and welcome to the Operations Center. Are you here to see your father this fine day?"

"Well, aren't you a happy man." Meghan displayed a bleak face to him. She'd rather be with her team in the thick of a mission, capturing CSD technology, than cooped up in the Operations Center with every guy mentally undressing her.

"Why, thank you, Miss Rhodes, and might I tell you how wonderful you look today and..."

"Where is my father?" Meghan said, still looking forward.

"He's sitting in his back office with several of the planners." The man leered at her up and down.

Meghan walked closer to the office. She heard the man swallow and knew he'd turned his head to watch her. She could hear him follow her but was at the door and jerked it open before he could stop her. Every planner looked back in annoyance.

Her father was staring at a paper spread over his desk. His slumping posture made her wonder if everything was OK with him. He raised his head and smiled at her.

"Hi, sweetie, it's great to see you," Dusty said quietly.

Every officer in the room stopped what they were doing and stared at Meghan. She looked around the room and noticed a guy she used to date was in the back, a man her father had hooked her up with. She'd discarded him when he talked not to her, but to her chest. Two of the officers, one on each side of the desk, quickly wrapped the large paper that was spread out on the desk. All the others, except the guy she used to date, turned their heads back at Dusty. He blinked in dismissal, and the officers headed toward the door. Meghan just felt icky as they walked past her and said "hello". She didn't acknowledged one of them with a response, she kept looking at her father.

"Come on in, honey, and please sit down."

Meghan walked over to the front of the desk, sat down in the chair, and then kicked her feet up on top of the desk. "What's with all the officers in here before?"

Dusty fisted his hands together under his chin.

"How are you doing today, my lovely daughter?"

Still playing by his rules, then. Meghan displayed a stern face. "That is enough, Dad, I am going whether you like it or not!"

"I am pleased you are going on this mission and I look forward to what you bring back." Dusty gave her a weary smile.

He *wanted* her to go? He'd never said anything like that to her—prior to every other mission, he'd begged her to stay. She looked down for a few seconds, raised her head back up, and thought it best not to ask what was different this time. He would never tell her the truth.

"Good luck, and I look forward to your return." Dusty said with a proud stare.

"Umm, thanks, Dad. You don't have any questions for me?"

"Nope, I sure don't."

She yanked her feet off the desk, stood up, and headed toward the office door. It would be pointless to ask his real reason for calling her here. Holding the door open, she stopped. "Are you going to be here when I return?"

"Yes, I sure will." Dusty leaned back in his chair. "I love you very much, my little flower."

Meghan ambled out of the Operations Room with her sweaty hands clenched to her sides. Her father had never acted this way toward her. She shoved down her troubling thoughts, though; there was quite the mission ahead, one that needed her full attention.

Feeling a need to hit the latrine, she took a left and hurried down a hallway she normally didn't use. When she entered, the stalls were empty. She stepped into the one at the very end—these were the most peaceful ones, in her experience.

Sitting in the stall, she heard two voices, muffled and echoing. She ducked her head down but saw no feet in the room. With her head tilted to the side, it became obvious the voices were coming from above. She looked up at the air vent, and wondered where the ductwork went. A shaft of light spilled through the opening, hitting the opposite wall of the stall. After pulling up her trousers, she stood on the toilet seat and looked through the screen covering the vent. Visible through the screen was a rack filled with cleaners, toilet paper, and brushes. She then remembered the time she needed more toilet paper in that bathroom—seemed to happen to her in every bathroom—and knew the closet was next door. Who would be in the closet talking, and what were they saying? From the sound of the conversation she could tell the closet door must be closed, it was muffled, and since the hallways were long and noisy, she would hear some of that. She stood on the tips of her toes, turned her head sideways, and pressed her ear up against the vent.

Meghan heard a man and woman whispering. The conversation centered on the woman's poor living conditions at the station. Something about sharing a room with three other women. The conversation then turned to what the woman was doing and how she was gathering information about a person of interest. Then the woman's voice got louder.

"At one point in time our idea was right on target. The information gathered was great but lately the person of interest has been just too busy to gather additional…" The woman's voice grew muffled again, as though she'd turned away.

Meghan held her breath and pressed her ear harder against the vent. It hurt, but curiosity—and duty—trumped the pain. The woman then said something about the amount of data taken from the person's computer recently being encrypted. She asked the man if he had the technology to decrypt the files. The man whispered, and Meghan caught only his last two words, "I understand," before he thanked the woman for the information. The woman then informed him she was heading to the bathroom.

Meghan heard the closet door open and smirked. She was going to identify that woman. She jumped off the toilet and ran to the sink. She looked into the mirror with anticipation.

The door opened and a woman in a chef's outfit scurried into a stall. Meghan decided to wait since, she'd seen only the back of the woman. The toilet flushed and the stall door opened. Meghan recognized the woman but didn't know her name. She was Dusty's new chef, one her father gee-gawked about all the time.

Meghan shot her an abrupt smile. "Hello there. I'm sorry, I can't remember your name."

The woman looked startled. "My name is Dottie. I've seen you around. Just don't think we were introduced."

"My name is Meghan. I'm a team member." Meghan talked faster than normal.

"Wow, a team! I heard there are only a few women in the teams."

"How long have you been working here and where are you from?" Meghan's deliberately aggressive tone sent Dottie scuttling back a few inches.

"I'm originally from West Texas and have been working in here for several months."

"How did you get this job?"

Dottie looked uneasy and kept her gaze fastened on her reflection in the mirror. "I was asked to come and help. My father used to be a team member—that's how I got this job." Her voice sounded lackluster, as though the words were rehearsed.

"Who was your father, Dottie?"

Dottie cleared her throat and cast an annoyed look at her while she was drying her hands. Her reluctance to divulge information spurred Meghan's interest, and Meghan leaned her hip against the sink, waiting. Finally, the other woman spoke.

"He was a team member, the same as the UTC leader, Mr. Rhodes." Dottie's neck vein rapidly pulsed. "How did you get a job here?"

"Oh, I just got recruited by some members and went through some of the training," Meghan said nonchalantly, despite the gnawing anger growing inside her. Her father had never said a word about Dottie's father.

The two stared at each other for a few long seconds before Dottie tossed her paper towel into a trash bin.

"It was nice chatting with you, but I have to get back to the kitchen."

Dottie headed out of the room fast, and the door swung shut behind her. Meghan stood there and wondered whom she was talking with in the closet. She'd wanted to ask her so bad, but she'd learned in training that you had to know a person before asking the right questions.

When Meghan headed back to the team room a minute later, the hallways had an abnormal silence and emptiness. This upcoming mission encompassed every team. Her team was going to be the last one to leave, and her hour was almost over. As she entered the motor pool, several members of her team were loading the vehicles. Stephan and Dirk were checking the power packs on the exoskeletons. She hoped she still remembered how to use that suit, since it was last year when she finished training in it. When she got to her vehicle she asked when they were heading out. The driver told her they were all set and should be heading out in a few minutes.

Meghan reminded herself again that this mission was important and required her full attention. However, her meetings with her father and his female chef within this past hour had made her uneasy, and they kept taking over her thoughts.

Chapter Seven

"Mona, where is Ihan? I need to talk with him."

"Hello, Gerald Bacon. I'm sorry, but Ihan is currently asleep and ordered me not to disturb him for another two hours."

"So I guess he's done harvesting. I'm very impressed because others are still busy working their fields."

"He finished six hours ago and the inspectors were very impressed, too."

Gerald inclined his head and rubbed his neck. "Since I'm his Security Controller, I'm overriding his order. Wake him."

"Please hold while I wake him, Gerald."

Ihan lay fully clad on his stomach, in a deep sleep. A rumpled blanket covered half his body. A dim blue light surrounded the recessed ceiling while a gentle noisemaker emitted soothing sounds of water to caress the room. Within seconds, the noisemaker's volume decreased and the dim blue light altered to white that brightened all the walls. The bed then vibrated, turning Ihan over onto his side.

Mona's red light grew brighter. "Wake up Ihan, your Security Controller ordered me to wake you."

Ihan slammed awake, sitting upright in the matter of a second. He rubbed his eyes, then yawned as he frowned back at his clock. Gerald's face appeared on the monitor at the end of the bed.

Gerald squinted and looked down. "Hey, dude, wake up. I have something important to tell you."

"I am tired and have another two hours." Ihan flung a pillow on his face as he fell back.

"Get that pillow off your face and listen to what I have to say."

"Go away!"

Gerald raised an eyebrow then smirked. "A pack of rabbits broke into your field and ate all your plants."

Ihan immediately pulled the pillow off his face and sat up, staring right at the monitor winking quickly.

"About time you woke up, man!" Gerald smiled.

"Very funny about the rabbits. You're a SecureCon, can you exterminate them immediately so I have breakfast?" Ihan yawned and rubbed his eyes. "What is the important item you have for me?"

"You are by far the first Agricultural Controller done with harvesting, and your goods just arrived at the processing plant. Your name is being spread around the city and I honestly do believe you will be number one in this year's rating. Anyway, I wanted to let you know that I will no longer be your Security Controller and that I will be replaced by Shaun Keller."

Ihan bent his neck back. "You mean the Shaun that controls the area south of here?"

"Yeah, the same guy. He will be security controlling the north and south areas around you."

"What in the world is the deal with that, Gerald? I mean how safe am I supposed to feel now?" Ihan shot him a sarcastic glance. "What happens if those damn rabbits bust into my field?

As he fell back on his mattress, Ihan shivered with laughter. After a few congenial seconds, Ihan calmed down and looked up at Gerald, whose face was red with suppressed giggles. Then Gerald's face sobered.

"You have to understand that I will physically be moving to a residence near Highland Park in a couple of days."

"Security Headquarters? What are you going to be doing over there?"

"I wasn't told. I was ordered for the move."

"After the last Security Controller was transferred, we weren't able to chat with him ever again. Is that going to happen with you?"

"Honestly, I don't know, but I will try my best to keep in touch with you."

Ihan furrowed his brows. "Take care, buddy. I will hit you up to be my partner in the next game."

"See you sometime soon!" Gerald grinned.

Once the screen went blank, Ihan looked around the room and thought about how strange this move was. But then, it didn't matter if someone was physically moved to another location. The communications system was accurate, even omnipotent. Even if Ihan's best friend Roger Bell moved, he would still chat with him like he'd never moved. His thoughts rumbled more. Gerald's moving didn't matter, but it still hurt for some reason.

After getting out of bed and walking into the kitchen,

Ihan grabbed a bowl of oatmeal out of the refrigerator and dispensed a squirt from the water line. He placed the bowl on the counter and pushed the one-minute button. He then saw red lines coming down that identified the direct microwave-laser current. Once the buzzer sounded, Ihan grabbed the bowl and headed to the table that was still full of boxes. He noticed a clean floor but the normal box area was empty. He assumed Mona had finished cleaning the floor but hadn't gotten around to the boxes yet. He sat down and ate his oatmeal, which tasted like apples and apricot—his favorite.

He then headed back to his bedroom to consider what his duties were today. With a sarcastic smile, he stuck his lower lip out and tapped his back. The day was empty. His duties were done.

Ihan knew he would soon have to clean the field since the timing was close to replanting the scheduled seeds. He remembered his tasking for removing the baseline of apples and replacing with a non-food item, cotton. This tasking disturbed him. Cotton planting would taint his soil, forcing him to replace the field if he was ever tasked to replant a fruit or vegetable.

As Ihan sat on his bed and stretched his arms high, he looked up against the wall, where Mona's camera was, and pointed at it. The lights dimmed and noisemaker got louder. "Thanks, Mona, and let me know if anything comes up." Ihan put his head down on the pillow and closed his eyes.

Mona waited until Ihan's respiration slowed, indicating sleep.

Back in the main room, robotic arms rose from the

floor, moving the boxes from the table and putting them back into the designated space. The dishwasher began, and a cleaner was sprayed along the counter, moistening the surface and evaporating quickly.

Laundry was Mona's next chore, but she hesitated for a nanosecond. She knew Ihan viewed her recent actions strangely. She internally debated waking him to explain. Mona then dismissed this thought, since an explanation would cause an alarm to be triggered.

CHAPTER EIGHT

The convoy sped along a desolate road leading to the team's drop-off site. Stephan kept his main focus upon his positioning system, sparing a brief glance at his watch. He'd traveled this route several times and it was by far the fastest; the convoy would arrive even quicker than he'd anticipated. For once, they'd had no slowdowns or setbacks the entire trip.

He twisted around and raised his eyebrows at the guy in the backseat monitoring his radar. The radar tech shook his head—nothing in sight.

Everything in the vicinity of the convoy was still, too. A few dried-up plants were blowing across the streets. The decaying buildings and signs made him realize this area was absent of any humans. That meant they'd entered the thirty-mile barrier, established many years back by the City-State of Dallas to keep away all infected people. UTC had eliminated many sensors in the past several years. A twenty-mile limit now existed.

Several miles down the road, the vehicles slowed down. Stephen grasped the door tightly, raised his head, and noticed they'd reached the dried riverbed, where the ground dropped sharply. The vehicles headed off the road to the left and dipped into the steep banks. When Stephan's vehicle reached the bottom of the riverbed, it picked up speed again, jolting over a path littered with stones and small boulders.

Within minutes, the positioning system alerted their arrival. He stopped his vehicle and made sure the convoy fell in behind. Stephan opened his door and crawled onto the roof of the vehicle.

Holding his body high, he circled his arms. The team turned off their vehicles and unloaded their gear. Jumping off the vehicle, Stephan walked back along the convoy to review his team. Everyone moved fast, and though some of the newer team members looked scared, they didn't slow down. When their vehicles were emptied, the team put their packs along their backs and started to line up in single file. Looked like his training had stuck with them. Stephan threw them a grin.

As soon as he got to the front of the line, he raised his arm and circled his hand before heading west along the riverbed. The heavy gear they carried would sap the team's energy, so he walked slowly. They had about two miles to hike into the staging area.

About forty-five minutes later, Stephan looked down at his mapping gear and knew they were just north of the staging area. He stopped the team and told them to rest. The team threw off their gear and sat down. Some of the members looked tired. Others took off their boots to check their feet. Stephan was amazed how such a short walk had drained his team, but he didn't comment; this was the first time they'd carried such heavy gear.

While the others enjoyed their break, Stephan decided to check for sensors above the riverbed. He tossed his knapsack to the ground and removed the sensor detector. He then extended the ten-foot pole and rubbed the thick layer of dust off the lens. After he walked to the riverbank, Stephan braced his back against it so he could stand straight and still. Once he raised the pole above the riverbank, he flipped the switch.

Waiting for the sensor results, Stephan surveyed his team. Dusty's warning about keeping Meghan safe rankled him. All the members were his responsibility, and he took their safety seriously. All of them had families, brothers, and mothers. He would make sure each of them made it through this mission. At the bottom of the pole, a red light blinked. Stephan pulled the pole down and collapsed it.

"What's the deal?"

"Well Dirk, the deal is not good, the sensors are active here. It looks like our planning session was wrong and we possibly were using old data. Bottom line is we will have to rethink an infiltration route, and fast. Hopefully a route that will lessen our exposure."

Stephan put the pole back in his bag and knelt down. He affixed his fingers to his temples and rubbed hard. This dry heat gave him headaches. He waved to his sides and heard the team shuffle closer. Stephan unfolded a map and placed a few stones along its edges to keep it from blowing away. After viewing it for a few seconds, his eyes widened.

"OK. This is our new infiltration route." Stephan's finger slowly brushed the route. The team concurred by shaking their heads. "Time to ensemble the exoskeletons.

Dirk and I will personally inspect your riggings to make sure assembly is correct. Make it happen."

Stephan then stood confidently and gazed into everyone's eyes longer than usual. The team looked invigorated as they jetted back to their packs and laid out the exoskeleton devices with grim efficiency. He bent down and unpacked his own bag.

Dirk, next to him, aligned his items in order. Dirk smiled.

"You ready for some assistance in putting that costume on?"

Stephan tilted his head. "From the most experienced. Of course."

Holding the weighted power belt around his midsection, Stephan wrapped it behind him and felt Dirk lock it together. He stood upright as Dirk attached the flexible steel leg components to the power belt. Stephan then held his arms out so Dirk could attach those. Then Dirk raised his shirt and affixed the medical assessment device to his skin—it monitored blood pressure and heart rate. Stephan lowered his arm components, and Dirk connected the machine gun units to both. On top of each gun unit, Dirk tightly slid the ammunition storage unit and wrapped the visible cable over the shoulder. Stephan then rested his arm unit on Dirk's shoulder and felt the squeeze of the foot units over his boots. This made Stephan two inches taller. He raised his arms over his head and watched Dirk inspect the riggings. Finished, Dirk smacked his rear hard. Stephan stumbled a few steps forward.

"Nice!" Stephan said sarcastically, squeezing his eyes

shut at the sting of the blow. "We'll see how your inspection results." He then raised one eyelid.

"Had to make sure you knew I was done." Dirk kept a serious face.

"Just get your belt on." Stephan shook his head.

Stephan then helped Dirk attach his exoskeleton. He inspected and tapped him lightly, at which Dirk gave a waggish smirk. Both of them checked the rest of the team members, inspecting their assembled outfits for proper attachment and electrical connections.

Meghan was Stephan's last inspection. He spent extra time on her exoskeleton, double-checking her boots and electrical connections. When he was satisfied all was as it should be, he tapped her rear and walked around to the front of her. He looked her square in the face and smiled encouragingly.

"Are you ready for the hike to the target?" He rubbed his hands together.

"Of course I am, and I think you can remember me beating you in the run we did last week." Meghan elegantly blinked.

Stephan squinted. "You would remind me of that, wouldn't you Meghan."

"Of course I would. You know how much of a trouble-maker I can be."

"True."

Meghan fidgeted in her outfit. "Why did you slap my butt and not all the others?"

"Because yours is softer and it wouldn't hurt my hand."

Meghan looked at him with mild contempt. "Real funny, smartass."

Once the team stood up, they got in their formation line and stared at Stephan expectantly. He studied his digital mapping device for a moment and set their location. The time associated with their current location was better than most of the missions in the past. They were performing well as a team. Stephan noted their current location and then plugged the coordinates where their target vicinity was.

Stephan chose two of the team members to be on point and maintain a considerable distance. If they were detected, the rest of the team could turn and head back. Those two members had the most experience in the exoskeleton suits.

The two headed out to the west. With each step they took, they flung a few feet into the air and fifteen feet forward. Stephan flexed his legs in his suit. It normally took a few days of training to just get used to the exoskeleton, but the suits had been a last-minute addition to the mission. He couldn't remember the last time he'd trained in one. Stephan threw that thought to the side. He would remember.

Staring down at his device, Stephan counted down the two minutes. Once he saw the twenty-second mark, he looked back at the team and raised his arm. The seconds hit zero, and he dropped his arm and started moving, gaze still fixed on the mapping device.

After the first step, he stumbled, then immediately threw his other leg down to maintain balance. He looked up and stuck his arms out for balance while he halted.

After turning his head around to look back at the team, all of them laughing. Stephan relaxed his muscles and shook his head. He couldn't believe he'd let himself become so focused on direction and timing again. During past missions, he'd been too focused on the details of missions, movements, and timing, to the detriment of his ability to be an effective leader. He told himself not to focus on specifics, just go with the flow of operations. He placed his foot forward, then the next, and began walking at a good pace.

Stephan heard each team member moving behind him. He increased his pace. Most of the members would be staring down at the ground and looking for obstructions that would potentially make them fall. After a few minutes, the team's steps and movements synched into a rhythmic pulse.

In the distance, the sky was clear and dark, with stars peeking down. The sun was just below the horizon and the team headed into the falling orange sunset.

A little while later, Stephan looked at his grid coordinate location and then checked his timing. He was shocked, but pleased, that his location was closer than his timing. After stepping along the riverbed for several more miles, he took the team up a ravine that flattened enough so the members could easily rise out of the shallows.

Stephan then halted the team. He checked the sensor detection device again and found them clear. In the short distance, Stephan identified a small hill, one they stayed behind. He felt confident because this was the location he planned for starting the attack. He pulled out his communicator.

"Point men, hold your current position at the foot of the hill and wait for us to arrive."

"Roger that, we have actually been here for a few minutes and are now drinking some Jack Daniels."

Stephan grinned. "Very funny, we'll be there shortly."

When the team arrived at the base of the hill, Stephan found the two point men drinking water and gnawing beef jerky. He clapped each of them on the shoulder, then headed to the edge of the hill to put out his sensor detection device. When Stephan walked back over to the group, he knelt down and looked at his timer. It was currently 1810 hours. The attack was scheduled for 1830 hours—end of evening nautical twilight. He then noticed the rest of the team stared at the two point men. Their mouths worked as though they were salivating.

"We're several minutes early. If any of you want to eat and drink please go ahead."

He considered the city wall he'd seen when he set the sensor detector. The vertical design of the wall interested him because at the top it curled out and faced the ground—virtually impossible to scale. Using the wall approach meant placing explosives. Blowing a five-foot hole a foot above ground would provide a large enough entry for the exoskeletons.

Stephan grabbed some venison jerky out of his pack. He took a bite, and then heard subdued explosions in the distance. Team members turned their heads to the right. Stephan pulled his device out and checked the time. Several members walked toward him looking confused and angry.

Stephan widened his eyes. "Ok guys, calm down and let's stay on our toes. Either one of the other teams got compromised or they attacked too early."

"What are we going to do now that the Dallas security will be on high alert?" A fidgeting team member demanded.

"We hopefully will start hearing other explosions so that all the teams will synchronize and mesh all the angles of the attack."

Stephan picked up his weapon. Most of the team already stood, and the others were lunging up in their exoskeletons. It was time.

"All of you grab your weapons and leave the supplies. This area will be the fallback location if we get compromised. Dirk, you and Jason grab the explosive bags and let's get moving."

The team hefted their weapons. Many turned off the safeties. They all lined up in formation, with the lead to the left.

"The two-member advance party will begin the low crawl once you get around the edge of the hill. Thirty seconds later, the main body will follow in the low crawl as well. The remaining two will stay here and monitor the rear for ground and air movement." Stephan tapped his sides and threw a forceful grin to his team.

When the two team members got to the edge of the hill, they got down on their knees and looked back. Stephan looked down at his timer—1816 hours—before he stuck his arm out and pointed his finger. The two turned their heads back to the front, got on their bellies, and began low crawling around the hill. In a matter of seconds they were out of sight.

The speed of those exoskeleton suits, in the horizontal position, impressed Stephan. He looked at his timer, moving his finger up and down. He then raised his head and saw Meghan standing third in the line. Her head was moving up and down with his finger. He smiled at her and she smiled back.

Once the thirty seconds mark hit, Stephan got in the front of the line and told the team to follow him. All got on their bellies and started low crawling. Members kept their heads turned to the side and let their helmets drag the ground.

Feeling the rocks drag along his ears bothered Stephan. He tilted his head up and saw the advance party reach the wall. Stephan kept his head high to observe them. Both members unloaded their bags and caulked the walls with glue. They then put the thermal detection device along the wall. A red light began blinking, indicating a room was behind the wall in that location. Stephan let out a thankful breath.

Shooting out his distance laser, Stephan ascertained he was one hundred feet from the wall. He halted and swung both his arms to his sides. Most of the team crawled around him in both directions and formed a line.

Dirk and another member kept crawling till they reached the wall. They took off their packs, rose to their knees, and pulled out the string-laden explosives. Dirk started sticking his explosive string on the lower left side and the other member on the right. After a few seconds both of them came together in the middle and up on their toes—they were the same height. They cut the strings, put the remainder back into the bags, and crawled back.

Stephan heard several distant explosions and gunfire. He then heard sounds of flying objects, all around, but none were near the team's position. A tapping on his back alerted him. Dirk raised his thumb on top of the explosive trigger. Stephan looked both ways again and yelled, "Put your heads down!" All the members slammed hard to the ground. Stephan looked at Dirk. "Fire it up."

Stephan felt the thump, and then heard the boom. His ears rang. When he raised his head, the smoke and dust settled, and a rectangular hole gaped in the wall. Trembling and numb, he raised himself to a standing position. "Move out."

A team member stood up, pointed his weapon forward, and ran toward the opening. Members to his left and right followed him in. Stephan then headed toward the opening. He felt Meghan behind him. When he got several feet inside the opening, he stopped to assess the room they'd entered.

Squinting, Stephen saw several monitors along the right-hand corner. An overturned chair lay on the floor. Stephan then realized the room was dark. They needed light.

"Disperse the lighting pack."

He saw Meghan kneeling on the floor with her opened bag.

"Already got that, Stephan." She pulled out a tube and pointed high. "Everybody duck."

Stephan bent down and put his arm over his face. He heard Meghan slam the button, followed by a loud shatter. Stephan cautiously looked up saw many lighting packs stuck to the ceilings and walls. The room was bright, its contents clearly visible.

Walking back to the corner where he'd seen the monitors, Stephan stopped by a desk. Underneath it were several CPUs, battery packs, but no central processor.

Stephan tapped his sides. "Meghan, trace the connector circuits to their source. I bet the central processor is either in the wall or up in the ceiling."

Meghan examined the systems, still on her knees. She turned them around and viewed how the circuits were fashioned and oriented. All the circuits were facing up. She looked up at the ceiling, then grabbed a rod out of her bag and extended it to its full length. Stephan wrapped his hands around the rod, covering hers. She grunted, then accepted his help with the heavy implement. They raised it to the ceiling, tapped several spots, and could hear nothing but hollow sounds. Then they hit a spot and heard a thump. He squinted and made out a small rectangular line around an area approximately two feet long and one foot wide.

Stephan winked at Meghan. "I believe we found it and it's located above our heads. We're going to need some help taking it down because I don't know how heavy this is going to be."

"Let's grab that laser cutter out of your bag and cut around those lines. We don't want to cut that thing." The lines of tension on Meghan's face relaxed, and Stephan suddenly had to work hard to keep his mind on the mission.

Meghan rummaged through his bag and pulled the

laser cutter out. He held it up and cut an inch outside of the lines. Another team member arrived and held his hands up. After the final cut, Stephan held his hand high as the ceiling board dropped. It thumped down on both their hands, and they braced themselves under the heavy weight.

"Way to go, people." They weren't home yet, but they were close. "We've captured our objective."

The box was eased down to the floor. An electronic clicking then commenced.

"Ihan. What is the problem and why are you moving me?" a bossy female voice demanded.

Stephan looked at Meghan. They both raised their eyebrows. A red light on the wall got brighter. Meghan grabbed the cut board from the floor and held it in front of the red light.

"What's going on in this room, and what happened to the last ten minutes?" the voice said.

Stephan looked down at the processor and noticed an antenna piece in the back. Meghan wrapped tape around the cut board, securing it to the wall. Then she looked at the antenna, too. He tapped her shoulder and crossed his hand in front of his neck. Meghan slid the antenna out, dropped it on the floor, and pushed the processor over a few feet. He was happy she'd understood. Stephan waved two team members over with a box. The box had lead-laced lining that would deflect any transmissions. Both members lifted the processor, placed it within the box, and locked it with a four-digit code. Once the box was lifted, Stephan followed the two members toward the opening.

"Stephan, get in this room. Now." Dirk yelled.

Turning back, Stephan saw a light moving in the back of the building. He ran toward it. In the doorway, he stopped and looked around the room. There were two team members on either side of a mattress pad. The pad was off the bed and against the far wall. He walked closer. The mattress was thrown back on the bed. Stephan flashed his light in the area. A still body lay on the floor, curled in a fetal position. He approached with caution and noticed that it was a male. He knelt beside the form and put his fingers on the neck to check the pulse.

"He's alive." He shook the man's shoulders and turned him over on his back.

"Who the hell is that?" Meghan said, rushing into the room with widened eyes.

Stephan slowly shook his head. "I don't know. He's alive but unconscious."

He got back on his feet and walking to the door, motioning for the team to follow him.

Meghan gasped. "Where are you going? We have to take him with us."

Stephen bent his head and bit back a retort about why women didn't belong on missions. "No we don't. We have the processor and that is our mission task."

"Didn't you hear the voice emanating from that processor? It must have been asking for this guy. If the processor is that technologically advanced, we're going to need him to get us into it."

Stephen scowled. "You bring up a good point, Meghan. Granted, taking the person back with us will be extra weight and will slow us down, but you're right, we will probably need him."

"That is if he stays alive," Dirk said with a smile.

"Right." Stephan pointed at Dirk and one of the other team members. "You two, carry him."

Dirk and the other member moved to the person's head and feet, bent down, and gently picked him up.

Stephan sobered at the delay. "We have to get the hell out of this building and back to the rally point." He slapped his legs. "Move out!"

They cleared the room, and he walked toward the entrance. Despite a few changes in plan, the mission was a success. He gazed the wall and was impressed how clean the blown parts were.

When he stepped out of the opening, Stephan turned his head to the right and left and counted the team members who were kneeling down against the wall. "Back to rally point!" The team members lined up and moved out. Stephan looked to the right and pointed at the member who was guarding the side. He ran behind the line.

When Stephan turned his head to the left he saw the last team member grinning at him. Just when he raised his arm to tell the member to move out, he noticed something moving on top of the wall, directly above the team member. He looked up. A SecureCon crouched atop the outward curve of the wall, its weapons arm angled down to target the team member below it. Stephan felt cold as he clenched his hands. He grabbed his weapon and raised it, taking aim.

The team member saw Stephan raising his weapon and looked above him. Multiple rounds fired instantly.

The weapon on the end of the SecureCon's arm spun like a circular machine gun, belching out numerous rounds.

A split second later, Stephan fired his weapon at the SecureCon. It leaped off the top of the wall, flew through the air, and landed about one hundred feet to the left of the team members. Stephan continued to fire his weapon. The rest of the team members scrambled to raise their weapons. The SecureCon opened fire at the rear of the team, who immediately dropped to the ground and rolled. Two members, in front, raised their weapons and opened fire. The SecureCon swiveled to stare at the team members firing at it. It took many rounds, but stood unharmed as it loaded more rounds into its gun canister.

The last gleam of twilight revealed a sliver of an opening on its neck. The wires along the body of the robot leading to the head were exposed. Stephan re-aimed his weapon and looked through the digital sights. The thermal sight showed the red outline of the wires going up the neck. He pushed the button, locked the sight, and squeezed the trigger. When Stephan lowered his weapon, the SecureCon's head was dangling to its side. Vast amounts of liquid flowed from its wires. Other team members continued to fire. One of the bullets hit the chest plate, and the liquid sparked and exploded. The entire top half of the robot flew into the air. Its legs wobbled, then buckled, and the robot crashed to the ground, sending up a plume of dust.

Stephan gazed at the disgruntled team. They looked healthy. He then saw the blood-ridden body of one team member, the man who'd been the last to leave the wall. No movement. He ran over and slid to his knees. Several rails attached to the exoskeleton were snapped and pro-truding outward. Stephan's fingers shook as he touched the man's neck—no pulse. Stephan pulled his hand back and bent his head down. Dirk slid to his knees.

"Can we save him, Stephan, or is he gone?"

Stephan looked up at Dirk and shook his head. With damp eyes, Stephan watched Dirk close the team member's eyelids. He looked back and waved over another team member. Once Dirk looked back, he put his hand on Stephan's shoulder.

"Boss, the rest of us are still here. We can expect another SecureCon soon. We must get out of here now."

Stephan nodded, his lips curling with grief. Dirk lifted up their fallen comrade's body, the tendons on his neck standing out with the strain, and carried it toward the rest of the team.

Stephan angrily looked back at the site. Their next return would be the city's destruction. He vowed that. With his pulse throbbing in his head, Stephan whirled around and caught up with the team, all of them moving at good speed. He hoped their return to base was safe.

Each time he looked at the limp, sickly form of the unconscious prisoner, who they brought with them at the expense of one of their own, disgust coiled into a hard lump in the pit of his stomach.

Chapter Nine

As he turned the shower off, Mayor Jerry Adams pondered his city's defense. He knew his security manager had the experience to thwart an attack, but could the man be trusted? A buzzing sound echoed through his residence.

Jerry pursed his lips. "Liz, please tell me why the annoying call buzzer is going off."

"Excuse the buzzer, sir. Your assistant, Roger Buss, desperately wants to tell you something," Liz said in a benevolent voice.

Shaking his head, Jerry wiped the towel over his legs. He stepped out of the shower and walked over to his sink while wrapping the towel around his waist. He pondered what was going to be said, second-guessing himself at every turn though he loathed this new self-doubt.

"OK, Liz, put him through."

"Sir, I have an update to our current situation."

Jerry aggressively rolled his hand. "Well, I am waiting to hear."

"Yes sir. We pushed away numerous UTC attackers that surrounded the city and have them retreating."

"And what is new about this? I've been watching for

the past hour and ordered our security manager to pursue those worthless coalition fiends. We need to know where they're headed."

Roger gulped. "One of the residences on the east side of the city was attacked and violated. I hate to say it sir but they stole a processor and the resident is missing."

"You mean to tell me that a sensitive processor was stolen?" He sounded too serene. "And we have no idea where that resident is?" Jerry bellowed. Much better.

He turned off the sink and stared out of the floor-to-ceiling window as though distraught. The city's skyline looked calm. He walked closer to the window, placed his arm against it, and bowed his head. When he'd stood that way long enough to reinforce the image of a man who'd been dealt a devastating blow, he returned to the monitor. Roger's face was composed.

"The SecureCon that patrolled that area was destroyed outside of the city walls. A city wall was explosively penetrated. When we examined the area, we noticed the resident was missing. We then reviewed outer wall motion sensor footage and noticed a body being carried. I ascertain it's that resident."

"So who is the resident?"

"His name is Ihan Duncan. He was going to be awarded the best Agricultural Controller of the year."

"Of course I know who he is. That man has been rated number two for several years. I just signed his award today. This is the first time the city has been internally attacked, and they hit the most productive agricultural area. I order you to get the External Security Unit together and chase, find, and recover that processor."

"What about that resident, Ihan?"

Jerry blinked. "Of course."

"No problem, sir, you won't be disappointed."

Jerry turned around and walked into the living room. The elegant archway was rimmed with gold. The natural hardwood floors gleamed. He headed straight to his silver-wrapped agarwood bar. He grabbed a bottle of Armadale Vodka and poured until the glass was full. Then he turned to stare out his three-story window at the city lights as he drank the whole glass.

"Liz. Make sure no calls get through for the next few hours, I want to lie down and take a nap."

"Would you like me to send in your standard comfort assistant?"

"Not tonight, Liz. I need to rest."

"No problem, sir, and I will dim the lights once you get in bed."

Jerry strolled through his expansive living room. He trailed his hand across silver-lined console with ivory jewel box and the Kinsale crystal globe that gleamed on top. He kept his eyes focused out the large window and looked across the city. He thought of how many advances he'd fashioned during his tenure. This recent attack might produce bad effects, especially in the eastern portion of the city, which sorely needed development. The possible disturbance to the residents living there made him hunch his shoulders. Jerry suddenly crossed his arms.

"Liz!"

"Yes sir."

"Get my assistant on the net now!"

Jerry turned around and returned to the bar. He

slammed down his glass and filled with vodka, then gulped the drink fast. He walked back to the window and drummed his fingers on the glass until Roger appeared on the monitor.

"What do you need, sir?"

"Tell me how many residents in the Mesquite area know about this attack. I expect you to say only a few."

"We did an evaluation for two blocks around the attacked residence. We determined that only the neighbors to the left and right were aware. The initial attacks on the west and south sides of the city were broadcasted, but not the area you are asking about."

Jerry smirked. "Make sure nothing gets circulated about that incident, and immediately move those surrounding residents to another area. Inform them that a security test was performed for their safety. The bottom line state of affairs is that we did this for them. Go forth and do it!"

"Yes sir, I will get our Internal Control Division on this."

"No, Mr. Buss. You will take the lead on this and make sure it gets done."

Roger raised eyebrows. "Excuse me, sir. You do remember that you tasked me to conduct the other important project. If I work both, I'm uncertain about projected timing."

"OK." Jerry hesitated. "I will appoint another lead, but I want you to make sure we are headed in the right direction. Monitor the media output."

"I will, sir. I would also like to remind you of the statement you will televise in a few hours."

Jerry raised his arm and crossed his hand in front of his neck. The connection turned off. He raised his eyebrow and waited for a few seconds before he sauntered to his bedroom. The Chinese furniture and decorations within the bedroom were arranged in an ornamental manner, bamboo within vases along the floor, gold-framed pictures along the walls, and teak furniture. Once he sat down on the bed, he turned his head and viewed a large curtain along the top of the wall. "Close the curtain, Liz." It slowly descended to the floor. The lights dimmed as Jerry sighed. He flopped back on the bed, closed his eyes, and attempted to fall asleep. But the statement he'd written yesterday plagued his thoughts.

CHAPTER TEN

Ordered to monitor the captive, Meghan grudgingly sat in her vehicle, giving his scrawny form an occasional cursory glance. He hadn't moved since they found him. Of course, being the only woman on the team, she'd been assigned babysitting duty. Her team had traveled roads that were little more than dusty tracks for several hours and finally halted for rest. Here, the road still showed traces of asphalt. She looked at her positioning system and noticed they were in Athens. Meghan thought of her father. He'd mentioned something about hamburgers in relation to this town. But that had been decades ago. Athens was as desolate and grimy as any other town in this godforsaken place. Her stomach growled anyway.

To give herself something to focus on besides her hunger or the pathetic prisoner, Meghan cleaned her pistol. She cherished the piece. Its shiny pink plastic edges along the grip always brought back the memory of her father presenting it to her on her fifteenth birthday. She slid the brush in and out of the barrel as she tapped her feet on the ground, whistling her favorite song, "Barracuda."

A foul smell overpowered her reminiscence. Now that

the convoy had stopped, and there was no wind circulating through the vehicle, it was more pungent. Swerving her nose, Meghan looked around the back of the vehicle. There were only a few boxes and some open food wrappers. Across from her feet, the captive lay in silence on the plastic sheet. He was so skinny that the arcs of his ribs stood out under the fabric of his shirt. What was wrong with the guy? What the hell did he do in his pants, Meghan thought. She cringed and shook her head.

She then looked down at her boots and noticed a dark glob on the outside of her right boot. "Great, my new boots are ruined." She grabbed a splintered stick from the floor, swiped off a little, and the bad smell got worse. She raised the end of the stick to her nose, sniffed, then threw the stick to the other side of the vehicle. "Oh! That is nasty!" Meghan stood up, opened the tailgate, and jumped out of the vehicle.

Meghan complained to herself with her hands on her hips. She was starving. She'd stepped in crap. She was considered not a full team member but the team child minder. She shook her head, whirled in a circle, and gave the vehicle a vicious kick. Dirk moseyed around the vehicle.

"What in the world are you dancing to?"

Meghan bared her teeth and snarled. "I cannot stand this crap!"

He responded with his trademark smirk, the one he usually saved just for her. With a rifle slung over his shoulder, he stood there grinning until she noticed his hands were filled with plump, green apples.

Meghan's mouth watered. "Where did you get those?"

"There's a tree about five hundred yards behind the building. It's the first green apple tree I've ever seen. I ate two of them back there and thought I would bring some for everyone." Dirk moved closer. "Do you want one?"

Meghan scuffed her soiled boot on the crumbling road. "Thinks he can make me a babysitter, then buy me off with apples," she muttered. Dirk sneered and headed up the stairs into the building, taking the luscious fruit with him.

"Wait for me!" Meghan trounced closer to Dirk, slamming her boot on the pavement. Once they stepped through the door, Meghan noticed most of the team members were unpacking the boxes, and setting up the computers and communication systems. Dirk bent his arms and laid the apples on the table. Three of the teammates looked at the fruit and grinned. They closed in on the pile and grabbed as many as they could. Dirk turned around, tossing an apple up and down in his hand, and walked over toward Stephan, who was sitting on a box typing into his hand-held computer. Meghan kept close.

"Stephan, when do you want us to bring in that body and processor?" Dirk said.

Stephan slammed his fist along the keyboard. "What is wrong with this thing?"

Dirk tossed an apple at Stephan. He raised his left arm and caught it, still staring at the computer screen. Meghan was impressed. Dirk shrugged, then knelt next to Stephan.

"We have two air sensors set on the rooftops to the

buildings situated to the north and south. A member is on duty for the next four hours placing road sensors in locations where we can view most of the streets in town that head this way."

"Thanks, Dirk." He bit into the apple. "Mm. Granny Smiths, my favorite. When I was a kid, my mother would bring me to an apple orchard and let me run around with a bucket. I would eat the whole day or until the bucket was empty."

Meghan found his emotional shift surreal. Stephan's clear-headed thinking and decision-making skills were all she knew. Even Dirk showed interest.

"Glad to see you smiling, boss. Is everything OK with you?"

Stephan's eyebrows rose, and he turned his head and smiled at Dirk. "I must say, Dirk, that is the most insightful feeling I have ever seen come out of you. I'm fine. But I need to understand what's going on with our current situation and how long we can stay in Athens until we make our next move. I haven't been able to communicate with base camp. It seems our communication system is active, just no connection."

"Are they aware of what we successfully retrieved from our attack?"

"I don't see how." Stephan looked at Meghan. "Have you been able to communicate with base?"

Meghan shook her head.

"I guess the worst probable case is Dallas somehow blocking our communications," Dirk said.

"That could be the case, but we won't truly know until we get closer. By the way, does Trinity Valley still have generators? We were told that many were still here and functioning."

"Roger that. I checked the two of them before I went shopping." Dirk grabbed his weapon from the floor and stood back up.

Stephan clasped his hands together. "Meghan." He stared deep into her eyes. "Did you bring in the captive?"

Meghan hunched her shoulders and widened her eyes. "No."

"Who's guarding him?"

"No one."

"So you disobeyed a direct order?"

"He smells like crap, Stephan. Who would take that?" Meghan glanced down at her stained boot, then quickly pulled her gaze back up to meet Stephan's.

She worked harder at looking forlorn, and Stephan finally shook his head. "Good thing I'm tired." He stared into his computer. "You and Dirk please bring that captive in."

"Roger that."

Meghan and Dirk headed through the door. She tapped Dirk's shoulder.

"What's up with our communicators? I've been trying to get a message out to a buddy of mine for the past twenty minutes, and it keeps getting kicked back. He's on the team that went to the north, and I would like to know his status."

"I'm sure he is thinking same." Dirk's posture stiffened. "Isn't he the guy you grew up with in San Antonio?" Yearning filled his stare.

"Yes." Meghan raised an eyebrow. This wasn't the first time Dirk sounded jealous. "Are you going to help me bring this passed-out guy into the building?"

Dirk gave a sudden wink and smiled. "I guess you're fed up watching this captive and ready to take a nap?"

"I'm tired. We've been up for over twenty-four hours, and sleep is my weakness."

"Well then, let's get this captive out of the truck and put him in that room."

Both of them hopped in the back of the vehicle and pushed the cot to the end of the open tailgate. As they carried the cot into the building, most of the team was quiet and stared the captive in the face.

They entered a room, and Meghan looked at Dirk as they dumped the captive on the bed. Dirk disassembled the cot, and Meghan grabbed a medical bag. She took out shot needles and a bottle of smallpox vaccine. Meghan rubbed the captive's pale left arm with alcohol, and injected the serum. Once she withdrew the needle, she placed a cotton swab over the site and taped it down. Meghan then contemplated the captive's dubious health. The bruised bump on his head looked painful, but it was minimal compared to other injuries she seen lately. Still, she couldn't help but feel a little sorry for him. He hadn't asked for any of this.

The torn flesh of their fallen team member, killed because she'd insisted they take extra time to bring the captive out with them, filled her vision. Blinking away sudden moisture in her eyes as she exited the room, she vowed to keep her emotions buried.

Meghan dropped to the floor next to Stephan and

untied her boots. She crossed her legs and began massaging her feet. Stephan was still on his computer mapping out his future routes and planning out different courses of action. He sighed heavily, then closed the lid on his laptop.

"Were you able to get him mended?"

"Yes. I sanitized his head wound on the ride here then immunized him in the back room. He is by far the lightest and most pale person I have ever seen."

"That is what happens when you are alone all your life. He probably has never physically seen another person. I don't know how we're going to handle his first encounter. But I'm sure you will be the best person since you are a woman. A good-looking one, by the way." Stephan kept a straight face. "That should make the first encounter comfortable."

Meghan lunged forward. "What are you talking about? I may be a woman but you damn well better remember I'm more like a man with boobs."

Stephan's deadpan expression cracked, and he laughed until he grabbed his stomach and shook his legs.

"That's so true. By the way, you look awful. You should hit the rack for some needed sleep."

"What about you? The last I heard you haven't slept in a couple of days."

"Well, the best way for us to deal with this Dallas captive is to set up some sort of system to monitor him in the room, that way our first communication will be what he's used to."

Meghan kept her eyes open with effort. "Good idea.

And then you want me to be the first to talk with him when he awakens."

"You are spot on with that one. Please get some sleep, and I'll get you when he awakens."

It had darkened outside and the interior of the building was dimming. Meghan noticed most of the team was asleep, some on the floor, a few on cots, the rest on tables. She yawned as she fell back on her cot and closed her eyes. Interacting with this captive kept bewildering her thoughts. The appropriate training and personal information was nonexistent, but she probably was the best choice—the captive's processor voice was female. She took a deep breath, and fatigue pressed down on her. She dozed off.

CHAPTER ELEVEN

Ihan opened his eyes and saw a bright light. He immediately raised his arm to shield his eyes. His head throbbed. "Ouch!" He lightly tapped around his forehead and felt a taped cloth.

"Mona? What in the world is going on here, and why is this on my head?"

He lifted his arm from his eyes and blinked. His residence refused to come into focus at first. Then the blurriness receded as he cupped his hand to the side of his face to block the light. He looked at the far wall, then sideways round the empty room. The one item he saw was a monitor that hung along the wall next to a door.

Mona remained silent. He was in a bed, but it wasn't his bed. Where *was* he?

The door had an imprinted design, nothing like the smooth, clean lines of his residence door. He put his hands down along his sides and raised himself up to the sitting position. Started turning and pulled his legs along side of the bed.

He noticed a whirring sound above his head so he looked up. A fan spun at a fast speed directly above his head. He shot up on his feet and sprinted over to the wall, making sure he was away from that fan.

Ihan licked his lips. "That is the first time I have ever seen a fan on the ceiling."

The pain in his head throbbed more. Ihan clinched his eyes shut and slid down the wall into the sitting position.

"Mona, where in the hell am I and why am I in so much pain?"

After waiting for a few seconds and not hearing anything, he looked around the room and thought of the potential move he was proposed a few weeks ago. That proposal was a move to a new location with the largest crop field in the city. Had he been injured during the move?

"Mona, where the hell are you!"

He quietly listened for a few more seconds. Unease crawled up his spine.

"Mona, you there!"

Meghan slept hard for a few hours, with the captive constantly in her dreams. Was it because she was ordered to watch him? Or simply because she wasn't sure how to handle him? She didn't know and kept her eyes closed. She was exhausted.

A few taps startled Meghan. She flipped over and pointed her gun. It was Stephan, watching her with a look of enthusiasm.

He nudged her weapon aside with his index finger. "Wake up, Meghan."

"What in the hell are you doing?" Meghan glared at

Stephan, then at her watch. Only four hours had passed since she fell asleep. She lowered her gun as the artery pulsed on her neck. "Are we under attack?"

"Come take a look at the monitor."

She jumped from her cot and hurriedly wrapped her blanket around herself. When she reached the table, she rubbed her eyes then looked hard at the monitor. The captive huddled against a wall, his gaze darting around the room.

Stephan widened his eyes. "He keeps asking for Mona. Do you have any clue who that may be?"

"Well, seeing how these people live alone and rely on their hard drive personas, it must be the designated name. It's no wonder that the persona is a woman."

"That's my rationale for designating you to talk with him to get him comfortable. We need to get good information out of him."

Meghan yawned. "I understand. Please make me some coffee because I think this is going to take a while."

Meghan pulled over a chair and sat down. She tightened her blanket around her shoulders and leaned over on the table to watch the monitor. After watching the captive for several minutes, Meghan noticed he was increasingly nervous. She wrote down on a piece of paper her talking strategy. One that would greet him, make him feel comfortable, understand his condition, and then get what they need from him.

Stephan brought over a cup of coffee, placed it on the table, and handed Meghan some headphones with a transmitter. He sat down next to her. She took a sip of the coffee, plugged in the transmitter, and put on the headphones. She saw the captive raise his head. He looked right at the monitor against the wall.

"OK, who is that on the other end? Please tell me where I am," he pleaded.

Stephan tapped Meghan and gestured to the monitor. The transmitter light was on. Stephan pressed the button and turned it off.

"Good thing we are quiet on this end. Are you ready?"

"Yeah, it's time to get this conversation going."

Meghan coughed, cleared her throat, and pressed the button.

"Greetings. I hope you are feeling better and in case you need anything, please let us know."

Ihan extended his neck. "I would really like to know why I'm in pain and in an unfamiliar place. Does this mean something nefarious happened a while ago?" He lowered his head and stared at the floor while he ran his fingers over the bandage on his head.

"You were injured and taken to a safe place where you will be looked at with care."

Ihan's hand dropped. He raised his head and snarled at the monitor. "Can you please tell me where I am and what happened to Mona?"

Meghan hesitated for second. She glanced at Stephan and raised one side of her upper lip. He nodded but wavered his hand from side to side. *Careful, don't tell him too much.*

"Mona is located in the vicinity but is going to be tested to see if she is OK. You have my assurance that once results are in you will be contacted. If you need anything, please ask and we will take care of it."

The up-and-down movement of Ihan's head made Meghan feel that the initiation was successful. She turned off the transmitter.

"When we get Mona set up and running we should be able to get what we need to corroborate future conversations."

"I agree, but we won't be doing anything with Mona until we run some security checks on its contents and activeness of the processor once we turn it on. Hell, the last thing we need is for this to have distant communications. I will take a few members and set that processor up."

Stephan stood up and walked over to the end of the room, waking two team members. They went into another room for a few minutes. As Stephan headed back, Meghan yawned again in the quiet room.

Most of the crew was asleep on the floor, some in cots along the wall. The team members must've been as tired as she was—all of them still wore their rumpled fatigues, and some had their hats and boots on. As Stephan sat back down on the chair, alarm spread over his face.

"That guy is in the bathroom, he hasn't escaped." Meghan said with a grin.

Stephen let out a deep breath, then he nodded. "Two team members are setting up the system. We need to attempt to get into that processor. Once they do the security check, and it's a go, I'll get back in there. The faster we get rolling with this, the faster we can get back on the road and find a signal so we can communicate with base camp."

"OK. By the way, Stephan, have you been able to get a signal on your communicator? This has been crazy and most of us believe we are either in a bad area for signals or something is being used to deliberately block us from communicating."

"Well, you are definitely the glass-half-empty girl, now aren't you." Stephan kept a straight face. "It's possible we are being messed with to cover something up. But if that were the case, we would have been hit by now. I recommend we focus on what we have with us and get some results. That way we will have some information to pass along."

"So what your saying is you don't know, and that we just need to stay focused?"

"Looks like your glass is getting full."

Meghan raised an eyebrow at him, and then shook her head. She went back to the monitor where she saw the bathroom door open. The cut on the captive's head was clearly visible, and not only was the bandage removed, but the guy was wearing a towel—he'd showered. She put the headphones back on and clicked the button.

"We hope you are feeling better now that you are clean?"

Ihan looked around the room, pausing for a moment by a small pile of clothing at the end of the bed. He looked along the floor, turning his head several times. Then he knelt by the bed and turned over the pile of clothing.

Stephen pressed the intercom button. "What is he looking for?"

"I have no clue, but something is off with what we

did. Let me ask him." Meghan clicked the button. "Is everything OK?"

"Yeah, I really appreciate the clothing but am curious to know how you got it into the room so fast."

Meghan looked at Stephan. He widened his eyes and shrugged. So it was up to her, then. After thinking for a moment, she raised her finger and grinned.

"You are in a newly renovated part of the city, one that requires many helping assistants to care for all our needs."

"I can somewhat understand that, but I can honestly say that I've never seen clothing such as this." Ihan stretched the shirt. "I don't understand the language written on the label."

Meghan watched him slide on the pants. The waistline was a couple of sizes too large The pants hung from his hips. The guy floundered into the shirt but then plucked at the fabric and stared at the bright orange pattern as though it was extremely strange to him. He kept staring at it while he sat on the bed and grabbed the socks. Another strange look came to his face when he put them on. His big toe was sticking out through a hole. He scratched his head and blinked at the monitor.

"Can you please tell me about this interesting clothing and why none of it fits? And why are you giving me shoes that have been worn and are too large?"

Stephan closed his eyes. She smirked and turned off the intercom again.

"What did you expect, Stephan, his clothing was in tatters. I had to throw it out. I got the clothes from the tiniest guy on the team."

"That explains Mexican symbols and Spanish wording all over the shirt. It looks like a Mexican tie-dye and that's Jorge, the loco team member."

"Yeah, I owe Jorge a big favor, and I'm sure he'll remind me of it every day."

Meghan reached down and pressed the button.

"Apology for the clothing. We received the wrong order, but knew you needed additional clothing. Please wear for the interim. I'm sure you are somewhat hungry and food will be brought to your residence very shortly. Please remember that there is a bottle of water on the shelving adjacent to the bed. We hope you drink plenty. In addition, we are working on getting Mona awake and running smoothly so that you will feel more comfortable."

The captive raised his head and looked at the monitor in confusion. He stood up and walked toward it. He got close and put his arms against the wall, on both sides.

"OK, I'm totally confused, and this whole situation makes no sense. Please put me through to Roger Bell."

"Sorry, but we cannot put you through to anyone as of yet. You are still injured and we are still monitoring on your situation."

"I feel fine and just want to chat with someone I know."

"Please just give us what you want Mr. Bell to know and we can pass along to him immediately?"

"Tell Roger to come on over and repair Mona because he knows her best. The last time Mona was fixed by someone other than Roger, her programming was tainted and Roger got very upset." Ihan turned around and walked over to the shelving, grabbed the bottle of water, and sat back down on the bed.

"Sorry but Roger is busy working other projects. He will not have the time to make his way over here, at least not for a couple of days. Do you want to pass along any other messages?"

"The only message I really want passed is how weird I'm feeling right now and how this situation is one I've never experienced. If you are not going to tell me why I am here, or where I am specifically, then what is the point, since I cannot even chat with someone I know."

"The food will be there shortly."

Meghan pressed the button. Then she walked over to her box, where she lifted the top and grabbed a meal. She got back over to the table and opened the plastic bag, spread out the food, and placed the smaller bagged items on a plastic lid. Standing up, and looking around, she noticed one of the team members across the room was awake, putting on his boots.

"Hey, I need your help over here!"

She waved him over. The team member ambled over, yawning and stretching his arms. He looked at the monitor to the left, which showed the captured man sitting on his bed.

"Wow, that guy is finally awake and moving around. Has he tried to bust out of that room yet?"

"That's not funny. You know those Dallas residents never leave their houses and that's the last thing he would do."

"Do we even have someone guarding his door?"

"What do you think I'm doing, you doofus!"

"All right, what do you want me to do?"

"Please do me a favor and bring him this food." Meghan lifted the plastic. "He hasn't eaten anything in quite a while and is probably starving. I will tell him to get something in the bathroom. When he walks in, I will lock that door, and that is when you hurry into the room and place that food on the bed."

"So you are going in with me to lock the door?"

"No. It's a remote lock and I have access to it from here."

Once he grabbed the food, the team member headed to the back hallway. Meghan checked the monitor to determine when she would inform about the bathroom. She determined that the time was getting close. She put the headphones back on and pushed the button.

"Excuse me, sir, your food is on its way. I need you to head into your bathroom to make sure your hands get cleaned."

Ihan looked up and thought about how attentive and controlling the watcher seemed. During his past medical checks and therapies he'd been closely watched as well. This woman was definitely a medical specialist, one that seemed to care more than past ones, who'd treated him very coldly. That bothered him. *Why haven't I seen a MedCon?* Then again, he was in the bathroom when all the items were brought into the room. It could be a fluke. He shook his head and pushed away his doubts. He was a top AgriCon. Despite the oddness of the move and his injuries, CSD valued him and was taking care of him.

He stood and walked into the bathroom. Once the

sink was turned on, the strangeness of all this hit him again. He turned the sink off and stood there listening. He heard the outer room door open, and some garbled shuffling sounds. He tiptoed toward the door and turned the handle, but it wouldn't move. The door was locked. He put his ear up to the door and heard more shuffling sounds. The outer door closed hard and fast.

Ihan pulled his head away from the door and walked back to the sink. He wondered what was going on in the other room and why he was locked in the bathroom.

Click. Ihan hurried to the door. After he turned the handle fast, the door flew open and slammed against the sidewall. He cringed. Then opened his mouth and slammed his teeth together.

Shuffling slowly into the room, he noticed the outer door was closed. He walked over and tried to turn the handle on the outer door. It was tight and didn't move. Turning around, he saw what looked like a plastic food tray and several brown plastic food bags lined on top of it. Ihan's intrigue drained away. He was hungrier than he'd ever been. He ripped open the bags and ate as fast as he could.

Meghan was cleaning her pistol and glancing occasionally at the monitor.

Stephan took a seat next to her. "Have we found this guy's name yet?"

"Not yet, but I shall get that soon, I know I will."

"Well, I just got back from the side room, and both those guys back there cannot get that Mona system running."

"I don't understand. Once you give it power then it should at least turn on?"

"It did turn on, but as soon as the connection was established, Mona jumped back and wouldn't let us in. I hate to say it, but this Mona is far more advanced than what we have to penetrate her. It seems as though she knows what software we are using to break in and she immediately counters all the infiltrations. She is too good for us, but if we link her to the monitor in that guy's room she may come right up. You know how sentimental those systems are for their possessors."

"That sounds like a plan, but I just don't think that idea is good right now. Obviously, this Mona knows she is not in safe place because she is on the defensive and has the techno teachings to counter all that stuff anyway. Besides, Stephan, if that guy were to realize his situation we could only expect trouble."

"Good call. I will tell those guys to pack the system. Once we get back to base camp, I hope our techno geeks can get inside her."

Meghan viewed the monitor. The captive had eaten all the food and was now sticking his fingers inside the packages. He scraped out the remaining morsels. Meghan then wondered how hungry this guy really was. It had been a day, or maybe more, since he'd eaten anything. However, Meghan could relate to the amount of stress this captive was under—after every mission she had a canine appetite.

Meghan grabbed another food package. She opened the pack and spread the little bags on another plastic cover. She then tapped the button.

"I see that you were hungry and ate all the food you were given. Would you like more?"

Ihan licked his finger and nodded his head at the monitor. He then looked at the bathroom door, and knew he would have to go back in there. What brought his food into the room sounded strange and piqued his curiosity. What type of robot was entering his room? He remembered talking with Roger about the new parts of the city, the ones that were tested by new technologies and ones that weren't known until they passed the testing. Ihan wondered if he could be in one of those locations. If so, was he being used as a test subject? The thought of his possibly being there, to test or recover, fascinated him.

There were stories of people being put into strange locations to test their personalities. The ones that passed the tests were promoted and ran sectors. Could this be the case? Or maybe this was the CSD way of testing new robots or systems to see if they were comforting citizens enough.

Ihan needed to know what he was a part of. He stood up and walked around the room before halting at the bathroom door. He opened it and knelt down to look at the lock—one that was large and had a thick sensor bolt. He then stood back up and walked over to the shelving, where he noticed many objects placed along the top shelf. There were picture frames, signs, and some extra floor tiles. He picked up a tile and felt its heavy and sturdy weight. He tapped it against the wall and it seemed pretty strong. Tossing the tile on the bed, he sat back down, and looked at the wall. He knew it was time to figure this out.

"Excuse me out there, but I sure could use some food and would appreciate more water."

"No problem. I shall send you some in a few minutes with a drink. I would like you to—"

"You want me to head into the bathroom. I know."

He looked over at the wall and slid a little forward on the edge of the bed to get in between the camera and the tile. He grabbed and kept the tile close to his side. Once he walked into the bathroom, he looked around the room to make sure there was no camera or monitor. He felt comfortable there was none and quickly placed the tile against the wall beside the door. The door started to close. He quickly got to his knees, grabbed the tile, and placed it along the lock area. As the door closed, he held the tile to make sure it would not drop.

Ihan then heard the movements in the other room. He felt his heart beat faster and could feel the veins in his neck throb. Was this the right move, the one that would get him to pass the test? The not knowing what was on the other side of the door was too powerful. It was now or never.

He grabbed the door handle and pulled it hard with all his strength. The door flung back at a high speed and slammed into the wall. Ihan stepped forward and looked into the room.

Meghan put the pistol down and wiped her hands clean with antibacterial wipes. She heard a loud scream down the hallway. On the monitor, she saw a blinking red light by the door symbol.

"Holy shit!"

She jumped to her feet and ran across the room toward the hallway. Most of the team members in the room grabbed their weapons and followed her. Once Meghan reached the door, she flung it open and ran in. To her right was a team member knelt beside the captive, who lay on the floor against the bathroom door.

"What the hell happened here?"

The team member squinted up at Meghan. "I thought you were going to lock that bathroom door."

"I did. How did he get out?"

The team member stood up. "I set the tray on the bed. I heard a loud scream, looked over, and saw this guy jump back. He hit his head against that door."

Meghan knelt down and checked the captive for any injuries. She lifted his head and felt behind for any cuts. No blood. She stood back up and put her hand on the team member's shoulder.

"You are probably the first real person he has ever seen."

Awed, the rest of the team gently picked up the captive and placed him on the bed. Meghan pulled over a chair and sat down. She heard Stephan outside the room.

"You got to be kidding me." Stephan walked into the room and pulled over another chair. He sighed. "Any idea what happened?"

"He somehow opened the bathroom door, saw his first genuine human giving him food, and passed out."

"How are we going to deal with this? We really don't have time for him to have a mental breakdown. We need to pack our stuff and get moving. One of the team members informed me a few minutes ago that a signal started sending a half hour ago. When he tracked it down he found out it was coming out of Mona. I immediately told him to just pull the power all together. Even though we pulled that antenna on Mona, I guess that system has an internal. I can only venture to say that we won't have much safe time left here."

"Well, I am not a psychiatrist, but I will do my best to be nice to this guy and at least attempt to make him feel comfortable. Besides, he is good looking. So hanging around him won't be that bad."

Stephan lowered his eyebrows, but then he chuckled. "You've got to be pulling my rod. This guy is pale, scrawny, and... Whatever, Meghan, do the best you can do. I need to get the team together so we can pack our stuff and get moving." He stood up and headed out of the room.

Moments after Stephan left, the captive moaned and rubbed his face. He opened his eyes and looked right at Meghan. He looked around the room and grunted. Then he curled his legs and pulled himself to the head of the bed, positioned himself in the corner with his arms clamped over his head.

Meghan smiled. "Hi there. I'm glad to see you are awake and hope you are not feeling any pain."

He placed his hand in the back of his head and whimpered.

"You are OK, and nothing bad is going to happen to you. You are not in any trouble, and I shall take care of you." Meghan grabbed a bottle of water from the floor and placed it on the bed. "Please drink some water."

His mouth fidgeted. "Who are you and why are you infecting me?"

"My name is Meghan, and I cannot infect you because I have been immunized for many years. You have also been immunized; I did that when you arrived here. What is your name?"

"Ihan." He looked around the room again, his eyes lingering on the open outer door.

"Ihan. That is an interesting name and definitely a nice one I haven't heard before."

"Where am I and why are you in the same room as me? Don't you know you are breaking city laws and probably passing diseases?"

"To be honest with you, and I hope you respect that honesty, you were taken from Dallas and are a few miles south of it. We brought you here to help us understand more about your city. Since you are no longer in it, the only laws that matter are Texas laws."

"You mean to tell me that you broke into the city and I'm no longer in it?" Ihan began cackling. "That seems a little strange. No one has ever stolen anything from Dallas, the most secure city-state in the combination."

Meghan bent her neck back in surprise. "You are definitely a bold person and one that has been infected with the Dallas disease!"

"What are you talking about, what is the Dallas disease?" He cringed.

"Oh, it's that nasty society you were born into. That city has contaminated your beliefs and existence. I guarantee you that nepotistic society tells you what they want you to know and you probably never hear the truth. The state is recovering from this disease and anarchy but keeps getting thrown back by the City-State of Dallas. Your city is forcefully taking Texas land, oil fields, and food by killing thousands."

Staring at Meghan, Ihan lowered his head then quickly raised it again. "You mean to tell me that you are testing my loyalty to Dallas? I am one of the best AgriCons in the city and have done everything that has ever been tasked to me. If this is some kind of loyalty game, then I'm done playing this and need to get back to my home. I have several re-cropping plans to write and—"

Meghan raised her hand, stood up, and walked around the back of the chair. "This is no game or test."

Dirk ran into the room and grabbed her arm, dragging her into the hallway. Meghan heard a ruckus. The whole team was running around and moving the boxes back out into the vehicles.

"I hate to interrupt your work with that guy, but we have to get moving. Both air sensors picked incoming aircraft headed this way, and we can only expect those ground attack robots not far behind. Grab that dude and get into the vehicle!" Dirk ran back to the main room and hefted two boxes onto his shoulders and headed for the door.

Meghan raced back into the room and gathered items into a bag she'd picked up off the floor. Ihan remained curled in a ball on the bed. He looked confused.

"Is there something happening?"

"I'm collecting your stuff. We need to head out of here now." Meghan held out her hand. All he did was stare at her hand. "Let's go!" She understood Ihan's uncertainty.

She reached down, grabbed his hand, and pulled him off the bed. As they slowly walked through the main room, Meghan made sure to focus on Ihan's stability. He was still weak and baffled. Meghan contemplated what Ihan must be going through.

After they got down the steps and closer to the back of the vehicle, Ihan abruptly stopped moving. He looked up into the sky in amazement. Meghan had plenty to ask of a man who never went outside, but she needed to get him into the vehicle. She pushed him hard, but he hesitated. Meghan stepped back with clenched fists. Then Dirk sprinted past her.

"Get that captive into the vehicle. We need to get out of here now!"

Meghan dropped her shoulder and slammed Ihan into the backseat of the vehicle. She locked the door and bustled around to her seat. The tires screeched, spraying up chunks of asphalt.

Chapter Twelve

Enthroned behind his nineteenth-century bamboo desk, Jerry video teleconferenced with the Chinese minister of commerce.

"Sir Minister of Commerce, the Textiles and Garments contract is one that we're overly pleased with and look forward to continuing the vast transfers on a monthly basis. The usage among the City-State of Dallas is greatly needed and we appreciate your delivery mechanism support. I recall when these transfer troubles started, but the delivery routes are absolutely secure, and you can count on my guarantee that all future safety is assured."

Jerry quickly looked to the screens on the right. His security minister looked calm and relaxed, but his commerce minister fidgeted and wiped a hand over his brow. He returned his gaze to the main screen, where the Chinese minister of commerce was chatting with other representatives. Their tones were calm but the verbiage had burgeoned. The Chinese minister shook his head up and down and looked back at the screen, addressing Jerry in Chinese. The translation came through Liz.

"Mayor Adams, the timing for contract renewal is soon. We must discuss the pricing change. It will increase due to the current market prices, which are greater than they were last year. I ask that you increase the oil amounts by one third." He inclined his head slightly before continuing. "Your oil is honored, and the Chinese government greatly appreciates your products."

Jerry tapped his leg under the table. "I ask that you let me promptly discuss this with my commerce minister, and I shall be right back."

The Chinese minister bowed his head, and Jerry pressed the mute button on the main screen connection.

"All right, Mr. Commerce, what's the deal with this huge increase? I don't see us greatly boosting our oil production in that short period of time." The minister's hand fluttered to his face again, and Jerry leaned forward. "You knew what he was going to ask. And you were afraid to tell me."

"S-sir, I really didn't expect a request for adding one third to the new contract. I knew it would be more, but not that huge addition."

Jerry drummed his finger on the desk. "And you figured I wouldn't understand the implications of that? You are a chicken, and I don't see you holding this position much longer."

"Sir!"

Jerry looked to the screen on the right. "Go ahead, Security Minister."

"Our Abilene, Midland, and San Angelo oil district boundaries are more secure due to the increased Secure-Con teams and greater technology. May I suggest you request an increase and addition of military technology to broker the deal, which should go smoothly since my earlier conversations with our commerce minister focused on China's escalating oil needs. If we do get an increase in military technology, we could easily take the San Antonio district, and produce more than enough oil to settle this deal."

Ah, yes. San Antonio. Jerry allowed himself a small smile. "That sounds viable. I appreciate your input. Liz, turn off our commerce minister's connection."

"Done, sir."

Jerry reached across the table, grabbed his glass of water, and downed the contents. He put the glass down and wiped his mouth with a napkin, then jabbed the mute button.

"I apologize for the short side talk but I wanted to confirm that our contract would be solid. I assure you that the additional oil amount you requested is secure. However, to ensure your goods are safely delivered, our military technology needs will also increase. Please let me know if the additional oil will confirm this deal?"

The Chinese minister looked over to his side and talk with others. The mute was on their side. Jerry didn't attempt to lip-read, because he didn't speak Chinese other than a few phrases of greeting. As the minutes went by, he thought about the past contracts he'd brokered and how crucial this relationship was with China, the world's only remaining superpower. The minister turned his head and look down for a moment as though preparing himself for a momentous speech.

"We agree with the terms and will greatly increase your weapons and technologies. The contract will be re-written and shall be sent to you in a few hours. Thank you for the honorable discussion, and I look forward to discussing our other contracts and agreements in a few days."

"Mr. Minister, *zai jian*, and thank you very much for our commerce relations."

The screen went blank and Jerry thanked the security minister before Liz turned off all the screens. The lights brightened and classical music lilted into the suite. Jerry stood up, walked out of the room, and headed over to his bar where he poured some vodka. He shot it down his throat. Enjoying the pleasant burn, he sprawled on his couch, kicked up his feet on the living room table, and watched his big-screen monitor display a beautiful beach, with waves crashing, and birds flying in the distance. The thoughts of all the deals and interactions with China were needed, but troublesome, due to the time he spent working with all the Chinese ministers. When he'd first taken office several deals failed because the weak Dallas ministers couldn't say no to the Chinese. Nothing upset Jerry more than Dallas looking weak. That display would reduce the city's effectiveness throughout the other city-states. Dallas was by far the largest and most successful city-state, it held the strongest society, and it was watched by others for advice and lessons learned. Jerry had a passion for his city-state, because of its economic influence and the affirmation of an external diplomacy of its own. His hands clenched and relaxed, clenched and relaxed, as he envisioned tentacles of power extending over the planet. The rhythmic motion empowered his focus. Then the music faded.

"Sir, your security minister would like to talk with you," Liz said.

Jerry rolled his eyes but knew he had to discuss the deal specifics in depth so that when the contract was sent in a few hours they could review it with the same thoughts.

"Go ahead, Liz, and put him through."

The monitor turned on and the security minister's face appeared. He was looking over to the side and discussing something with others until he noticed his connection was on.

"Sir, I apologize for interrupting you, but—"

Jerry rolled his finger. "I understand the importance of this deal. We need to go over the specifics."

"Actually, I need to discuss with you the latest information we received in relation to the stolen technology and the resident that was captured." The security minister swallowed hard. "We learned that the processor was turned on for about fifteen minutes and we got its location. It's approximately fifty-five miles southeast of here in Athens. I ordered the External Security Unit to immediately engage and retrieve what was stolen. There are currently two air and three ground units who are en route or currently at that—"

Before the idiot was through speaking, Jerry slammed his fist down on the desk. "How dare the UTC attack Dallas and steal our technology?" he roared. The security minister's cringing made him feel marginally better.

"How many processors were taken?" he demanded.

"J-just one, sir."

"What are the odds of retrieving that item while killing the bandits who stole it?"

"It depends on how soon we can evaluate the specific disposition and composition of the enemy. Once that is determined, we can evaluate and determine the best course of action."

Jerry shook his head. "That will take way too much time. Go ahead and eliminate it all. We can survive without that processor and eliminate the chance of UTC gathering information from it."

"What about Ihan Duncan?"

Jerry grimaced. "If he survives, then please bring him back and clean him up."

"Yes sir, I shall pass the order."

Jerry lifted his arm in a dismissive wave. The monitor turned off and the music got louder. He pushed his head back against the couch and focused on clearing his mind.

Political machinations always exhausted him.

Chapter Thirteen

As the convoy emerged from underneath a devastated bridge, Stephan looked down and saw the signal strength was strong. New technology that surrounded Athens must have blocked the signal. He picked up his communicator, went to the drafts section on his system, and pressed send. The information he'd been unable to send for the past several days would finally make it to base camp.

Inappropriate communication problems tended to bug the snot out of Stephan. The base camp always replied with numerous questions. Stephan ignored responding, knowing his duty was finished.

In the backseat the team member in charge of the radar system swore. "Uh, boss, we have two air objects, probably UAVs, heading our way quickly."

Stephan shot his head up twisted in his seat. "Let me see that screen."

The team member turned his screen. The objects on the display were close, within normal attack distance. A missile should be showing on the screen, but none was.

Stephan jabbed his finger at the team member. "Keep your eyes on that screen and tell me if anything in their movements change."

Turning back around, he surveyed their route. The densely tree-lined road was straight. The harsh sunlight would reveal every movement the convoy made.

The team was too vulnerable here. Stephan grabbed his communicator. "Drivers, spread the vehicles apart. Make it harder for them to pinpoint us."

Of the corner of his left eye, he saw a flash near ground level. A split second later, the missile slammed into the lead vehicle. The driver of Stephan's vehicle braked fast and hard. Stephan flung forward, and his arm hit the dashboard hard. The lead vehicle flipped and skidded on its side, flames licking up around it. Tires screeched. The two vehicles collided in a sickening crunch of metal, and then another impact jerked him back into his seat.

Meghan had watched Ihan throughout the ride. She smiled as he stared at the sunrise, and the scenery above the wayside. She didn't have to imagine the thrill he must be experiencing in his first trip outside the city—unguarded astonishment was evident on his face.

An explosion flipped the lead vehicle. Her vehicle slammed on its brakes. Her heartbeat intensified, and her seat belt cut a diagonal line of pain down her chest. When the vehicle stopped, Ihan sat gape mouthed, his head bent to the side, looking out the front windshield. The front door opened, and Dirk jumped out of the vehicle. Bullets immediately slammed against the side of the vehicle. Dirk dove back into the driver's seat. He grabbed the door handle and yanked the door closed.

"Holy shit!" Dirk said.

Meghan squinted in the direction the bullets were

coming from. Three objects sped toward them through the woods. One cleared the tree line. A SecureCon. Dread paralyzed her. The SecureCon turned its head back and forth as it moved at even greater speed.

Dirk snatched his communicator and screamed into it. "We are being ambushed and I highly recommend we keep moving forward!"

He held his communicator close to the side of his head for a second.

"Stephan, over?"

Meghan cautiously rose to peer out the side window. In Stephan's vehicle, the driver bent down to his right. Bullets slammed into his vehicle. Stephan had his head bent forward. He wasn't moving. The driver shook him with no apparent response. He picked up his communicator.

"Dirk, Stephan is out cold but looks like he's fine."

A rush of relief flooded Meghan.

Dirk gave a hoarse cheer. "All right, everyone put the pedal to the metal and follow me. We have to encircle the hit vehicle and grab the wounded."

He slammed down on the accelerator and cranked the wheel. The vehicle swerved around the others and screeched to a stop by the damaged vehicle. Two other vehicles came in close behind. Team members jumped out of their passenger-side doors. Dirk looked at Meghan in the backseat.

"Stay put and watch that captive."

She dropped her hand from the door handle and slouched back into the seat. Dirk crawled out the passenger door and ran over to the damaged vehicle. Three other team members jumped out of their vehicles and opened cover fire with their weapons over the roofs of their vehicles.

The SecureCons slowed down, but continued to fire. A loud knock slammed Ihan's door, and he jumped. A sweaty team member was bent over outside. Meghan immediately reached across Ihan and opened the door. The man outside shoved a wounded team member into the vehicle, across Ihan's lap, and Meghan helped pull the body in. The door slammed shut. As the weight of the man came crashing down on Ihan's lap, he grunted. "Ooph!" The wounded man's blood pour over Ihan. He struggled to get his hands out from under the body. Meghan raised the body, and Ihan pulled them free. His face froze in panic.

"Don't worry about it, Ihan, we will be out of here soon."

Dirk and another team member climbed back into the vehicle and closed the door. Sweat poured down his forehead. Dirk pulled his communicator off the dashboard.

"Let's get the hell out of here."

The tires screeched again as vehicles spun to top speed. Meghan reached into her pockets but couldn't find her communicator. She bent forward, feeling the floor around her feet. Her fingertips brushed against the communicator under the seat in front of her. She grabbed it, wiped off the dirt, and blew the dust off the control screen.

"Is Stephan still unconscious?"

"Yeah, he's out cold and his head is leaning against the window," Stephan's driver said.

"Whoever is monitoring the radar system please tell us where the UAVs are?"

She heard the line open, and a team member cleared his throat.

"I see three airborne blips on the screen, one is to our rear, one is on the east, and the other is west."

"What's their distance? Are they within a mile?"

"The two to our east and west are roughly eight hundred feet. The one to the rear is a little over a mile."

Meghan bent forward and tapped Dirk on the shoulder. "What is the employment radius on those mobile jammer devices?"

Dirk widened his eyes. "A mile and a half. Great thinking, Meghan."

"How many of those devices do we have?"

"At least two in the vehicle. In the orange box behind you." Dirk hesitated for a second. "Just to remind you, those jammer devices tend to work when they want to. And they only have an hour capacity."

"That will at least give us enough time to get out of this mess."

Meghan jumped around and grabbed the orange box, pulled it toward the back of the seat, and opened the lid. The two devices were covered in a thick layer of bubble wrapping, which she peeled away. A handle jutted out from each device. She looked at the five numbered buttons on the handle.

"Dirk, what is up with turning this thing on?"

"It has a cipher trigger. The dates are zero, four, zero, one.

Meghan chuckled. "April Fools Day? You are quite the comic."

"Make sure you toss that device out the window, because once you press the code, you'll have ten seconds before it goes off and fries every electronic device in this vehicle."

"All right. Let me tell the team." She grabbed the communicator and touched the team button. "Listen up, ya'll. I am going to turn on one of those jammer devices and toss it out the window. Make sure ya'll keep the speed, and this techno grenade should hopefully get us safely to our next location."

She opened the door a crack. As soon she the pressed the numbers, she tossed the first jammer device to the side of the road. She looked back and saw it bounce on the pavement then roll into a grass ditch off the road. She slammed the door, turned around on the seat, and knelt, staring out the back window. Dirk laughed, and she turned her head to see him grinning at her in the rearview mirror.

"I don't know what you are looking at, Meghan. That device won't explode. It will just send out the jamming signal."

Meghan settled back on the seat. "How we supposed to know this grenade works?"

"Patience, my lady. Give the radar man a call and ask him to tell you what he sees in a few seconds. If this device does go active, then he should at least see UAVs either go off course, or just dive down to the ground. The Secure-Cons should just stop moving. They might fall over."

Meghan pressed the communication button. "Radar

viewer, I need you to monitor those UAVs. Let us know of any changes if you see them."

"Will do."

The injured teammate's neck was bleeding tremendously. Meghan looked for her emergency medical kit, then realized she'd left it in the building. She bent over and slightly turned his head so she could see where the blood was gushing. Below his chin a shard of metal, pierced his throat at an angle. She thought of pulling it out, but if the metal was adjacent to the jugular, it might tear it open more than it already had. She looked in the back of the vehicle but couldn't see any towels or rags.

"Any of you up front have any rags or towels?"

Both shook their heads no. She needed something clean to stanch the flow of blood, or this guy could die. She whipped off her jacket and pulled her shirt up over her head. Then she chewed on the seam to create a tear and ripped the garment in to several strips. Meghan then noticed Ihan's full attention was focused on her bra. Looked like being raised in isolation had no effect on a man's fascination with boobs. She smirked at him.

"Grab these two cloths and hold on to them while I wrap the other one around his wound."

Meghan handed him the cloths. She then unscrewed the cap on the water bottle and poured it over the wound area before wrapping the cloth around the man's neck. She grabbed the other pieces of cloth from Ihan's hands and continued the wrap until she ran out. As she put her jacket on, Ihan was still gawking at her breasts.

"You can now check the proverbial block that you've

seen parts of a real woman's body. But don't ever think you'll see another part of mine."

Ihan's complexion turned red, and Meghan turned her head to the front. Her communicator beeped.

"The jammer is working. The east and west UAVs are going around in circles. The one to the rear of us is dropping altitude fast. Good job, Meghan" the team member said.

Chapter Fourteen

The vehicle rocked and jolted, and the sound of gravel pinging up against the undercarriage woke Stephan. He opened his eyes. Treetops flew past the window—the vehicle was moving at a fast speed. He turned his head, and the driver gave him a thumbs-up.

"You OK Stephan? You look like shit."

"At least I feel the way I look." Stephan rubbed his temples. "What's going on and how long have I been out?"

"About twenty minutes. Those damn robots ambushed us. You slammed your head into the dashboard when we rear-ended the vehicle in front of us. Dirk took charge and had us block the burning pile of metal. We were able to get the bodies out."

Meghan? Stephan sucked in a breath. "How many?"

"Three of our brothers are dead. Two others are seriously injured."

Stephan put his head back against the seat. He'd tried to prevent something like this from happening. The thought of three team members being killed escalated the pain in his head. He continued to rub his temples, to numb the throbbing. Good thing Dirk had been there to take charge of the situation and recovering the bodies from the wreck. He trusted the guy. Stephan lifted his communicator and looked at the GPS. Palestine was only ten miles away, and the team needed a rest stop. He pushed the button.

"Attention everyone, I just awoke from my painful nap. We are about ten miles from our next stopping point. We will stop quickly and help the wounded. Let me re-emphasize that the stop will be quick, because we need to avoid another attack like the last one."

"We are so glad you are awake and hope all is well," Meghan responded. At the crackle of her voice over the communicator, his pulse thundered in his ears unexpectedly. "The two that are wounded are pretty serious and they need to see a doctor fast."

Would have been great if you took charge as well, Stephan thought as Meghan talked. He shook his head, knowing he didn't have the full picture of what had happened. He then reconsidered stopping in Palestine. They'd stopped there a few missions back, and CSD tracked past routes. Better to get the wounded straight to base camp.

He called off the stop and told his driver to take the convoy lead. He wanted to travel an obscure route to San Antonio. The vehicle passed the others and pulled in front.

Several hours passed before Stephan spotted the exit sign for Giddings. The convoy needed to stop and refuel in order to make a straight drive into base camp. In addition, Giddings was close to the safe zone—it hadn't been attacked in the past year.

Passing communications to base camp from here

should present little risk, and they'd be awaiting news of Team Eight's success. He pressed the message browser. It was clear—no responses from Operations Center. He closed his message browser and went to the secure communication channel with an alternate encryption code, one held by only three in each team. He pressed the connection button to alert the Operations Center and waited.

A beeping became apparent on the operations center screen. The communications officer sat up straight and checked the signal to make sure it was legitimate. The large screen on the wall displayed that the signal was approximately one hundred thirty miles northeast of the base camp, moving at a good speed. The identification code was Stephan Grabowski, Team Eight's leader.

"Mr. Grabowski, this is Operations Center Control and I can read your signal five bye."

"I can read and hear you the same. Look, I need to know if you received the three messages I sent to you this morning."

"Roger that. They were passed to the appropriate personnel within the center."

"OK, then why haven't I got any replies?"

"We have been told to keep the communications past the one-hundred-fifty-mile radius down to a minimum. That's all I know—I just got on shift a few hours ago."

"Put me through to the Operations Chief."

"They are all in a meeting."

"Well then, go get one of them!"

"I've been told that the meeting is important with no interruptions."

"Please explain to me what is more important than this mission and the teams conducting it?"

"I fully understand and am just following orders."

"Then go tell the Chief I'm the one who told you to break the orders!"

"I will have the operations chief get with you as soon as the meeting is over."

"Bullshit! You will do it now or I promise you will be the one to bury the three dead we have!"

"OK, OK! I'll go and tell the Chief."

Putting the headphones down on the counter, he looked over and saw his co-worker shaking his head. However, orders not to disturb operations chief didn't matter, communications officer was a team member who knew most of the support personnel in the Operations Center never went out on a mission. He walked down the booth line and stuck his middle finger up as he passed his coworker.

When he reached the conference room door, he knocked a couple of times on the door and stood there for a few seconds. He knocked again. The door opened, and an operation officer scowled at him.

"Why are you knocking on the door? You were all told this meeting was not to be disturbed."

"Sir, I have Stephan Grabowski on a secure connection and he needs to talk with the Operations Chief."

The operations officer rolled his eyes. "Just tell him he will be contacted when this meeting is over."

The officer nonchalantly started to close the door. The

communications officer pushed past him into the room and stopped in front of the Operations Chief.

"Sir, I am sorry for the interruption but Stephan Grabowski has something important to discuss right now. He is on a secure connection."

All the personnel in the room looked over at the Operations Chief, who bared his teeth and clenched his fists. He stood up and pointed his finger.

"You tell that Stephan…"

Dusty, seated next to the chief, grabbed one of the man's fingers and bent it the wrong way.

"Sit down." Dusty widened his eyes and applied more pressure. "Now."

The operations chief inhaled sharply, and as soon as his finger was released, thumped back down into his chair. Dusty stood and walked toward the door.

"You all continue this important meeting and let me know the outcome when I return."

The communications officer held the door open as Dusty walked out. He stomped toward the communications desk and looked up at the big screen, where Stephan's location was pinpointed. "Giddings! They're only a couple of hours away." Dusty sat at the desk and pulled the headphones on.

"Stephan, is that you?"

"Dusty, yeah it's me. Have you read the three messages I sent this morning?"

"I sure did. We are anxiously awaiting your return with the goods, so we can get the ball rolling. How's Meghan?"

"That's not why I'm calling. We need air support for the last leg of this return."

"What are you talking about? There is no air support in the area."

Stephan grunted. "We have three squadrons of UAVs and we need a lift!"

"All squadrons are on an operation near Midland."

"You got to be kidding me! How could you send the entire fleet to one operation when you have your lead team with the acquired package and no support? We already got attacked and are expecting another one!"

"I would send you a backup team, but they're all employed."

"We have four dead and two severely injured members who might not make it to base camp."

Dusty clenched his fists. "What do you want Stephan, sympathy? I suggest you read the dictionary because the word sympathy is between the words shit and syphilis! All teams are being hit and some aren't going to even make it back. Those were the teams who distracted the enemy and made your mission more successful!"

A few grudging seconds passed.

"Fine, Dusty, we'll make it back to base camp and provide the acquired goods."

"You keep my daughter safe and tell her I'll have her favorite duck cooked for her when she gets back."

Dusty flicked the connection off. The communication officer rubbed his neck as he watched Dusty walk away.

After the convoy passed a curve in the road, Stephan looked far down the straight portion of the track ahead and saw nothing that looked dangerous or out of the ordinary. He leaned back and stared out at the empty sky.

"Hey boss, is everything OK? You know we have some aspirin in the back and one of the guys in the back can pass it up here."

Stephan sat silent for a few minutes. From the backseat, an arm came forward and tapped him on the shoulder. He took the aspirin. The driver reached under his seat and produced a bottle of tequila.

"If you down that aspirin with this love juice, I guarantee it will speed up the pain reducer."

Stephan then grabbed the bottle, raised his eyebrow, threw the aspirin in his mouth, and tilted the bottle vertically into his mouth. The level of liquor in the bottle dropped fast. The driver reached across, grabbed the bottle, spun it back over, and held it on his lap.

He smirked. "There is no need to compromise your decision-making skills by getting slammed."

Emitting a burp of some bass and duration, Stephan blinked. "I really needed that, thanks."

Frustration was a tough feeling to conceal. One that Stephan reminded himself, all the time, not to let his teammates witness. It was a sign of weakness, one that would hamper his leadership. And it wasn't his place to question his superiors in the company of others. The proper military etiquette, to not challenge a person's rank, maintained order—but that didn't mean he had to like the person.

Stephan's hatred for Dusty seemed to mature more every day. The anger had started when he learned of his father's death. It swelled immensely when he became a team leader, having to speak with that family killer on a daily basis. That family killer's daughter was nothing like her father. That puzzled Stephan. How that family killer would give his treasure to a person, who's father was killed on his team, was perplexing. Was it payback or atonement? Driving his confusion deeper was Dusty's assertion, on numerous occasions, that Stephan was the best and most trusted team leader in UTC.

Could his facade of respect for Dusty stay intact? Time was the essence adhering to UTC success. He believed that. Stephan clenched his jaw and his fists against his impatience—waiting for the right moment to revere his murdered father.

CHAPTER FIFTEEN

Their breakneck speed along pitted roads numbed Ihan's legs. The gory smell of scorched flesh from the injured man made Ihan queasy. Meghan reached over and placed her fingers on the man's neck as she stared at her watch. Her look seemed anxious and increasingly sad. Her thought of this man's condition couldn't be good.

Ihan squirmed in his seat as he remembered his own recent injury. He'd tripped over a sharp metal rail inside his residence pod, and blood gushed from his leg. Mona immediately told him to go to the shower and wash the wound, then apply pressure to stop the bleeding. He relied on Mona for these basics.

The thought of not being with Mona, or knowing where she was, formed a deep sadness in him. He watched Meghan steady the man's head when they hit bumps in the road. Her face was turned toward the window, away from Ihan.

"Is this man going to be OK?"

Meghan turned her head slowly to stare at him, a stunned look tightening her face.

"Do you mean you actually care for someone other than yourself?"

Ihan sat motionless for a few seconds, looking down at the man, then back to Meghan. He smiled, not wanting to make her feel bad for being unable to understand—how could she, when she'd grown up in barbaric conditions?

"I can see how much you care about his health, and that is something I've never seen before, at least physically."

Meghan raised an eyebrow. "Makes sense, seeing how you never experienced any tangible interaction, but I must say you still have lots to learn. That look on your face makes me believe you are beginning to understand how camaraderie is so important to us and how it makes us survive."

"Would you do the same for me if I got hurt, even though I'm not on your team?"

"Of course I would, Ihan. You are a human being and not some robot, like you're used to."

Ihan jerked his head backward. "What do you mean? Mona cares for me greatly. She would do anything to help me."

"OK, Ihan. It's time for you to get real. I'm going to share a realistic viewpoint with you, so try to understand why you need to work with us from here on out. Mona is a computer who's been programmed and told to serve Dallas through you. By no means does that mean she is there specifically for you. She was created and placed with you to make the service matters get accomplished. Do you honestly believe she keeps your personality and everyday actions to herself?" Meghan pointed her finger at him. "She is not there for you. She is there to make sure you do what you're supposed to get done and would rat you out if you didn't. Your despotic leadership plays you like a fool!"

Ihan stared at the injured man's neck. Meghan became fascinated with her watch again. Ihan glanced back and forth, confused.

"If you have the freedom to do whatever you want, then why are you here with a team that is being run by someone else?"

The seconds were up. Meghan pulled her fingers from the man's neck. She took a deep breath and shook her head. His pulse was weak and at thirty-two beats for the minute.

"I was directed to be on this team, but I volunteered to do what I am doing. I chose." She gaped at Ihan. "You were brought up, placed into your residence, and are working in a field because someone else decided. Not you. That is the difference, and it's called freedom. You were kept alone and told what they want you to hear—that way you do what they want you to."

Why is she telling me this, Ihan thought, I talk with friends all the time. "We are kept alone because of health and disease."

"That was cured decades ago, so don't even go there, Ihan!" Meghan swung her head away. Ihan didn't know what to say, so he watched the scenery go by. CSD had reiterated, his entire life, how severe the smallpox infection was. Hence the justification and rationale for the residence partitioning law. His eyes became damp. His lips started to tremble. *I don't know what to believe.* However, he felt fine, could detect no pain or sign of an infection.

He looked at Meghan and reminded himself how healthy she looked despite the shadows under her eyes. Had his life of solitude been a lie? He stomped his foot down on the vehicle floor. That thought was too much to deal with right now. He needed to focus—he just didn't know on what.

He saw a large building with an oval running track next to it. Then some houses. Women with scared looks gathered their children and ran indside. On some roofs men sat with weapons, while others dropped to their knees and pointed at the convoy. There was no mistaking the vacant faces with eyes that seemed to look beyond everything; the dirty, disheveled clothing; and the constant emotionless gestures among the men.

The vehicles slowed down as they drove past a small child standing on the side of the road. The child had torn clothing and only one shoe. As the vehicle passed, the boy's placid expression never changed. Then the convoy stopped, and Ihan heard some conversation emanating from a few vehicles ahead of theirs, but couldn't understand the words due to their dullness. It was as though the heat had sucked the life from everyone around here.

Meghan leaned forward. "Hey, Dirk, what town are we in?"

"This is Giddings."

"I don't remember ever going through this town."

"Stephan is taking an alternate route to conceal our location from the enemy."

"What is up with the townspeople and the checkpoint we are stopped at?"

"I would recommend you get your gun ready just in case this goes ugly."

Meghan drew her pistol. "I don't understand."

"The citizens will defend themselves. They don't even trust the towns next to them. You know as well as I that most towns are on their own."

Her eyes widened. "I knew, but I didn't think it was as bad as this."

For all her tough exterior, Ihan saw something vulnerable in Meghan. But when he leaned toward her, intending to comfort her in some way, her scowl pressed him back into the seat.

The vehicles started to move again. Rugged men stood behind the crossed barriers, holding guns and looking suspicious. Once they passed the barriers, the vehicles sped up. Ihan turned his head back to look at the barriers, where the men remained with those chilling emotionless stares.

"I thought you took care of these people, Dirk?" Ihan said.

Dirk sent him a condescending look through the mirror.

"Maybe we would if Dallas types, like yourself, became peaceful Texans again. We could all get along and help civilize these poor people you keep stealing needed goods from."

"Hey, hey!" the other teammate in the vehicle yelled, and smirked at Ihan.

Ihan turned his head and looked back out the window.

Meghan slowly turned toward Ihan. What was he thinking, now that they'd pulled him from the only life he knew? He seemed inquisitive, but considerate. The verbal path they were taking was leading him into new thoughts, but those thoughts were still in question. An individual with Ihan's past would normally not care about others, would fight against all attempts to change—his safety always in the forefront. Yet instead of struggling, he had asked questions. A person with an open mind is about the only one who would ask questions. At least questions that lead people to understand the other's background and viewpoint. Could that lead a person to change? That was the question, and the answer wouldn't be known until proof was provided.

Another question nagged at her: Did she want him to change?

Chapter Sixteen

Dirk drummed his fingers on the steering wheel as he kept his eye on the blinking fuel gauge. Gas pumps were close, he just hoped they contained some. When Stephan signaled the vehicles into the station, Dirk pulled in and parked, stretched his legs, and watched team members bound out of their vehicles with plastic gas containers. Someone stomped up behind him, and he recognized the heavy tread as Stephan's.

"How are the two wounded doing?" Stephan said.

Dirk stretched his arms and shoved down the burning emotion welling in his chest. It wouldn't do anyone any good anyway. "Mark is in the back with Meghan. He's losing too much blood—probably won't last much longer."

Another team member walked over. "Tony is doing fine. He wrapped his own leg and gulped down a bottle of scotch. He'll be out cold for the whole trip back to base camp."

"All right, fellas. I promised the residents here in Giddings plenty of supplies for the fuel, but they said they don't have much left. They haven't received any shipments in quite a while. I'm sure that stopped when CSD took over Houston area refineries. Let's all get the legs stretched for a few minutes and get these wounded back to the doc's."

Dirk opened the back door and Meghan hopped out. Both grabbed the wounded teammate, placed him the rear of the vehicle, and asked the other sitting in the passenger seat if he could watch him. Meghan opened Ihan's door. She tugged Ihan's arm and asked him to get out of the vehicle. Ihan stumbled—his legs were swollen and probably numb.

"Thanks, Meghan." Ihan ducked his head blushed to the tips of his ears.

Meghan gave the captive a look more serene than Dirk had ever seen on her face. He knew Meghan was under lots of stress, whole team was. He just hoped she would deduce Ihan into believing he was cared for. Dirk snickered to himself—Ihan was covered in blood and now that his blush had faded, his face was pale and slack with shock. What a wimp.

"Why don't you walk over to that water hose. You need to clean some of that blood off you." Dirk jabbed his finger in the direction of the hose. "After that you can get into that old store and use their bathroom."

Meghan pointed to the water hose too, as though she thought the prisoner needed extra encouragement. Her limbs moved with easy grace as she led Ihan to the water and turned the dial. Water rushed out of the hose. "Go ahead and pick it up," she coaxed. Ihan bent down and tentatively sprayed his arms. Dirk smirked at Meghan. She blinked back at him. What did *that* mean?

Dirk knew his legs needed circulation. He walked

around the front of the gas station and looked both ways. A few vehicles drove through the streets and people walked in town. Giddings was more populated then most towns they'd traveled through.

He noticed a van stopped at the checkpoint. A clean and well-dressed man hopped out of the van, open his side door, and handed the residents boxes of something. The van then moved along and headed toward him. Dirk felt down his side, tapping his holster, to make sure his pistol was there. He thumbed the bottom of the clip to make sure it was full, then brushed along the grip to the safety knob. He pushed it forward so the safety was off.

As the van got closer he noticed there were three oriental men inside. The man sitting in the passenger seat pointed at Dirk and kept turning his head to the driver. The van slowed and pulled over to the side in front of Dirk, who kept his hand on his pistol. The passenger and side doors opened. Two men jumped out, one walked over to Dirk, and the other reached back into the van and came out with a camera. Their bright yellow vests bore a Chinese flag and with "News" emblazoned below it. Damn foreigners.

"Hello sir." One of the men shoved a microphone in Dirk's face, babbling a stream of heavily accented English. Dirk thought he said something like "I am Chen and request your honor with an interview. Your name, sir?"

The presence of Chinese newscasters could mean only that an attack by CSD was imminent.

"What honor are you requesting?" Dirk kept a straight face.

Chen turned back around, tapped his mike, and held it up in front of Dirk again.

"Chu`ang!" He looked into the camera. "Good evening. We heard of the recent United Texas Coalition attack against the City-State of Dallas and would like to know how your team is doing and if your attack was successful."

Dirk raised his eyebrows at Chen. "What do you mean by attack?"

Chen put the microphone down, spun around, and pointed his thumb down. The cameraman slanted the camera while Chen turned back around.

"Sir, we know you are a member of the United Texas Coalition and that you must be returning from the attack that recently happened in Dallas. I can see your exhaustion and the weapon your carrying. By no means can we harm you. We are reporters and just want to show the world your current situation."

Dirk continued to stare at Chen, squinting. "I have nothing to tell you and I suggest you move along."

He spun around and walked back to the building. Chen dropped his arm, letting the microphone dangle. Dirk heard the van doors open and close. The engine turned on and the van sped off. Dirk halted, turned his head, and watched the van take a left and then park several hundred feet away. The people in the van then stepped out and set up their equipment again.

His gut feeling told him the reporters had an agenda beyond covering the story of the attack on CSD. *Something fishy about to happen here.*

Dirk stood by the gas pumps and kept his elbows close

to his sides. He'd cultivated his calm, cool, and collected persona that impressed the entire team. Tragic events had taught him to take all situations seriously. He knew these things harmed his friendships, but the habit was ingrained. Most teammates never delved into closeness with him.

Stephan sauntered over to Dirk and stood next to him looking across the street.

"What's going on?"

"See those Chinese newscasters across the street setting up their stuff? They came by here and asked me how the attack on Dallas went. Those damned Chinese are marplots. You know as well as I, they're sided with Dallas. They have stones, asking me questions."

Stephan bared his teeth. "They're a bunch of pain-in-the-ass media vultures. It kind of makes me wonder why we can't rescind those orders that say we can't hurt them. Another one of Dusty's political diatribes that keep us from ending this mess."

Dirk glanced at Stephan. "Well, I guess that's your take on Dusty. I recommend we hurry on getting the vehicles gassed up so we get the hell out of here."

Two of the team members, behind the building, were leaning against one of the vehicles eating venison jerky and sharing a bottle of whiskey while the setting sun transformed the bleak landscape into gorgeous scenery.

One of them tipped the bottle to his mouth and took a long, satisfying pull. "Boy, the last time we saw something this beautiful was back when your sister came by to visit us in our locker room."

The other team member slapped the other's chest. "You fucker! That girl is still in puberty, which verifies you are a child molester."

"We get what we can get. Hell, who knows how long this life thing lasts."

They laughed, glad of the camaraderie at the end of a tough mission, and the bottle changed hands again.

To their left were several old trash bins, strewn in a line, in front of the bushes and trees. A strange sound became noticed, something shuffled behind the bins and a stomping seemed farther. The two men turned their heads fast. One put the whiskey bottle back on the vehicle, and both raised their weapons.

"What the hell is that?"

"Sounds like something is moving in the tree line."

"Let's fire it up to be safe."

"Hold what you got. If Stephan hears us fire and we kill some raccoon then we'll get our ass kicked for the ruckus."

One of the men reached down and grabbed a rock, brought it back behind his ear, and threw it hard. Tensing, they waited for a few seconds but didn't hear a thing.

The second team member smiled. "Dork."

The first man picked up a larger rock. He tossed underhanded and listened as it hit one of the trash bins hard. It made a loud thump. Instantly, the rustling sound increased in volume, and the men raised their weapons. Between two of the bins, a dog came rushing out, looked at the men with its tail down, and then skulked off to the right behind another building.

"That was some dog-looking raccoon. Damn!"

Relaxing again, they lowered their weapons.

Another movement drew their attention to the tree line. A SecureCon flew through the air and flopped on top of the trash bins. Bright flashes burst from its arms. Bullets riddled the bodies of the two men. The violence of the impact threw them on top of the vehicle, and they slid off the edges to crumple lifeless on the ground.

Meghan pulled out sanitization cloths in the bathroom, and heard gunfire. She was midway through her urine cycle. "Go figure!" She tried to flex her internal muscles to speed the cycle along, but it just kept going at a steady rate until it voided completely. The bullet sounds got closer and faster. She heard the pounding of ammunition against the outside wall. "Oh, forget this!" She threw the cloths on the floor, quickly pulled her pants up, snapped the buttons, pulled the zipper, and closed the belt. Leaning against the wall, she grabbed her weapon and put her hand on the doorknob, took a deep breath, and turned it quickly while leaning back against the wall. Once the door fully opened she pivoted and rolled headfirst out into the hallway. She got on her knees and pointed her weapon down the hallway.

Ihan sat on top of a stack of boxes next to her. He stared down the hallway before turning his head with his typical bewildered look.

Meghan grunted. "Get down off those boxes and get behind me!"

Ihan jumped off the boxes and sat down against the wall next to Meghan. His knees and feet protruded from behind them. She grabbed the edge of the nearest box and pulled as hard as she could, but the box didn't move.

"Grab the back of those boxes and help me push them out from the wall."

Reaching back with both arms, Ihan grabbed the end and pushed while Meghan yanked with one arm. The boxes moved a little but were heavy. It was enough—Ihan's feet were behind the boxes.

Dirk ran to the back corner of the building. He thumped his back against the wall, his weapon held vertical, and took a deep breath to calm himself. He then pointed his weapon out and spun around the end of the wall.

In front of Dirk, the vehicles were aligned in a row. A firing SecureCon spewed ammunition to the left, and to the right a team member's body sprawled on the ground, motionless and drenched in blood. Farther down the vehicle line, another SecureCon fired rounds into the front of the far building. The rest of the team was pinned down across from it.

He crouched and ran along the right side of the vehicles. He glanced into his vehicle. Looked empty. He took a few steps, looked in the back, and saw the wounded man lying motionless. He grabbed the rear door handle and swiveled into the backseat. He opened the lid of the box and took out the last jammer device. Another deep breath cleared his thoughts. He typed the code into the device's handle. He rolled back out of the vehicle, looked up to get his bearings, and tossed the device.

Ihan gazed at Meghan as she pushed his feet behind the boxes. Out of the corner of his eye, a swift-moving shadow got larger along the wall. A SecureCon thudded to the end of the hallway, its gears squealing as it turned toward them. Ihan's eyes widened. His heartbeat raced. Meghan was exposed in the middle of the hallway. She jolted back, hit the wall, and froze. She stared at her weapon but didn't move. The SecureCon clanked down the hallway.

Meghan sat still against the wall, her face a pasty white. The SecureCon was almost on top of them. He squinted and focused on the monitor mounted in the chest plate. *That's Gerald Bacon!* Outside of Dallas. Why? The fear and anxiety Ihan had lived with for days vanished. He felt only a numb curiosity.

Ihan stood. He jumped in front of Meghan, holding his arms out to his sides to shield her. The SecureCon halted and pointed both of its firing arms.

He tipped his face up to the monitor on the Secure-Con. "Gerald Bacon."

The SecureCon stood steady and brought both of its arms back as a camera zoom squealed.

Ihan leaned forward. "I know it's you, Gerald!"

The SecureCon's eye light flickered. "Ihan Duncan, is that you?"

"Yes it's me. You can see my face and recognize my voice."

"Why are you here and how are you still alive?"

Ihan lowered his arms and took a step toward the SecureCon. "I was taken from Dallas a few days ago.

Gerald, they lied to us. We are contagion free. That's the reason I'm still alive, it was cured!"

"A technical persona was stolen. I have orders to get it back no matter what."

"You mean Mona." A flare of anxiety burned in his chest. "She was stolen?"

"If you were taken, then I'm sure it's her."

"Where is she, Gerald?"

The screen on the SecureCon flicked and got fuzzy. In a matter of seconds, it went blank and the SecureCon's upper torso bent over.

"Gerald. Where is Mona?"

Ihan stepped closer to the SecureCon. Meghan yelled, "Ihan, get away from there!" She trotted fast, pulled him to the rear, and fired her weapon at the SecureCon. Ihan ducked with his hands over his ears. The SecureCon fell backward and slid to the floor.

"Let's get the hell out of here!"

Ihan stared at the SecureCon. He couldn't believe it was Gerald. Meghan grabbed his arm hard enough to hurt and towed him down the hallway and out the door. As he stepped outside, Ihan closed his eyes. The light was overwhelming. After a few seconds, he squinted and noticed a couple team members drag a damaged SecureCon over and toss it on top of another.

Dirk stared into Meghan's eyes, ignoring Ihan as he trotted toward them.

"Are you OK?"

Meghan stared at the SecureCon pile. "There's another one of those robots in the hallway next to the crapper."

"Really?" Dirk waved a couple of team members over. They ran into the building. "What happened in there?"

"When I finished doing my thing, I walked into the hallway and saw a SecureCon at the far end. I shot it up and we got out." Meghan's face was calm and confident; she stood upright with her shoulders back.

Ihan felt confused. That's not what had happened. He opened his mouth as he squinted at Meghan. Dirk tossed a glance at him and rolled his eyes before returning his attention to Meghan.

"Wow. That's what I call timing, Meghan. Another few seconds and you could have...well, you're here and that's all that matters. Right?"

Meghan's shoulders drooped. She sent Ihan an un-readable look. "Right! I'll bring Ihan into the vehicle, and then we need to get the hell out of here and back to base camp."

"Roger that. I'll tell Stephan and get us out of here."

Two of the team members carried the SecureCon out of the building and threw it on top of the others. One threw an incendiary grenade hot on top of the pile. "Fire in the hole!" The bright flames smoldered as the metal popped and split. The team members headed back to the vehicles.

Meghan stared out the window. Ihan sat beside her wondering why her attitude had turned solemn. He looked behind him and saw the injured man's body lying still, his complexion even paler than before.

"Why haven't you checked the man's pulse since we got back in this vehicle?"

Meghan slowly turned her head, looked at Ihan, then

turned around and saw the man's body in the back. She spun around and pressed her finger to the man's throat while looking at her watch. She moved her finger several times and finally let her hand slide away from his neck. She bent her head down and fell back into the seat. Ihan didn't know what he should do or say. Meghan started to shake as tears flowed from her eyes.

Ihan felt helpless. The reason she was feeling this way made sense to him. If this was Mona he would know what to say, but Meghan was not Mona in any way. He felt something inside of him, an unfamiliar feeling—a copulative feeling!—that overtook his thoughts. He leaned across the seat, grabbed Meghan's shoulders, and pulled her closer. She bent forward and put her head along his shoulder. Awkwardly, he wrapped his arms around her, and she let out her tears.

The front door opened, and Dirk leaned inside, hesitating before he swung into the driver's seat. He grimaced and blasted a smile toward Ihan before taking his seat. Ihan didn't think the smile was real. Once the vehicle turned on, Dirk pressed down on the gas pedal.

Meghan pulled her head back from Ihan's shoulders and wiped her eyes on her jacket. She blinked several times, looked at Ihan with a watery smile that was definitely real, and then pushed him back into his seat. He slumped back and stared ahead at the road, trying not to notice the concern on Dirk's face when the man checked on Meghan in the mirror every ten or twenty seconds.

"You de-stressing yet?"

"I'm fine, Dirk. By the way, I heard you tossed that jammer. Thanks for the timing on that. I owe you one."

The cold stare returned to Meghan's face. Ihan wished he could be that calm. The shooting pains in his stomach continued to increase. Not knowing where he was or what he was doing was tying him in knots. He found himself contemplating ways to escape and return to the only home he knew. He pushed the idea aside. This current path was uncertain, but he felt safe with the UTF team, though he didn't know why.

CHAPTER SEVENTEEN

Stephan's vehicle wove through the laterally staggered concrete barricades leading into UTC underground facility in San Antonio. The team followed the signs to the main entrance checkpoint and halted. Cameras atop thick metal poles scanned the vehicles for electronic signatures. Once the scan completed, the sign turned green and two heavily armed guards walked out of their concrete shacks to verify the team codes in all vehicles. The last set of barriers, a row of four-foot metal blocks across the road, bent forward and slammed into the ground. The guards waved the vehicles through into the dark oval entrance.

As the vehicles angled down the curved road, they traveled deep into the facility. The road leveled off at a depth of two hundred feet, and opened into the Coalition's large motor pool. The large concrete structure echoed with sounds and smelt musty. Several UTC support and medical personnel emerged running from a hallway, pushing two gurneys. Stephan jumped from his vehicle and directed them to the rear of the convoy. He walked fast to join the medics as they pulled out an injured team member whose pallid skin worried Stephan more than he liked to admit. The medics transferred the member to their gurney and wheeled away at a brisk trot.

"Hey, wait a minute!" Stephan jogged closer to the gurney and grabbed it, halting the medics. One of them had a mournful look on his face.

Stephan's belly tightened. "Is this guy going to make it?"

The medic looked down at the team member.

"Sorry to say sir, but this gentleman is deceased. From the looks and inner temperature, he has been for a while."

Stephan closed his eyes and breathed in heavily. He took his hands off the gurney and bowed his head. The medics looked at each other and frowned but started pushing the gurney toward the hallway. Moving his eyes to observe the body, Stephan noticed more medics drop from the last vehicle. He crossed his fingers as his thoughts filled with grief to the point where he felt numb. After he reached the end of the vehicle, a medic waved across the room to a few members who stood by the second gurney. Another team member lay on it, motionless and pale.

"He didn't make it either," Dirk said quietly. "A bullet got him at Giddings."

Dirk leaned against the front of the vehicle. Stephan walked over and stood next to him.

"I just cannot believe this, Dirk." How had it gone so wrong?

"Neither can I. Just try to remember that all of them died for a reason that means a lot to this cause. You did one hell of a job leading us into that city, and we all believe those captured items will help us kick that Dallas ass."

Stephan forced a grim smile and a wink. "Thanks."

A man entered the room with his arms out and let out a loud whistle. Dusty—who else down here would have such blatant disregard for fallen team members? Stephan clenched his hands into fists.

Dusty heading toward Meghan, who had just grabbed her bags from the vehicle. She flung them on the floor as Dusty firmly hugged her. The thought of that man putting his hands on a woman like Meghan made Stephan feel ill. Dirk looked Stephan in the eyes, and Stephan could tell he wasn't hiding his bitterness well.

Dirk nodded toward the payload vehicle. "How about we grab those captured goods and bring them in to the secure room?"

Stephan didn't move or take his focus off Dusty. Dirk stepped in front of him, grabbed his arm, turned him around, and walked him around the other side of the convoy. Two of the team members stood next to a vehicle and placed items from the vehicle into their bags.

"Hey guys, why don't you get those bags later and help us take in that processor and Ihan guy," Stephan said.

"Sure thing, boss."

Both team members dropped their bags and jumped into the back of the vehicle to push the box toward the tailgate. Once the box was halfway over the edge, Dirk held it upright while the team members jumped down and grabbed both ends of the box. He stepped away, and they carried it toward the hallway. Dirk walked to the next vehicle, opened the rear right door, and grabbed the prisoner's shoulder.

"Let's go, Ihan."

Ihan stumbled out the door, and Dirk had to hold him up so his scrawny legs wouldn't collapse under him.

"Where are we going?" Ihan's eyes were huge as he gazed around the vast motor pool.

"Just follow me."

Stephan let Dirk lead Ihan around the vehicle. He kept his eyes on Dusty, who still had his arms around Meghan and raised his head as the three walked around the back of the vehicle. Stephan locked eyes with Dusty for an instant and then turned his head. The last thing he wanted was sympathy from his father's murderer.

"Stephan! Welcome back and congratulations on your successful mission," Dusty said.

Stephan walked past him, his face stiff and emotionless, looking directly ahead. A ton of impatience distracted him. Dusty was the last man he wanted to deal with. He didn't know how to handle Dusty after this tumultuous mission. Dusty pulled away from Meghan, took a few steps forward, and waved his arm.

"Stephan!"

Stephan eyed the door to the tunnel leading to his quarters. It would feel so good to keep walking, to show the bastard just how little respect he had for him. But the repercussions of that would interfere with his personal mission, so Stephan halted and turned back toward Dusty, keeping a tight rein on his emotions so his face wouldn't betray him again.

The seconds that passed while Dusty closed the distance between them stretched out like hours. Each smug, overbearing step drilling deeper into Stephan's pride. Then Dusty stood in front him, his teeth bared in a lying smile.

"Welcome back from that successful mission and sorry to hear about the losses. You have a scuff on your forehead. How are you?"

Stephan kept a straight face. "I'm fine."

"I noticed a small, pale individual Dirk was moving along, and that makes me question the reasoning behind that capture. But hell, if those clowns have personalities, it might be beneficial." Dusty sneered. "Did you manage to capture that Dallas computer so I won't have to taunt you too much?"

Stephan closed his eyes to keep himself from snarling. Any mission could end in death for any of the team members. They all knew that. He reminded himself that today's losses were nothing like what had happened the day his father died, because Stephan was nothing like Dusty. A sudden hallucination of shooting Dusty flung through his thoughts. Aware of his loaded pistol at his side, he clamped down on the urge with iron control. This wasn't the time.

Silence reigned for a moment, and then Stephan said, "I really must be getting to my team room, so if you please, allow me to depart."

He swung around toward the hallway and headed through the door. Dusty's silence grated at him.

CHAPTER EIGHTEEN

Ihan spent a cold, lonely night locked in a small room in the UTC base camp. His situation hadn't improved by the time he opened his eyes the next morning. A fluorescent light bulb in the middle of the concrete ceiling cast a harsh glare over bare concrete walls. He couldn't detect vents or windows. At the end of the room was a steel door with what looked like a slide-opening portal in the middle. He remembered being brought into this room last night by two men who escorted him away from Dirk, but he'd been to fatigued to pay attention to where he was.

His legs ached but felt jittery at the same time, so he decided to stand and stretch them. The floor was cold against his bare feet as he drew each knee to his chest a few times, and then jogged in place. His muscles loosened up a little. Maybe someday he'd get used to living in Meghan's world, with all its physical exertion. Maybe he'd even enjoy it.

The doors hissed open. Ihan halted and turned his head. Two enormous men rushed into the room and directly at him. They smashed into him and threw him to the floor. Ihan's buttocks hit the concrete, and then the back of his head slammed the ground. His head went numb. His vision blurred. Unintelligible voices echoed. Hard, rough hands yanked Ihan to his feet and dragged him out the door to another room across the hallway.

The men pressed Ihan down hard on a metal chair and rammed him forward against a metal table. The light was vastly brighter and made Ihan squint. The two men walked out and slammed the door, and Ihan cautiously raised a hand to rub the back of his head.

The room was colder and much smaller than the one he'd spent the night in. A large mirror, mounted in the wall rather than on it, took up most of the wall before him. The light dim, ever so slightly. Out of the corner of his eye, he noticed a large, muscular man stomp toward him from the corner of the room—his face had a mean look and his skin was reddish. The man bent down and pushed the metal table into Ihan's chest, forcing him and the chair backward. The chair slammed into the wall and a split second later, Ihan's head did as well.

"Tell me the password to that processor!"

With extreme pain ringing his head and chest, the only response Ihan could make was to feel queasy and force his eyelids wide open. The man pulled back the table and slammed it into Ihan's chest again. Ihan felt a snap. Vivid pain exploded in his ribs, and he gagged.

"Tell me now or I will kill you!"

The sensation of his throat getting filled made Ihan open his mouth. He vomited onto the table. The large man jerked his hands off the table and leaned back.

"That's nasty."

He angled forward and slapped Ihan's face. He then

seized his chin in a crushing grip so Ihan had no choice but to look straight into his eyes.

Ihan didn't need previous experience with being killed to understand these were the eyes a man who enjoyed coldblooded, hands-on homicide.

A smaller man entered through the door. He tapped the shoulder of the larger one, who flailed Ihan's chin before releasing it. The large man grumbled an obscenity and headed toward the door.

Ihan leaned forward on the table, blinking in confusion and pain. The smaller man stood nearby, inquisitively staring at him.

"You are OK now that I sent that violent man away. You won't have to worry about him anymore." The man's soft voice penetrated the fog of Ihan's pain. "My name is Charlie and I am here to help you. I don't know who let that bad man in here."

Ihan wanted to feel relief, wanted to believe this man. He straightened in the chair, but the motion made him lean to the side and vomit again. Charlie slid the table back, and when Ihan toppled forward, he ran around the table and grabbed Ihan's shoulders, placing him back gently.

"Good lord, you don't look good at all. Let me help you and make you feel better."

Charlie took a few steps across the room and grabbed some things off another table. He turned and placed a pitcher of water, a towel, and a glass on the table in front of Ihan. He poured water onto the towel and gently wiped Ihan's face before filling the glass and putting it up to his lips. After a few sips, he set the glass down.

"Why don't you just let me know what the password is to your processor? If you do, I guarantee you'll come to no more harm." Charlie's eyes looked calm.

"Why are you asking me for a password?"

"Because we need to get into your processor. It's very important, Ihan. Your giving us the password will help us survive."

Ihan's lip trembled. "Survive? Survive what?"

"There is an evil city force out there that wants to kill us. They will do anything to hunt us down and kill us."

"What city are you talking about?"

Charlie raised an eyebrow. "Come on now, Ihan, you know which city I'm talking about. City-State of Dallas misguided you and lied to you your whole life. They probably didn't tell you that Dallas has been sending out all its robotic forces, the SecureCons, after us."

Ihan wrapped his arms around his sides to put some pressure on his sore ribs. He closed his eyes and took a deep breath. "If I have been misguided, then how would my processor help you?"

"Because that processor is the one who is conducting that misguidance and is the one who knows the truth. The truth about who is killing us."

"If I had a password, I would give it to you. But I really don't understand what you mean by a password."

Charlie's smile dropped. His face turned bitter. "I see how it is. I will go get you some pain medication and some food for your empty stomach. I will be back shortly."

After the door closed Ihan let out a big breath and cringed at how sharply the pain throbbed in his ribs. One might be broken. He might have internal bleeding.

The door flung open and the brutish, muscular man stomped in, growling out evil sounds. Ihan shielded himself with his arms. The man violently pushed the table aside. He grabbed Ihan's ankles and pulled him straight off the chair. Ihan thumped hard to the floor. The man crouched over him and slapped his face back and forth until he thought his neck would snap.

"Tell me that password now or I will kill you!"

Ihan moved his mouth but couldn't make sounds, couldn't breathe past the ache in the center of his chest.

The man twisted his fist in Ihan's shirt and yanked him to his feet. He spun him around and threw him. Ihan flew in an arc across the room and hit the far wall. He crumpled to the floor. He lay motionless, able only to sob. And watch the man come at him again.

Behind the man, Charlie entered the room, a plate of food in his hand.

"Get out of the room now!" he yelled, and the large man turned and walked away. He stopped at the door and turned around.

"Just tell me when, and I will come back here to kill that piece of shit!"

"Just get out of here now or I will have you thrown in jail," Charlie said mildly.

The large man grunted and slammed the door. Charlie put the plate on to the table and ran over to Ihan.

"I am so sorry that evil man got back in here. Are you OK?"

Ihan's eyes felt like they would burst any moment, and he could barely see through the tears flowing down his face. He coughed hard, and when he covered his mouth with his hand, his palm got wet. He lowered it and saw blood dripping from it.

Charlie grabbed Ihan by the arms, helping to pull him up, but Ihan shrugged away from him. He stood, queasy, and swayed. Groping at the wall for stability, he stumbled over to the chair and sat down. The towel lay on the floor, and Ihan bent forward and reached for it. Charlie was quicker and raised the towel. Ihan snatched it from Charlie's hands, grunting with the effort.

Charlie looked Ihan in the eyes.

"I can see how much pain you're in and I really want you to feel better. All you have to do is tell me the password, and I can promise you that evil guy will not come back in here." He stood tall. "You have to understand that I am your watcher, the guy who is protecting you from that violence, but I just don't know how long I can watch you if you don't tell me soon. I mean, think about it, I cannot stay in this room twenty-four hours a day. I have to sleep and attend to my personal activities. You see how much I protect you from that guy when I'm here, but when I left to get you some food and water, that guy sneaked back in here. Just tell me the password, Ihan, and you can get some rest."

Ihan dabbed the moist towel on his stinging face and studied Charlie's expression. Something about it seemed fake, like the way Dirk had smiled at him when he had his arms around Meghan.

"Can I ask you a question?"

"Sure, Ihan. Ask me whatever you need and I will do my best to answer."

"I cannot understand what the point of this is. I

mean, when it comes to being asked a question, I always answer with the truth." Ihan coughed. Pain flared in his chest, and he tasted blood. "You keep asking for some password, but if I knew that password I would tell you right away, especially if I knew I was going to get beaten for not telling it."

Charlie grimaced. "So let me know what it is and I will—"

"Charlie, please stop! That thing you are talking about is Mona and she is a computer personality that adheres to my voice and commands. I have never known of any password, it is just my voice." Ihan wrapped his arm about his ribs.

Charlie stood up and walked over to the table. He pushed it over toward Ihan, mercifully stopping before it came in contact with his chest, and removed the plastic covering from the food plate.

"Please finish wiping your face, eat some food, and drink some water. I'm going to step out of this room to take care of some items, but I promise you that evil guy will not return."

As Charlie walked away, Ihan brought the towel to his face and felt the pain. He dropped the towel to his lap and took a deep breath. He looked down at the food on the plate, but just couldn't stomach it. He gingerly wrapped his hands around the water glass and sipped as fast as he could, ignoring the sting of the water in his lacerated mouth.

Ihan still didn't know where he was, and though he knew Charlie and the man who had beaten him so brutally wanted him to help them access Mona, he didn't trust them. He honestly didn't know what their motivation was. He *did* care about Meghan and wondered why she wasn't with him. Ihan shook his head. All he'd seen since being taken from CSD was violence, constant death, and frightened looks in everyone's faces. Meghan has a compassionate look in her eyes, one Ihan had never seen before. He hoped to see it again.

Chapter Nineteen

Classical music jarred Meghan awake. She shoved the sleeping goggles off her eyes as the volume of the music increased, grating along every exhausted brain cell. Across the sleeping quarters, a team member was wiping his back with a towel. Meghan bent over and grabbed a plastic ball from under her bunk. She fired it across the room and it hit his back. When he looked over his shoulder she tapped her ear, but he just bumped the volume up again. She pulled her blanket over her head.

The musky scent of Dirk's cologne joined the barrage against her senses. Great. She felt pressure on her big toe. It increased, and she pulled the blanket off her face. Dirk stood at the foot of her bed, pinching her toe.

"What is up with your weird foot-grabber fetish?"

"Howdy, Meghan." He gave her a laconic grin. "Sorry to disturb your beauty sleep, but it's time to head down for the post-mission interview."

Meghan bolted to a sitting position. "What the hell time is it and how long have I been asleep?"

"It's sixteen hundred and you've been out for approximately twenty-four hours."

Meghan stretched her arms over her head, yawning.

Give her another twenty-four, and she could sleep that away too. She rubbed her eyes in an attempt to wake up a little more. Dirk turned his head to the side. She looked that way and saw nothing out of the ordinary. Cool air brushed her midriff. She looked down and saw her shirt was rumpled, exposing her navel. Funny, she hadn't pegged Dirk as a prude. She rolled her eyes and brought the blanket up higher. By no means was she indecently attired—she always slept in the team room with the men, and she knew better than to titillate them. Being a female team member was hard enough even when they thought of her as one of the guys.

"Ah, come on, Dirk, I'm sure you've seen a woman's skin before." She pulled the covers higher anyway.

Dirk turned his head back smiled. He was a good guy, for sure—morally upright and always comported himself in a mannerly fashion around women. When they left for a mission, though, he was a warrior, and acted that way, as he left base camp. Meghan smirked as Dirk stared at her midsection.

"Earth to Dirk, is everything all right in that brain of yours?"

Dirk shook his head and looked Meghan in the eyes.

"Yeah, all is good." Dirk cleared his throat. "Just get awake, clean, and make sure you hurry to the conference room."

Meghan watched Dirk walk out of the room. She threw the blanket down and swung her legs off the bed. She glanced the room and noticed the rest of the team had left—she was the late one again. No one telling her the time of the event had become the norm, and it pissed her off.

In the shower, Meghan braced her hand against the wall and moved her head back and forth in the spray of hot water for a while before she got down to the business of scrubbing off the mission dirt and sweat.

The team kept themselves at a platonic distance from her—none more distant than Dirk. The only time he ever looked at her was when she asked him questions or Stephan ordered him to work with her. Not that he was any closer to other members. But in recent times, Dirk interacted with her more, seemed more sociable with her though still reclusive with others. Her mouth popped open. *How did I not see this before?*

Meghan turned the shower off, grabbed the towel off the rack, and headed back to her locker. To take her mind off the alarming shift of Dirk's sentiments, she thought of Ihan. After Dirk took him away, she'd been pulled in other directions by her father. Ihan was just a prisoner, and a scrawny one at that. She shouldn't even care what had happened to him. Still, she wondered where he was. How he was doing in what must be a frightening new world. It didn't matter that she shouldn't care, she felt strange not knowing Ihan's status.

After Meghan got dressed, she hurried to the Operation Center.

"Hey there," her dad said. "Glad you finally decided to show up. Please take a seat at the table and let's get rolling with this."

The team was sitting around the table, with Dusty at one end and Stephan at the other. She closed the door

and took a seat near the end of the table next to her father.
Dusty took a sip of water.

"Just to reiterate my thanks for your wonderful mission, I do plan on throwing y'all a dinner after this meeting and hope y'all like the tasty beverages we just got in yesterday. We have home-grown whiskey from Kentucky."

All the team members grinned and slapped one another's shoulders in anticipation. Looking to her left, she smiled at Dirk, who smiled back, but when she looked down the table at Stephan, he was sitting there with his head down, showing no sign of emotion whatsoever. Dusty cleared his throat.

"This two-pronged mission success is by far the preeminent accomplishment of the Texas Coalition, and one that will increase our motivation due to our understanding that Dallas is vulnerable to our proactive approach. The timing between the Dallas and Midland attacks confused our enemy and that is because those conventional farts never had to deal with two simultaneous attacks. Taking out their largest oil refinery and fields, which they stole from Texas, and gathering great intelligence on their internal systems will lead us to our overall victory. We will bring this great state back to normal."

Stephan raised his head and looked at her father. His eyelids narrowed to slits.

"Where is the processor currently located, and please tell me you haven't attempted to break into it yet?"

"Good question, Stephan. A few hours after you brought it here, I had a team of technological analysts look at it."

"Just tell me they haven't already tried to enter the processor. We attempted a few days back with no success, and it transmitted a signal that gave away our location."

"Unfortunately, they have attempted but still haven't found a way in."

Stephan shook his head. He slammed his fist down on the table. The rest of the room was silent as every member stared at Stephan.

"What kind of internal communication problem do we have here? This is our first post-mission meeting, and this is where you're supposed to get that kind of information. Have you checked to see if that processor sent out a signal?"

Dusty's smile drooped to a straight face. "Well, they did catch a small indicator emanating from that processor but since then no worries, because it was moved into a safe room where..."

Stephan bared his teeth. "Great, now our location has been compromised!"

"Calm down, Stephan. That signal strength was weak, and I was told there is no way it could have transmitted that far." Dusty stared at Stephan. "I know you're upset about this, but your team was exhausted and needed rest. The fact that we have the golden ticket to Dallas means they will focus on us. The way I see it is that Dallas knows they are vulnerable and not as secure as they once were. This obviously means carte blanche impromptu attacks upon us, which will open their vulnerability."

Her father reached under the table and pulled up a bottle of whiskey. He plopped it down on the table before smiling to the team. He then pressed a button on the table. In a matter of seconds, the door opened and waiters rolled pushcarts laden with bottles and glasses into the room—the team erupted in cheers.

Dusty beamed. "You veteran warriors, the ones who will bring this great state back, go forth and drink copious amounts of whiskey and enjoy the celebratory dinner. God bless you all!"

The team all stood up and walked toward the pushcarts. Country music started playing, and many within the room shook hands and tapped one another on the shoulders. Stephan jumped up and grabbed a bottle of whiskey from a cart moving past him. He opened the bottle and drank from it while others slapped him on the shoulders.

Meghan felt her father tap her arm. She smiled at him and put her hand on his. He led her over to the corner of the room. Dusty blinked away telltale moisture from his eyes and rubbed her shoulders.

"How are you feeling, my beloved daughter?"

"I'm fine and I can see you are talented in knowing how to conduct morale-building festivities. How in the hell did you get the whiskey?"

"A good father knows how to surprise his daughter with astonishing gifts. A woman your mother grew up with is now living in Kentucky, and I keep in contact with her. She misses her as much as we do. She sends her regards, plus is on our side to getting our state back in order."

"The next time you talk to her, please tell her I send thanks as well." Meghan's mood turned serious. "I must say that I agree with Stephan's comments about your messing with that processor before ever chatting with us in regards to what our experiences are. Within a matter of moments after it transmitted that signal, we picked up detection and aerial vehicles headed directly for us. I just don't think we know how advanced and technologically superior that city-state truly is—and that could lead us into a tragedy."

"I can understand your thoughts and feelings about this but I must tell you that this has been thought of for quite some time. Think about it, Meghan, we have been dealing with and combating that nasty city-state for many years. We do know how technologically advanced they are, albeit due to sucking it up with China and letting them dictate CSD domestic matters." He chuckled. "My true scope is bringing this great state back in order, but these city-states are allowing foreign governments to suck all our resources, and that is anti-American."

"It doesn't matter, Dad. The point is, you are not communicating with the team that brought you the processor. Stephan is a great leader, and I'm proud to be on his team. And now I can understand why he either dislikes or distrusts you. You need to do a better job of keeping him in the loop and listening to what he says."

Dusty smirked. "Got you. I'll keep Stephan more in the loop."

"You promise?"

Dusty raised his hand up and put his index and middle fingers together.

"Scouts honor promise."

Meghan shook her head with a smile while Dusty

opened his mouth and put his teeth together for his trade-mark overboard smile.

"You are a goof, Dad, and I do love you. Oh, by the way, where is Ihan currently at and is he safe?"

"Ihan? You mean that skinny and pale guy your team captured from Dallas?"

Meghan raised her eyebrows. "You don't know his name? I guess I thought you would have been told by now."

"Things have been busy lately and my head is spinning in many directions."

"So where is he?"

"He's down in the secure wing of the complex, and they're still working him. I'm due an update within the next hour."

Meghan's emotions started to ache. "Update? Secure wing? Dad, what in the hell is going on?"

"We found that to get into the processor, we need a password. That looks like about the only benefit he has for us."

"So what you're saying is, he's being interrogated."

"You could say that. What's with that frown on your pretty little face?" He touched her cheek with his finger, and she impatiently brushed it away.

"How do I get into that wing?"

"Meghan, you don't want to go down to that wing. Stay here and enjoy the drinks and dinner."

"Fine, I'll find it myself."

Meghan threw her hands down as she turned away. Her father grabbed her shoulder.

"Where are you going with this? Why do you have such an interest in this guy?"

"Dad, Ihan is a good man who was born into that city-state mess. He doesn't deserve to be treated like this."

Her father's face rumpled in bewilderment. "What are you saying?"

She realized what she'd said and how he might have perceived it, but the thought of Ihan's being mistreated or abused gnawed at her. She deemed Ihan's personality as not one of evil but one of openness and intellect. *Why am I so worried about Ihan? Why can't I get him out of my head?* She looked up at her father and tried to think of the proper wording to justify seeing Ihan. Dusty placed his hand lightly upon her shoulder.

"Meghan, are you OK?"

Just ducky. "I hardly ever ask you for favors, Dad. Do you remember the last favor I asked of you when I was a teenager and it took over a week before you finally said yes?"

Dusty smirked. "You mean the pouting, screaming, throwing things around the house, and not eating anything I cooked for you?"

Meghan looked away. "OK. That may have been a bad example but the point is, I hardly ever ask favors from you."

"Let's use this example of my caving in and allowing you that favor." Dusty gently tugged her chin forward. "You run out of the house, meet up with this boy across the street, get lost with him down by the river. I don't see or hear from you in twelve hours, I form a neighborhood team and search for you for another twelve hours, and finally find you under a tree lying in this guy's lap."

"OK! Really bad example and let's just forget that debacle now." Meghan inhaled deeply and let out a bunch of air in a quietly blown raspberry. "I was designated by Stephan to take the lead on Ihan. Once we captured him, I spent many hours interrogating him myself. I can honestly say that he doesn't know any password."

"Come on, Meghan, you are not a trained interrogator. I know you well enough to say that you're not the one who could get valuable information out of a stranger."

Meghan stuck out her jaw. "I don't have to be a trained interrogator to understand what Ihan said. He doesn't know how to lie. You know as well as I that their society is one of control and physical isolation. They communicate via a network and their processors monitor all discussion. Their reclusive lifestyle would drive people insane, and that is the reason why their internal processors were created—to help them live with some sense of contentment and sanity. Ihan chatted with his processor, named Mona, throughout the day. CSD technology is advanced enough for verbal recognition and biometrics. So why would he need a password? I guess you need to rethink your interrogation, because it's technologically Stone Age."

Her father's eyes bulged. Then he started to laugh.

"You are a flabbergasting woman, Meghan. I commend your thoughtful approach. You certainly make me proud to be your father and continually keep me flexible trying to understand you. I should make you our technological philosopher."

Meghan stood quietly, concentrating on staying serious as her father giggled and held his tummy like a big toddler.

"Come on, Dad. Before you hurt this good man, please let me talk with him and earn his trust once again. I do believe Ihan will help us by getting into Mona."

"What makes you think that guy is trustworthy? "

Meghan raised her arm to her father's shoulder as he had done to her a few moments ago.

"You can trust *me*."

Her father pursed his lips. He nodded. "All right, Meghan. I'll let the guards allow you into the wing."

Meghan leaned forward and kissed his chin. "Thanks, Dad. I love you!" She turned around and headed out the door while the rest of the team continued eating and drinking along the table.

Stephan noticed Meghan heading out the door. Dusty stared at his daughter then grabbed his communicator and spoke into it for a few seconds. A team member handed Dusty a drink. The old murderer smiled Stephen's way and raised his glass. Stephan kept his face tranquil but he raised his glass and downed the whiskey in one gulp.

Dusty strolled the room in a cordial manner—team members and operational staff raised their glasses as he passed. The rest of the room continued to chat about the mission's good and bad times. Stephan cringed when Dusty stopped next to him.

"You mind if I take this seat?"

Stephan stuffed a cracker in his mouth and chewed it instead of answering. He nodded yes, which he knew

Dusty would interpret as "No, I don't mind." The chair skidded back, and Dusty sat next to him.

A staff member serving the table asked if they wanted more whiskey. Both men nodded, and their good-sized glasses were filled to the rims. Stephan leaned forward and slugged back a few inches to feel the whiskey sting his throat. Dusty grinned and raised his glass high.

"Congratulations on the mission's success! You never cease to amaze me, how first-rate your operational manner is in the conduct of your missions. Your team members and this coalition commend you. To be honest with you, I really wouldn't want anyone else performing these special missions. Here's to you, Stephan, the one man my daughter respects!"

Stephan had just filled his mouth with crackers. He stopped chewing and turned his head to look at Dusty. He swallowed, the dry crackers scraping their way down. *I could reach up and slap the glass out of his hand before he knew what hit him. Or pick up his glass and toss his own whiskey in his face.* Stephan raised his glass and tapped Dusty's before they both took good sips. Dusty laughed and landed a good-natured slap on his shoulder before snatching a cracker from his plate.

"After you get some rest and finish your after action review, we need to discuss our next operation." Dusty said.

Stephan's neck ached as he felt his pulse increase. "Did you get my report on the inadequate body armor and how my team member died due to Dallas' newfangled ammunition?"

"That was discussed the moment after you sent it. I

immediately inquired as to a plan of how we can combat this difficulty. After many pitches and opinions, I learned from our new delegate that the latest body armor has been tested to repel any form of small arms ammunition. He is currently working on getting us permission to obtain them."

Stephan stiffened in distrust. "Who is this delegate?"

"I approved an interaction a few weeks ago through many conversations with the Indian Defense Department, who—"

"The Indian Government? So what you're telling me is that a delegate is currently here with us?"

"Yes, he arrived with four others a few days ago from Mumbai."

Stephan leaned forward and stared into Dusty's eyes.

"Four days ago. What is the purpose of this? How can we trust anyone in this phase of state unification? And now it's been agreed we'll allow a foreign government to assist us—what path are we heading down?"

"No worries about path direction, that was decided when we got word Dallas created an accord with China. Hell, now we have to fight a city backed by a country."

Stephen grunted. "Why India?"

"They are currently in a cold war with China, and both are siding with whatever unsigned nation is out there. The bottom line is, we have to counterbalance whatever gets in our way."

"Let me ask you a hypothetical question. If India

sends more troops, then will China? You're putting us in the middle of their fight, not ours."

"That is not my intent. The Indians only sent Assam Rifles combat advisors."

"All right, if we can get a hold of equipment advancements, then we have that going for us. My bottom line is, the sooner we get rid of the City-State of Dallas, the faster we can eliminate these other matters."

Dusty smiled. "Touché! But I'm in charge, and that is why I made this decision."

Stephan stood out of his chair and pushed it hard into the table. Dusty raised his eyes.

"Where you going, Stephan? You didn't even finish your whiskey."

Stephan stomped out the door.

CHAPTER TWENTY

Meghan opened the elevator door and peered into a gloomy hallway on the second floor. A musty smell lingered in the air. With her hand over her nose, she walked ahead through the dark hallway. Farther down the long corridor, bare light bulbs dangled from the ceiling—it looked as though the corridor distance was thinner.

After several steps, a brighter light emanated from an opening to the right side. She approached it and saw a steel door at the end of another hallway. Glancing both ways, she proceeded with caution and stopped before the door. A buzzer sounded. She looked back over her shoulder and noticed red sensor light jetting across the hallway she'd just passed through.

Once Meghan arrived at the steel door, she noticed a palm-sized rectangular glass bubble projecting from the otherwise bare wall. A bright red line traveled from the top to the bottom. "Identification confirmed," a simulated voice announced.

The door opened, revealing a bright hallway that was chilly and smelled clean, though a desk on the left side looked filthy and was strewn with heaps of dishes and wrappers. A guard with his feet on the desk was reading a book. He paid her no attention. She decided to walk around the desk.

From the corner of her eyes, she saw a distant door open. A blond man emerged from it and locked it behind him. He looked both ways and headed toward the guard desk with his hand raised in greeting. The lights within the corridor dimmed slightly. Meghan looked down at her watch—it was the nightly hour of light reduction for underground living. Goose bumps prickled her skin. She knew the environment in the facility and wondered why her emotions were on edge. The blond man got closer.

"Miss Rhodes. It's a pleasure to meet you. My name is Charlie, and I run this interrogation cell." He reached his hand out. "Mr. Rhodes called me a few minutes ago and told me you wanted to see this interesting man your team captured recently. I must say, he is an information hider, but we are close to finding the password."

Meghan felt her blood pressure rise, and her posture tightened. She knew she had to keep a professional demeanor. The annoying display of confidence and authority on Charlie's face amplified her distrust—and increased her fear. However, she'd been down this road before; the insensitive approach was the only one to take with a man like Charlie. She shook his hand.

"Nice to meet you, Charlie. Please tell me the status of Ihan."

"Sure. He's been asleep for an hour. We decided he needed some rest after the intense interrogation techniques we've been using for the past several hours."

Meghan clenched her fists briefly, then forced herself to relax. "What were you ordered to retrieve from him?"

"The password to his processor."

"Password?"

"Yes. We were told that the processor you captured was technologically advanced to the extent that we couldn't get into it with our current techniques and tools."

"Did you know that Ihan was already interrogated by me, at a location on our way back here?"

Charlie grimaced. "No, we sure weren't informed. I would really appreciate your letting me know what you got from him. That will give us either a different approach or a way to enlarge yours."

"That may be, but first I need to physically see him."

"No problem. Follow me."

The walk down the hallway was intolerably slow. Meghan stared at the back of Charlie's head, her fingers clenching and releasing, clenching and releasing. She envisioned plowing her fist into his skull. If he had hurt Ihan—

Charlie put his finger onto the terminal by the door. The sensor beeped and flashed a red light. He stepped back as the door opened.

"After you."

Meghan walked through the door into a shorter hallway. Two closed doors lined each side. The first two were solid, and the last two had windows. She looked through one. The floor was littered with food dishes, clothing items spread about, and many tables with Tasers and injection needles along the tabletops. Meghan took careful steps and eyed the floor so she wouldn't trip. Another door opened. A large man came out of the room carrying cups and a pitcher of water. He shoved aside debris on one of the tables and placed the new items on the table, and turned to face her. Charlie came to her side.

"Meghan, this is my partner, Gary Doyle. Gary, this is Meghan."

Gary extended his arm and put his hand out. Had this man given Ihan injections? Used a Taser on him? Meghan forced herself to shake his hand. He picked a few items off the floor and headed toward the entry door, kicking aside rubbish as he went.

"Is everything OK?" Charlie said.

Meghan shook her head. "Everything is fine."

"Sorry for the dirty hall. We were going to clean this up but obviously you arrived before we tackled that."

Meghan stared through the window. Ihan lay on a bare mattress against the far wall. The room was white, and the only other object in the room was a toilet chair along the right wall. She held herself back from busting through the door. Keeping calm in appearance was her only guarantee Charlie would let her in to see Ihan.

"As you can see, Ihan is fast asleep but we shall get back with him in a matter of minutes. Both Gary and I feel we're close to getting what we need." Charlie said.

Meghan kept her head still as Charlie leaned forward.

"Would you like to go in the other room so I can bring you up to speed on what we know?"

Meghan lowered her head and stared at the floor. Her arms jerked as she fought the instinct to take Charlie down so she could get to Ihan. She raised her hands and pressed her palms against the cool glass. Her vision seemed subtly sharper and sweat prickled along her hairline. She drew a slow breath and released it.

"Please open this door and let me see Ihan for a few minutes."

Charlie jetted his head back. "I don't know about that Meghan, it's against regulations."

"Regulations?" She dropped her arms off the door and slowly turned her body to face Charlie. She leaned forward and the skin on her forehead tightened.

"That is how we operate and—"

"You either let me in the door or my father, Dusty Rhodes, will convict you for not assisting me!"

Charlie's gaze darted to his watch. "What is it you want in there?"

"Just checking his physical status and that's all you need to know."

"OK." He glanced over his shoulder. "But I can only give you five minutes."

Meghan smirked. "That'll be enough."

She judged the window's height from the floor. She then looked around the garbage covering the hallway floor and spotted a steel tray leaning haphazardly against one of the table legs. It would do.

She dragged the chair toward Ihan's cell and grabbed the steel tray.

"Open the door." Meghan blinked at Charlie and added, "Please."

Charlie frowned at the chair and the tray. She raised an eyebrow at him, daring him to question her. He huffed and stuck his finger on the terminal. The door automatically opened.

Meghan dragged the two items into the room. She dropped the tray on the chair and looked around the room. She noticed a visual sensor within a plastic bubble attached to the far wall.

"Thanks, Charlie. Please close the door and give me some time."

Meghan mimicked a smile as Charlie closed the door. She bumped the chair against the door and placed the steel tray on top, blocking the window. She then reached down and grabbed a strip of toilet paper, jumped onto the toilet seat, and draped the paper over the plastic bubble, taping the sides with a strip of medical tape from the roll in her pocket. Meghan noticed no other optical sensors as she inspected the room. There was nothing she could do about the audio sensors. She sighed deeply.

Meghan stepped closer to the bed and studied Ihan. He lay curled on his side. Dark reddish marks ran along his waist and ribcage. A lump swelled out from his neck, with many others on his chin, and around his eyes. *Why the hell did those bastards do this to him?* Anger and sadness overwhelmed her thinking. She felt herself breathe heavy and her vision blurred. She rubbed her eyes and her hand came away wet. Suddenly, tears flowed down her cheeks as if she were a rookie again, reacting to her first taste of violence.

Meghan reached down to Ihan's face and tenderly dragged her fingers along the rough red scrapes there. He didn't respond. She slid her hands around his shoulders and gently turned him on to his back, and his head flopped to the side and settled against the hard mattress. Overhead, the air vents rattled, and chilled air poured over the mattress. Goose bumps rose along his skin, and he began to shiver.

Meghan was agonized over what she should do. *First things first because Ihan needs it.* She shuffled down near the end of the bed, bent down to her knees, and brought her hands together. She then closed her eyes, bent her head, and whispered a prayer.

"Meghan?" Ihan whispered.

Meghan looked up to see his bloodshot eyes. She put her hands down on the bed and jumped up before placing her finger in front of her mouth. She bent over, a smile curving her lips as her mouth came close to his ear. "Don't say a word. We're being listened to in here." She pulled back a little. "I apologize for what has happened to you, and I plan on getting you out of here soon. You don't deserve this." Meghan straightened up and watched Ihan smile.

"What were you doing at the foot of the bed?" he whispered, tilting his head to the side.

"I was praying for you."

His forehead furrowed. "What is that?"

"I was asking Sister Mary Gervais to look after you."

"Is that your sister?"

Meghan sat there for a few seconds trying to understand what Ihan meant, and then it dawned on her. He'd been more sheltered in Dallas than she'd realized.

"I guess you could say that. Sister Gervais was a loving nun that I grew up with. She is now in heaven looking after me. I guess she has become my guardian angel because I can sure feel her presence in my down times."

"What is a nun?"

"She is a Catholic woman who is committed to life-long vows. Sister Gervais helped me understand the true meaning of morals and religion."

"I don't understand religion."

Meghan smirked. "That's OK, Ihan. Just know that Sister Gervais is now your guardian angel. I can assure you that she will be there for you and will help me at least get you out of this situation." Meghan stood up and looked down at Ihan. "Can you walk?"

He sat up, and his face contorted. After he panted for a few seconds and then nodded, she reached behind his back and pushed him forward. He slowly heaved his legs off the bed while Meghan placed her arms under his. She pulled him to his feet. His grunting efforts and weak stance worried her, but she swung his arm over her shoulder and shuffled him the short distance across the room.

Meghan pushed the chair aside. The tray clattered to the floor. She slowly opened the hallway entrance door.

"What the hell are you doing?" Charlie yelled.

Two guys scurried down the hall toward them. She looked both directions and didn't see a way out. The only exit door was beyond those two. She clutched Ihan's waist and lowered him gently to the floor. Then she stood tall with her fists raised.

"Stand aside because I am taking him out of here."

"The hell you are!" A cruel grin spread over Charlie's face.

He swaggered toward her. Meghan ducked behind him, flung her arm under his, and cupped her hand behind his neck. She reached in front of him, gripped his chin with her other hand, and gave his neck a sharp upward twist. She felt the sickening crunch of the vertebrae dislocating, and she lowered him to the floor. His legs and arms flailed for a few seconds until they went limp and his eyes shut. Meghan pushed him aside and got back on her feet.

Gary shouted and lunged at her, swinging his fist. She jerked her upper body back before darting forward and kicking her leg out low to the side. Gary's knee distended backward and he screamed and fell to his side. He landed hard. She jumped forward and kicked him hard in the face. He went limp. Unconscious.

Meghan panted as she stood in her fighting stance. Heavy footsteps thumped nearby. She rushed down the hallway and slid to the doorway, where she pressed her back against the wall. A security guard sprinted around the corner, and Meghan slid her foot out. The guard tripped and slammed into the wall. She sprang forward while he was regaining his balance, spun her body around, and hit him square in the face with the back of her hand. He crumpled to the floor and didn't get up.

Meghan stood silently for a few seconds. She looked over her shoulder and down the hallway and saw nothing but a desk. They would remain undetected for a minute or two more. Her face immobile as a statue's, she returned to Ihan, who was sitting where she'd left him and staring at her in awe. When she reached him, she took a deep breath, crouched, and pulled him to his feet.

"Hang on tight to me and take it easy. I'm taking you to a safe place. We have to move fast."

As she assisted Ihan down the hallway, Meghan dialed Dirk on her communicator.

Dirk sat next to other team members cleaning his pistol and putting the parts back together. The gunpowder smell was pungent, but he enjoyed that smell—kept him motivated. His communicator beeped. He picked it up and saw Meghan's ID number.

"Hey, Meghan. What's going on?"

"I need a favor from you and I am going to need it two seconds ago."

"What's the deal?"

"I need you to meet me at the elevator down the hall from the team room and escort me back."

"What for?"

"Just please meet me there!"

"Roger that and heading there now."

Dirk placed his pistol down on the table. The other team members continued to clean their weapons and tell jokes. He picked up a clean cloth and wiped his hands down.

"Hey, guys. I'll be right back." Glancing at his pistol, he added, "You know what happened to the last guy who grabbed this without my permission."

The members smiled as Dirk headed out the door. He whistled down the corridor looking at all the people walking by. He then noticed a guy drinking from an aluminum can with Hindi lettering that looked like scribble. *I've seen many of those lately. Guess the Indian goods are flowing into Texas faster than ever.*

He then arrived at the elevator door. He looked up at the indicator. It flashed floor two—four to climb before it reached his level. He didn't have clearance to go below floor three, and he didn't think Meghan did either. What was going on down there? The door opened, and Dirk's jaw dropped as he saw Meghan holding a swollen and bloodied man.

Ihan.

"What in the hell happened down there?"

She half carried Ihan from the elevator, staggering under his weight. "Help me take him into our room."

Dirk put his arms under Ihan's legs and back. He carried him to the room with Meghan at his side. Once they entered the room, the door closed and Meghan quickly pressed the code to lock it. Dirk placed Ihan on a cot near the lockers. Meghan looked dizzy. She sat down in a chair and shook. The other team members stared at her with confused looks. Dirk tossed a blanket over Ihan and spun around.

"Meghan!"

She raised her head and looked at him.

"You know I have a ton of questions, but just let me know—what's on floor two?"

"It's the interrogation cell."

"OK. I take it they headed in the wrong direction seeing how we were never asked?"

"Look at him!" Meghan pointed at Ihan. "They beat the living shit out of him for a fucking password!"

"Calm down, Meghan." Dirk walked over and sat down next to her. Fear skittered in her eyes as she glanced at the locked door. He let out a long breath. Meghan cared too much about Ihan, and Dirk could see only trouble in it for all of them, but she'd asked him to help. He didn't want to embarrass her by treating her like a girl, so he didn't touch her. "Once those assholes know I am in the room with you, they won't try to break in."

She leaned her head on his shoulder, flooding him with unexpected warmth.

"Thanks, Dirk."

CHAPTER TWENTY-ONE

The woman under Jerry's sheets giggled and stirred in his arms. Jerry relaxed to his uttermost as he enjoyed the power of having any woman he wanted available at his beck and call. Suddenly, he brushed aside her hands. The music had been playing a few seconds ago, but now he didn't hear a thing. He clamped his hand over the woman's mouth an instant before Liz beeped to get his attention.

"Jerry, is that you?" A man's voice sounded on the speaker.

Jerry rolled his eyes and got nervous. A woman in his bed was the last thing a city resident needed to see. Jerry pushed the woman farther under the sheets, and off the bed. He then popped his head from under the sheets and raised himself higher against the headboard.

"Who the hell is that?"

"Sir, it's just Roger Buss."

Jerry raised his arm and ruffled his hair, then patted it down. Keeping his eyes on the screen instead of on the naked woman with her mouth open in indignation, he pursed his lips.

"Liz! Mute that sound."

"Done, sir."

"Close that camera angle so it shows just my face."

"Yes sir."

The camera slowly focused in on Jerry's face, which he kept motionless. Out of the corner of his eye, he saw the woman crawl along the floor.

Jerry displayed a tense look for the camera. "How dare you let that person in without my permission!"

"Sir, he is your personal assistant and you gave him permission to alert you."

Jerry rolled his eyes. "Whatever! Just turn that mute off."

The red light to the left of the monitor glowed, and he smirked a little because the closest Roger had ever come to touching a woman was donating sperm in a sterile room.

"What can I do you for, Mr. Buss?"

"Sir, you told me to inform you when our special packages arrived from China. I verified that all four CSS-25's are intact, and we also received the instruction guidance for their setup and deployment."

Jerry raised an eyebrow. "Which one is the CSS again?"

"The short-range ballistic missiles that you agreed upon getting several weeks ago."

Jerry squeezed his eyes shut as he thought. How was he supposed to remember which missiles did what? He had people for that. "Get to the point."

"You do remember this matter sir? You agreed upon it during our last special project meeting?"

He nodded. "Of course." His confusion dissolved.

"That's right. Those missiles are the extremely pricey ones. I suppose you were able to handle the budget?"

"Yes sir. It took me days to launder the money through our special channels but we are covered."

Geez, this line had better be secure or Buss's stupidity would bring the whole thing down around Jerry's ears. "That is all I need to know about the money. Where are those things located?"

"They are currently heading to the Flower Mound area and should arrive in a few minutes to the complex we completed a few days ago."

"How long will it take to set things up?"

"I'm unsure as to the specific timing but I guess it should take us about a week."

"OK. Just keep me updated on the status."

"Yes sir. I plan on informing you throughout the process."

"That's enough, thanks."

Jerry looked over at the glass bubble protruding from the wall, and swung his thumb downward—the video screen went blank. He bent over the bed and looked along the floor. His female companion was nowhere in sight. So, she wanted to play hide-and-seek, did she? He then smiled and tapped the bumps in the rumpled bedding. He lifted the sheets, looked under them, tossed a few pillows, and then puckered his mouth not finding the woman.

As he rolled off the bed, Jerry wrapped a sheet around his body and headed toward the closet. He opened the door and stared in once the light automatically turned on—nothing. Clever girl. Grinning with curiosity, Jerry then walked out of the room and stared down both ends of the hallway. "Come out, come out, wherever you are!" He listened, then walked into the living room and stood there for a few seconds.

"Liz!"

"Yes sir."

"Where did that woman go?"

"She left a few minutes ago."

Jerry stuck his lips out. "Why did you let her out?"

"I wasn't ordered to keep her here."

"I need to change that." Jerry raised his voice in frustration. "From here on out, Liz, please don't let that woman leave without my permission."

"Yes sir."

Jutting his chin out, he looked over at the large windows and noticed dark clouds in the distance. He shuffled his feet toward the windows, still holding the sheet around his hips. With his arm straight out against the window, he stared at the clouds and watched as they flowed around each other at a faster than normal pace. The cloud spheres extended down underneath an incoming storm, it kept Jerry staring in amazement. He wondered if he'd ever seen such a display of raw power before.

The storm was heading in from the west, and it turned his mind westward.

West of CSD lay Midland, where the recent attack, one that had severely damaged the largest oil refinery and halted production. The idea of the city-state and oil refinery being attacked dominated his thoughts and made him consider how he was going to keep the production pace that was intended to mature his society. *That damn Texas Coalition is a pain in my side.* Knowing any future actions would have to be voted upon made him consider the options he needed to win the hearts and minds of the Dallas citizens. "I will make getting their support a priority," Jerry promised himself.

He spun around and headed to the bathroom. He stepped into the shower and reached for his body wash. Nothing came out. He shook the container, turned it upside down, and squeezed hard, watching drips land on his hand. He turned his head he tossed the container across the room. It hit the wall and landed in the trashcan.

"Liz! I thought I ordered a whole box of body wash last week?"

"Sir, I will track down the order's current location."

Jerry stood there staring at the wall and waited for a response. He shook his head back and forth in frustration. He realized how busy he'd been lately due to all the internal and external city actions. Work had been overwhelming his thoughts. He then heard a click.

"Sir. The current location for the ordered item is at the Highland Park distribution center."

"That is the one closest to here?"

"Yes sir."

"How long has it been sitting there?"

"According to the database, the ordered item has been there for two days."

"Two days! I live right down the street from that center and it's just sitting there?"

"Yes sir."

"So what is the reason?"

"Can you explain your question, sir?"

"Oh, come on, Liz. During your search of the location

I assumed you would have tracked down the reason why my body wash has been sitting there for two days."

"I apologize sir. I didn't, but will get you an answer here shortly."

"Before you do that, I want you to display the current transportation status."

"Yes sir."

Jerry walked out of the shower and placed his hands under the sink faucet. The water flowed as he rubbed his hands together. He flung a towel around his waist and headed over to his workstation. Once he sat down in his leather chair, he looked over at the monitor and watched the current transportation display zoom into his neighborhood. Green lines displayed along the streets. He then focused on the Highland Park distribution center and followed the green line, which passed his location.

"Liz!"

"Yes sir."

"From what I can see on the display, the routing network looks fine with no troubles."

"You are correct, sir. The routing network in our city sector is confirmed to be operational."

"I realize there are currently some problems in other areas of the city, but I placed a priority of actions upon this sector. Please check the status of the distribution center."

"Yes sir."

The bottles of Armadale vodka sitting on the table started to shine out of the corner of his eye. The sparkly display emanating from the crystal glasses and the bottle brought him a moment of thoughtful happiness. A click sounded.

"Sir."

Jerry looked back at the monitor and saw several internal areas within the Highland Park distribution center. The upper right panorama showed several RepairCons working around an internal delivery line. There were several sparks of light and constant movement of gadgets.

"Tell me about it, Liz."

"As you can see sir, the internal delivery line broke down two days ago, and it was ordered several minutes after that incident to replace the whole line since the current system is antiquated."

Jerry rolled his eyes. "Yeah, yeah. When can I expect to smell better?"

"Excuse me, sir?"

"Getting that order into this residence!"

"Exact timing of the delivery is unknown, sir, but the repairs are expected to be completed in a few hours."

"I guess I will just have to deal with my stench."

"Sir. You have an older container located in your linen closet. You ordered me to leave it in there a year ago and it's located on the floor below the towels."

Jerry walked over to the closet and opened the door. He squatted down and raised a small stack of towels, which he tossed onto the floor. There sat a bottle of body wash.

"Good call on remembering that one, Liz."

"Yes sir."

Jerry grabbed the container, kicked the towels to the side, and headed back to the bathroom. A metal arm rose from the floor and speedily ran down the hallway to pick the towels up and replace them on the shelf. The closet door was closed and the metal arm jetted back under the floor. Placing the container along the ledge inside the shower, Jerry turned around and stood there for a few seconds.

"Before I forget, Liz, I need you to send out a message to the city council. Let them know we will need to meet quickly in order to generate a rapid voting proposition. Make sure you enunciate in the message the need for speed because this involves future security concerns."

"Yes sir."

After his shower, Jerry sat in his dining room. The table was set with an ivory-colored willow fabric tablecloth, gold candlesticks, silver flatware, and crystal glasses. Jerry ate a tasty meal, as he looked at the large screen set in the wall. Today's vista was blue with a sunny background and waves crashing ashore. The classical music was thunderous and clear and echoed against the far walls.

He stared at the crystal pattern engraved in the glass and mentally reviewed the deal he'd initiated with China, and how they dominated the negotiations. China practically told him what he was going to receive and what he would benefit from it. The wheat and corn amounts they demanded were large, almost too large to handle, but after a few weeks the citizens' long hours and motivations solved the shipping timeline. The furniture, crystal, silverware, and modern electronics were sorely needed, and distributed, but the diminutive amount of goods made Jerry look like less of a leader than he was. *This is a beautiful glass though.*

The music volume decreased. "Sir. Mr. Roger Buss is on the line for you."

"Put him through, Liz."

Jerry pushed his plate forward, dropped the silverware to the sides, and stood. He grabbed a glass and walked over to the bar, where he slammed the glass on top of the bar and poured some Armadale. Out of the corner of his eye he saw the monitor brighten and recognized Roger's face.

"Mr. Buss. Welcome back with the good news."

"Good evening, sir. I do have some good news for you tonight. First of all, I just want to say the vote has been tallied, and the yes vote is ninety-eight percent. As for the city council, they wanted to state that their support for your plan is one hundred percent and they do back your strategy." Roger smiled.

Jerry poured more vodka into his glass and stared out the window while he drank it. He turned around and walked into the living room, where he sat down on the couch. Roger waited obediently while Jerry absorbed the implications of his news and finished his drink. He flung his feet upon the table and wrapped his hands behind his head.

"That is good news! Now tell me, what questions were asked?"

"The special plan we designated several months ago has come to successful completion. Domestically, the citizens and city council have all agreed that the aging wall along the eastern zone is fragile but only two councilmen asked why the Mesquite area portion of the wall was the weakest and never got an upgrade two years ago.

Jerry rattled the cubes in his glass. "And what were they told?"

"The same justified answer we determined with the plan two years ago—that we ran out of supplies, which we did, and that the budget amount ran out. I was asked why we didn't reallocate funds to finish the remodeling. I told them it was because they wouldn't allow it in their focused budget plan, the medical facility upgrade."

"What was their response to that?"

"They accepted that, sir, and actually showed a little guilt for the recent attack."

Jerry smiled and nodded his head. "Outstanding."

"Sir. I commend you on such a successful domestic plan."

Jerry jumped to his feet and walked over to his desk across the living room. The monitor rose from the desktop and he looked at Roger as he sat down. "Tell me about the other plan."

"Yes sir."

Roger's face tilted down, and a hybrid image map of San Antonio came up on Jerry's screen. On the top right corner of the map was a blinking, red-circled image. Immediately the image focused down, and the map zoomed in to the circled area, to the northeast of the city. The image blinked again and zoomed in further to one-hundred-meter resolution. Once the image focused and cleared, a red dot blinked on smooth ground dotted with bushes and small trees. Over to the left of the image was a paved road that led to a dirt road . . . that led to nothing. It dawned on Jerry that a road didn't simply end. He pressed the screen to zoom into that area and saw concrete barriers on top of another paved road that was covered by what looked like vegetation. Jerry put his fingers on the screen and pulled them across. The image rotated and came to an almost horizontal perspective—the image showed the entrance.

Damned clever, but not as clever as he was.

"You mean to tell me they have been hiding underground like a pack of diseased rats?"

Jerry tapped the screen and Roger's picture came back.

"Yes sir. We have assumed for a long time that's how they were hiding, but we couldn't designate specifically where it was. I think they have done a great job masking their location and I do commend them."

"All right, Roger. Now I can understand your excitement about those missiles. Are you certain those things will work when the target is underground?"

"I was told by our Chinese representative that the warheads have deep penetration technology and can blast several hundred feet into the ground."

"Sounds good, but let's hope our first attack will be successful. That way we won't have to answer any inquiries from outside observers."

"Yes sir. By the way, I wanted to update you on that plan and how successful I think it will be. We have been vulnerable to jamming devices for many years, but I can now tell you we received new technology that can counter that."

Jerry squinted his eyes. "And that is?"

"I have SecureCons out there right now setting up data link focused transponders, that will strengthen our signals. We have tested those a few times and found them to be successful. Our only problem is the limited amount of those transponders we currently have."

"That's not good." Jerry rolled his eyes.

"Actually, sir, the units we have are being placed in direct line with the target. We should have just enough to reach the target."

Jerry sat back in his chair and looked up on to the ceiling, shaking his head in bafflement.

Roger cleared his throat. "Sir, is everything OK?"

"Yes. I just cannot believe it took UTC this long to finally attack that location we designated along our outer wall. Those idiots should've done this sooner. I was literally getting tired of waiting."

"No problem, sir. We can now eliminate our threat and make our city safer."

Jerry raised one eyebrow. "Let's hope!"

CHAPTER TWENTY-TWO

Dirk tensed as security officers banged on the team room door. He watched Meghan's body jolt back and forth with the efficient slam of the magazine into her pistol. The other team members looked wary but continued to play cards. Meghan reached over and tucked the blanket against Ihan's side—he was passed out on her bed—and then she jumped to her feet and walked in tight circles, a perturbed look crinkling her face.

Dirk widened his eyes at her. "Sit back down and try to relax."

Her cheeks flushed, and the swell of emotion that implied worried him. A loud beep emanated from the door. Meghan halted and raised her pistol.

"Come on, you fuckers. I dare you to bust through that door!" She leveled the weapon to a man's chest height and cocked the hammer.

Dirk stood and walked toward Meghan a lot more patiently than he felt. He raised his arm and gently touched her shoulder. Cringing, she pulled back and swung her head around with a snarl etched on her features. Dirk bestowed a calm look. *Please listen for once, Meghan.*

"Just take a seat. Please."

"If they push that buzzer again, I swear I'm going to bust out of here and shoot their asses!"

Dirk chuckled. "Why, so they can throw you in stockade?"

Meghan threw an angry look his way. "I have no patience for this!"

"Look, Meghan. I can understand why you're upset. Hell, I would probably have done the same thing once I found out what was happening to our captured item. Those ignorant fools a few floors down were not doing the right thing. You're right, and we will need Ihan to get into that processor."

"Captured item!" Meghan plopped down on a chair and wept.

Dirk walked over and knelt down in front of her. He put his hands on her knees and angled his head to look up at her face.

"Just please try to calm down a little."

She raised her head and stared at Ihan. "He is more than just some captured item. He is an intelligent man with an open mind, one that could truly help us get this state back."

Dirk saw the solemn look on her face. He turned his head and looked at Ihan lying faceup on the bed. He recognized where Meghan's thoughts were heading now, and the intensity of her loyalty to the captive confused him.

"Dirk, please. Make them leave him alone." The corner of her mouth trembled.

He looked into her eyes. Unfamiliar numbness showered through him. "All right, Meghan. I will get those clowns out there to stop bugging us."

Dirk stood to his feet and headed toward the door. The communication button blinked and beeped.

"This is your last chance to open that door!"

Dirk rolled his eyes. He had to be crazy. He should just open the door so they could take Ihan and get into the processor using whatever means they wanted. But he'd told Meghan he wouldn't let that happen. He pressed the button. "This is Dirk Young and I suggest you take it easy."

"Hey, Dirk." A pause ensued, as though they were conferring. "We didn't know you were in there. We were ordered to get that stolen man back, so please open the door and turn him over."

"Hate to tell you guys, but he's not going anywhere."

Dirk looked back to notice Meghan's eyes widen. A smile came to her face, followed by a wink. His heart beat a little faster than it had before.

"That's not what you were supposed to say, Dirk!" The guard cautioned.

"Yeah, but that's what I'm sticking with."

He grinned at Meghan.

Stephan walked down the darkened hallway and heard heavy footsteps getting closer. He looked behind him and saw two fully armed men marching toward him. Stephan stepped to the side, and they continued on down the hall and turned to the right. As he rounded the corner a few seconds later, the two armed guards flanked his team door. Stephan approached, making sure to stand against the far wall.

"You guys mind telling me what the hell you're doing?"

The lead guard looked back. "We were ordered to take back the man that was stolen earlier."

Stephan raised an eyebrow. "Stolen? What man are you talking about?"

"The Dallas prisoner your team captured several days ago."

"What the hell are you talking about?"

"Your female team member busted into floor two a few hours ago and wounded three personnel. She has that captured man in this room."

"Meghan Rhodes? Why the hell would she do that?"

"Good question, sir."

Stephan flickered his hand. "OK. Stand down and let me deal with this."

The guard shifted uncomfortably. "Can't do that, sir."

"What do you mean you can't?"

"The head of security ordered us to get that man back with no distractions."

"Distractions! I am the team leader and have full authority for that room. All four of you back away, and I will get that man."

The guard's gaze flickered. Then he pushed out his jaw and raised his weapon. "I don't know about that, sir."

"Listen. We are all in same organization and there is no need for this to be violent. Just back away and let me handle this."

The guards looked at each other with hesitation, and

then stared at the head guard, who took a deep breath and waved his hand up and down.

"Lower your weapons, guys, and take a few steps back. Sir, you have a few minutes to get that man and turn him over to us."

Stephan smirked. "Good plan."

He stepped forward, pressed the code, and stuck his eye in front of the iris recognition device. Nothing happened. He pressed the code again and heard a beep with a red light. Stephan took a step back. "What the hell?"

He pressed the communication button.

"This is Stephan, please open the door!"

"Howdy, Stephan," Dirk Young drawled. "I will open the door if you promise to be the only one coming in."

Stephan looked over at the head guard and raised his eyebrows. The guard closed his eyes and shook his head with the look of discontentment.

"You have my word, Dirk."

The light went green, and Stephan pushed open the door. After he walked in, Dirk slammed the door and pressed the lock code into the door panel. Stephan looked around the room and saw Meghan perched on the edge of a chair, toes on the floor, knees bouncing. Next to her, Ihan lay silent on her bed. Across the room, two team members studiously concentrated on the cards in their hands, though they wore expressions of mild shock. Dirk walked in front of him and sketched a flippant salute. The dumb grunt had to know what kind of hole he'd dug himself into, and his casual attitude made Stephan want to open the door and let the guards have him.

"You mind telling me what the fuck is happening in here?"

Dirk grinned. "We're just relaxing and throwing a party."

"Very funny."

Stephan leaned around Dirk to get a look at Meghan. For the first time ever, her shoulders were slumped and her head hung down. She looked like a dog that had been kicked by someone it trusted.

"Meghan, what's wrong?"

"Look at him, Stephan." Her voice cracked, and she pointed at Ihan. "Those fuckers beat the living shit out of him and for what!"

Stephan walked over to the bed to verify her assessment. Ihan's face had a boot print on it. He pulled the sheets down and saw severe bruises in various stages of healing, and red welts along his upper body. She hadn't exaggerated. He let out a long breath.

"Who the hell did this?"

"The interrogation bastards!"

Stephan closed his eyes. "You mean those dudes on the second floor?"

Dirk cleared his throat. "You know about that floor?"

"Yeah, I know about those buffoons."

"Why don't the rest of us know about them? I've been in this coalition for a lot of years and this is the first I hear about this."

"Calm down, Dirk. There's a reason why that counterintelligence group's existence doesn't get put out. I'm not going to defend them, but their mission has done some good."

Meghan shot to her feet. "Oh really. Well, look at Ihan and tell me what good is that?"

Stephan tipped his gaze at her tearstained face. "I can understand what you're saying. This isn't the first time something like this has happened. Lack of communication hurts us and creates disorder."

Meghan stepped closer. "Were you asked about Ihan and what we learned from him before we even got back here?"

"I'm only playing devil's advocate here, but what we heard from this guy wasn't worth anything."

"What are you saying, Stephan? Look where we took Ihan from and the lonely life he was brought up in. There is no way he would have told us anything. We had to first tell him where he was, that he was safe, and that we are here for him." Meghan's gaze enkindled as she glanced over at Ihan. "I may not be the sharpest knife in the drawer but at least I know what it takes to make a person comfortable. Look at what we know so far: that processor is more technologically advanced than what we have to exploit it, and Dusty has already sent that Mona to the technology office. You see where I am going with this? We may not be the experts but by no means were we asked what we learned.

"That's what I meant when I said communication disorders. I provided our situation reports and when I was debriefed I answered all the operational questions accurately. "

Meghan scratched her head. "Accurately! Come on,

Stephan, what is accurate about Ihan's personality and thoughts?"

Stephan grinned. "That's kind of what I'm saying Meghan. I am with you on this. The questions I was asked were square pegs being put into a round gadget."

"So you know what I did. Are you with me on this?"

"Meghan, I was with you from the beginning." He touched her sleeve. When she jerked away, he let his hand fall back to his side.

Why did she always push him away? He had to concede, though, she had a point about Ihan.

Stephan turned and walked to the door. He pressed the communication button.

"Security guys. This situation is handled, so I suggest you go back to what you were doing."

"I don't think so, sir. Either you bring that man out or we will go in to take him!"

Dirk tapped him on the shoulder.

"You mind telling me what you're doing?"

"Relax, Dirk. I'm only pissing that guard off. We never got along anyway."

Stephan typed a code into the communication panel.

"This is the Operations Center."

Stephan winked. "Please put me through to Dusty Rhodes."

"Sorry. Mr. Rhodes is in a briefing."

"This takes priority. I have four guards outside my team room and they are about to break in and die."

"They are about to do what?"

"Just put Dusty on the line."

"Yes sir!"

Stephan pulled over a chair, sat down, and crossed his legs. He watched Dirk and Meghan stare at him, then each other, before they settled and sat down.

"Stephan, is that you?" Dusty rumbled.

"Howdy, sir. Yes it's me."

"You mind telling me what your situational crap is?"

"I guess the bottom line is that I have that Dallas man locked here in our team room. I'm letting him recover from that shit beating he's been through for the past couple of days. He's no good to us if you hurt him any more."

"So what are you saying?"

"Let us take care of this guy and get the information we all need."

"Is Meghan in there with you?"

Stephan smirked at Meghan. "She is sitting right here next to me. I must say, Dusty, she sure did chew me out for taking this guy earlier and is quite the coalition patron."

"OK, Stephan. I'll call off the guards, but you are now being held accountable for retrieving the needed information from that guy."

"Will do, Dusty."

Stephan reached over and pushed the button.

"What was that for, Stephan?" Meghan said, her eyes wide.

"Ihan is now yours, Meghan. Go forth and get us what we need." Let Dirk try and top that.

Stephan stood and opened the door. When he got into the hallway, he tapped the guard on his back and commended him for his duty as they walked down the hallway.

Chapter Twenty-Three

Meghan loved her team's cooperative spirit and the shared vision of becoming the premier team—thoroughly prepared, properly equipped, and highly motivated to reach their goal. Meghan engrained that vision in her thoughts. She decided to head to the dining facility to pay back Dirk and demonstrate to Ihan the sense of loyalty that made Team Eight a tight-knit unit.

She then noticed Ihan's face blush as he turned his head and grunted with the effort to rise to a sitting position. She bent forward and lifted his shoulders, but he let out another weak grunt before his body went limp and fell backward on to the mattress. He opened his eyes, and she smiled.

"Just keep still, Ihan. You look exhausted and need to rest more. Dirk will stay here and protect you while I get you some chow." Meghan looked over her shoulder and shot Dirk a questioning glance. He wrinkled his features in mock agony and clutched his stomach with both hands. "No worries, Dirk, I'll get you some chow as well."

Meghan tapped Ihan's leg as she stood up and walked out into the hallway. The other team members went back to throwing cards down.

As Meghan entered the dining facility, she paused to admire the food islands, which were newly decorated with pumpkins, gourds, and wheat stalks. Low-volume country music pulsed throughout the room. Meghan grabbed a food tray and placed bowls and plates on it. She walked around the food islands, scooping out potatoes and squash. She made sure to heap larger amounts on Dirk's plates. His appetite surpassed many. The seasonal smell inspired a grin as she tapped the floor with her boot. She grabbed some turkey and chicken.

Meghan knew her father had ordered these seasonal decorations and foods—it kept up morale and brought smiles to the soldiers' faces. However, it also brought respect from all that served him.

As she placed the food tray down on the counter, Meghan looked around the room, and despite the guilt she felt over the horrors of Ihan's interrogation, a wave of happiness flowed through her body. "Why am I feeling this way and what the hell am I thinking?" It dawned on her that the recent hardships she'd experienced meant little compared her father's and her team's thoughtfulness for her. She shook her head and picked the tray back up, making sure she had enough for Ihan and Dirk. She added a few extra rolls, then picked some juice cartons and plastic cutlery. Backing up, she bumped into someone and apologized before heading for the desserts.

The sweets always brought high spirits, and Ihan needed that. She turned to her side and looked down to where the desserts normally were, but the silver island was empty.

"How are you doing today? If I remember correctly,

your name is Meghan," a woman said. She was wearing a white chef's uniform with a long and tall circular white hat. Meghan recognized her from their meeting several days earlier.

"Hi there and yes, my name is Meghan. We met in the women's bathroom."

"We sure did."

"I didn't catch your name."

The woman gave her a smile that bordered on flirtatious. "My name is Dorothy, but please just call me Dottie."

Meghan nodded. "Thanks, Dottie. Could you point me to the desserts?"

Dottie did, and Meghan carried the heavy tray to the relocated dessert island. She put a few cakes on the tray and headed for the door, hesitating for a few seconds to make sure no one was striding quickly through the doorway. However, a figure appeared. Meghan looked up and saw Stephan.

"Hey, Meghan, you chow thief."

"Real funny, Stephan."

"Where you going with all that?"

"Back to the team room. This chow is for Ihan and Dirk."

Stephan gracefully hopped to the side and bowed as Meghan shuffled past the doorway. Just as she left the dining hall, Meghan noticed she'd forgotten salt and pepper. She knew that Dirk would give her foul looks, and blame her for not thinking of him—he exploited those events whenever he had a chance.

"Ah crap!"

She turned around and headed back to the dinning facility. As she headed toward the counter to get the salt and peppershakers, she noticed Stephan talking with Dottie at the entrance to the kitchen. She halted and stared in the open for a second, and then picked up the pace and headed over to the counter. Snatching the salt and pepper, Meghan raised her eyes and noticed that Stephan had moved to stand closer to Dottie. They were focused solely on each other. Meghan smirked, recognizing her chance to add to the good-natured ribbing that was as much a part of her team's cohesiveness as their training and dedication were. *This is juicy intelligence and I need to spread this to the team.* Stephan raised his arm and placed it upon Dottie's shoulder, as he bent his head and chuckled. "Oh, this is good stuff." Meghan murmured. Her team relished any opportunity to pick on each other—it kept their motivation and high spirits. She lifted her tray and headed out the door.

As Meghan entered the team room, she placed the tray softy on to the table. She put her hands upon her lower back and stretched backward while grunting. She then stretched her arms out and shook them for a few seconds.

"Boy oh boy, that trip sure kicked your ass." Dirk smiled as he oiled his pistol.

"Yeah, well, some people around here eat enough to choke a mule." Meghan winked at Dirk as she walked over to the bed. Ihan lay quietly with his eyes shut. The severe beating he received sure would take time to recover from. She then took a seat and looked over at Dirk.

"How long ago did Ihan fall back asleep?"

"A few minutes after you left."

Meghan leaned back and put her hands behind her head. "Oh, by the way, I got some good intelligence for you."

"What good stuff do you have?"

"Guess who I saw flirting with a woman in the dining facility?"

"Come on now." Dirk put his pistol down. "You know I'm not good at these kind of questions."

"Just take a wild guess."

Dirk rolled his eyes. "Dusty."

Meghan's neck flushed. "My father hasn't been with a woman since my mother passed away."

"Well then, I guess his man pipes are truly rusty."

Meghan widened her eyes. "Who's the other guy we have never seen with a woman?"

"You talking about me? Because if you are, then that's good intelligence since I don't have a clue what you're chatting about." Dirk smiled with his teeth together.

"That is true now, isn't it?" Meghan hastily blinked. "No. I'm talking about Stephan. He was flirting like crazy with that woman named Dottie in the dining facility."

"Dottie. Who's that?"

"That woman who is the new chef in there."

"Oh, that one. I remember Stephan mentioning something about her many moons ago. She's your father's designated chef."

"Really? I almost forgot she cooked for him."

"Stephan mentioned a few weeks ago that Dusty would stare at her ass as she walked around the room."

Meghan raised one eyelid. "That does make sense then. The reason why Stephan's all over her."

"You may be right with that one."

"I know he doesn't care for my father too much. Getting with the woman my father stares at all the time would be Stephan's internal revenge."

Dirk raised his head. "That could be."

Meghan then looked over to Ihan and wondered how he was feeling. She also wondered how she could get him back to feeling comfortable and somewhat secure. Helping him recover from his injuries was her tradecraft. Making him feel comfortable was her concern. Meghan felt certain she couldn't trust anyone outside of her team. Not knowing how things were outside of their facility concerned her a great deal. She didn't know the latest on CSD forces or whether her facility was in danger.

She then shook off those concerns, knowing her boss was Stephan. He was a good guy who always kept abreast of the current situation and informed the team of troubles. He wouldn't let them down.

Chapter Twenty-Four

Stephan walked into the Operations Center, where all personnel were focused on their computers, and the bark of tense conversations blasted through the room like shock waves. On the large screen on the far wall, several team identification icons inched across the digital map. A screen to the right showed live coverage. A team convoy traveled at a good pace with transportation trucks between its military vehicles.

Stephan crossed his arms. He hadn't been informed of the current situation. The team icons drew closer to San Antonio, heading north. This piqued his curiosity.

"There you are!"

Stephan looked over and saw Dusty heading his way with his eyebrows drawn together and his upper lip curled. Dusty looked tired, and slouched a little, but that only meant a military operation was in progress.

"What's happening here?" Stephan said.

"A major transshipment order is on its way."

"From what I see, you have six teams out there."

"Correct. Those teams were designated to make sure those goods arrive safely. They should be arriving here shortly."

Stephan took a deep breath and looked at the screen. "Why weren't we informed of this?"

"You know as well as I that your team is not suitable for any operation right now. You recently provided this coalition with its greatest treasure and paid the price greatly. It will take some time before your team will be back up to speed and able to head out of here, due to the lack of manning and equipment recovery." Dusty pointed his finger into Stephan's chest. "Besides, your recent rescue circumstance brings many future matters into question."

Stephan slowly turned his head toward Dusty. "Trust me. We can handle that situation better than anyone else."

"I'm specifically holding you accountable for that, Stephan."

Feeling his heart rate increase, Stephan closed his fists together and looked around the room without paying attention to anything other than controlling his urge to bring Dusty to justice. A burst of piercing conversation dragged his attention to the screen.

"Operations Center, this is Team Three. An aerial vehicle three miles west of our location launched a missile. It landed approximately five feet to the rear of our lead vehicle. We have no casualties, but that vehicle is currently replacing a rear tire. Convoy continues in motion and we just passed the town of Devine. Over."

"Roger that, Team Three. What is enemy UAV's current status and location? Over."

"We destroyed that UAV a few seconds after its detection. We currently don't detect enemy within the area. Do you currently have any long-range detection, over?"

"Negative, Team Three. There are currently no detections within your sector. Over."

"Roger that. Team Three out."

Dusty shook his head. "Those goddamn UAVs. What a pain in our ass!"

"Dusty. You mind telling me what the deal is with this convoy?"

Dusty cleared his throat. "This convoy is transporting the most needed, and utmost technologically advanced, weaponry the coalition has ever ordered."

The old goat must enjoy making him beg for every scrap of information. Stephan stroked his chin as though the two of them were having a casual exchange. "What specifically are they?"

"A new highly advanced man portable surface-to-air and surface-to-surface missile package. These missiles can detect and target any objects that are driven by remote connections. What makes these missiles so extraordinary is that they are a foot long, six inches wide, and only weigh about a pound. And hold your hat, Stephan, these tiny missiles' maximum effective range is three miles!"

Stephan raised his eyebrows. "A missile weighing a pound can go three miles?"

Dusty nodded. "Amazing pieces of equipment. These weapons have been utilized for many years but we finally reached a deal to get them."

"Let me guess, you got them from India?"

"Good guess. We utilized our Mexican connection to ship them here as long as we assured them the protection from Laredo to our location."

"So, let me guess again, Dusty, India is now forking

over those missiles just because you're letting them into our coalition."

The older man shrugged. "You could say that."

Stephan folded his arms. "Actually, in my opinion, India is now utilizing us as a surrogate force to tackle China's expansion into Texas. I have one question for you." He stared deep into Dusty's eyes. "What are we going to owe India once we take down Dallas and restore this state?"

Dusty kept his head still for a few seconds then slowly turned toward Stephan and smiled.

"Nothing, Stephan. We will owe them nothing."

Stephan lowered his eyes then turned his head to look up at the screens. His temples began to throb. *What Dusty said about this transaction with India sounded truly one-sided. How dare he make such a huge decision without asking team leaders? This deal doesn't make any sense.*

Stephan thought about how he was going to deal with India when he took charge. *How many repercussions will I receive for cutting India off with any future interactions? China will be cast away from Texas when I eliminate that city-state. That is a plus, seeing how it makes logical sense for India's decision to send military advisors.* The rumbling of thoughts kept flowing through him.

Dusty coughed and cleared his throat. "Can I ask you a personal question?"

Dusty's eyelids remained low and he swallowed repeatedly. The show of emotion immediately made Stephan suspicious.

"Excuse me?"

"How is my daughter doing these days?

"She's doing a great job for the team."

"I'm sure of that, Stephan. She is a focused woman." Dusty's eyes dampened. "Please let me tell you how scared I've been lately and I desperately need to get your opinion because my daughter has always been very open with me. She has never been afraid to share her loving and angry emotions with me. She started talking to me many years ago, when she was knee-high to a grasshopper. I brought her to this beautiful lake during the beginning of fall, the leaves were beginning to turn colors and that beautiful glass-like smooth water was so peaceful." Dusty smiled. "Ever since that moment she has truly been an open flower. For these past several weeks I really haven't heard a peep come out of her, and she doesn't come by and see me anymore. I have to call for her and that upsets me. I don't know how long I can take this."

"Have you asked her why?"

"Not directly, no, but I have asked her many other questions and she just gives me one-liners. Have you noticed any differences in her lately?"

"No."

Dusty's shoulders dropped down and his face seemed sadder than ever before. This was potentially Dusty's one weakness, a way to exploit him out of his power and show the rest of the coalition how weak their elected leader has become. Then again, this emotional weakness could be used to make Dusty break down and cry in front of the staff, a minor payback but one that sounded enjoyable to say the least. *What the hell am I thinking?* Stephan strained to get back his focus. Not just for Dusty, but also for his loyal and valued teammate, Meghan.

Dusty grabbed Stephan's shoulder. "I just don't understand what might be happening to her."

Stephan ground his teeth. "Tell you what, Dusty. How about I ask her to come talk with you about this so she'll know you have a problem. I just don't understand why you haven't asked her yourself."

Dusty lowered his head. "I don't think I know how to, Stephan. I never had to before. She always came to me."

"Calm down, Dusty." He slipped his shoulder from Dusty's grip. "I'll make this happen."

Dusty grinned. "I sure do owe you one."

"You sure do." Stephan smirked as he walked away.

CHAPTER TWENTY-FIVE

To begin the process of accessing Mona, Meghan knew it was time to make Ihan feel comfortable. She pulled a chair over and sat next to his narrow bed. His eyes were still bloodshot, but the dark circles around them had lightened a little. She lightly grabbed his chin, and slowly moved his head side to side. All his scrapes were a healthy red, and his bruises were turning yellowish instead of their original angry purple.

"How are you feeling?"

Ihan coughed. "I'm feeling better, Meghan. Thank you for freeing me from that . . . place earlier."

Meghan smiled. "I assume you would do the same for me if I were in that nasty place."

Ihan moved his eyes and focused slightly beyond her. Meghan twisted and noticed Dirk standing in front of his locker wearing a towel around his waist. He held a toiletry bag and stared at her while water trickled down his face. Meghan rolled her eyes and turned back to Ihan. He smiled and raised his hand slowly at Dirk. She looked back again to see Dirk not respond to Ihan, but wink at her before he opened his locker.

"Of course I would help you, Meghan. Nobody should

go through something like that." Ihan looked around her again. "Did I do something to offend Dirk?"

Meghan raised her brows. "Of course not. Why, do you feel something is wrong?"

"He really doesn't say much to me."

Meghan put a smile back on her face. "No worries, Ihan. Dirk is by far one of the best men I know. I trust him more than anyone, and he would put himself on the line to protect not just me but you as well."

"Is that because I'm being watched by you?"

Meghan swallowed as she sat back in the chair. She looked over at Dirk, who grabbed stuff out of his locker and continuously glanced her way. She wondered what Ihan was trying to say and how he really felt about Dirk.

"I don't think so, Ihan. Dirk cares a lot, but just doesn't show it all the time."

"I understand, Meghan." He stared at her with a knowing smile, almost as though he wanted to make Dirk—oh, crap.

She returned his smile, placing her hand on Ihan's shoulder for a moment. She turned her head to check Dirk's facial expression. He looked away and went back to grabbing stuff in his locker. *You've got to be kidding me.* Why did she have to know about this now? And why did she have to care so much? There were more important matters to think about. Meghan shook her head and quickly put this contemplation into the back of her head, protectively walling it in.

She looked back at Ihan with a calm face, put both her hands upon her knees, and sat up ramrod straight.

"I am sure you are hungry, Ihan, and I brought you plenty of food that will bring energy back into your system."

Meghan jumped out of her chair and hurried over to the table. She placed utensils upon the plate, folded a couple of napkins to the side, and poured water into a glass. She then stopped for a few seconds, stared past the plate, with the glass in her hand. She gently placed the water glass down and spread both her hands upon the table.

She hadn't planned on having Dirk or Ihan interested in her romantically, let alone both of them. Her experiences with Dirk were ones of laughter, protection, loyalty, and professionalism. Those experiences now felt strange to her because feelings toward Dirk just weren't clear anymore. She could feel his presence across the room, and one heavy-lidded gaze had the power to grab her attention. Deep in her heart, Meghan knew that Dirk had the kind of personality that could make her happy and feel secure. But he also had the power to crush her feelings. He was a professional soldier, and going by what she'd heard of his past, he knew nothing else.

She turned her thoughts to Ihan and nearly groaned. Like her life had room for feelings for a man they'd recently captured. Worse, those feelings were ones of contentment and adoration. She hardly knew this man at all. *Why am I feeling this way?* She shook her head and looked back down at the plate. *I need to stay focused!*

Meghan reached down and grabbed the plate. Before she turned around, she made sure her face was serene before walking back to the bed. She let out a deep breath and headed toward Ihan. Dirk headed her way.

"Good luck with that guy, and I wish you the best." Dirk continued past her, his voice toneless and his smile stopping short of his eyes.

When she arrived at the bed, Meghan sat down and placed the tray on her lap. She quietly gathered her thoughts. Ihan propped himself up on the bed and slid backward against the wall, a grimace creasing his face. Meghan reached behind him and turned the pillow upright so he had some comfort when he leaned back.

She gently placed the tray upon his lap. The last thing she needed to do was hit any of his sore spots and add to his pain. As Ihan looked down at the food, a joyful look came to his face. He reached down and grabbed the fork, lunging into the dish, and stuffed his mouth. His hands flew to his cheeks, and his eyes watered.

"Take it easy, Ihan! I know you're hungry but you have to take it slow due to your injuries."

He chewed again, slower this time. Meghan leaned forward with a grin.

"I want to talk with you about Mona."

Ihan stopped chewing and looked her in the eyes. "Is she OK?"

"I know you're worried about her, but I can assure you she's fine."

Ihan swallowed. "When can I see her?"

"Soon. You have to eat and feel better before I can take you to her. The last thing you need to do is pass out around here. The floors are pretty hard." She winked.

He stared straight ahead, his face paling. He slowly

placed the fork on the plate and sat straight back against the pillow.

"How am I to believe it will be Mona and that she hasn't been messed with?"

"Because I just said she's fine."

Ihan looked down to his lap and took a deep breath, blinking fast. Meghan felt her pulse increase. Didn't he believe her?

"What's the deal with you, Ihan?"

He gazed at her solemnly. "Don't take offense to this, Meghan, but I just cannot stop thinking of when I first met you. I really wouldn't call it meeting you, just hearing your voice through that system. You made me believe I was still in Dallas."

Meghan sat back in the chair. "I see your point. You have to trust me, though. I'm not deceiving you with this."

"Then why are you bringing me to see Mona?"

"To show you my honesty, Ihan, I will let you know the truth." Meghan looked around the bare room. "We can't figure out how to talk with Mona, and the last thing we want to do is damage her by trying to get the information we need."

Ihan raised an eyebrow. "What information?"

"About Dallas."

"Why?"

"So that damn city won't continue to exploit the people of Texas and keep us from bringing back this wonderful state."

"Mona can't help you with any of that. I am the one she looks after."

Meghan scowled. "Come on, Ihan. You know she's directly connected to the Dallas universal processor system. We need you to ask her some specific questions about Dallas."

"I will do my best, Meghan, but I really just need to make sure Mona is OK."

A loud beep sounded as the door swung open. Stephan walked through, headed directly toward his locker, and opened it. He pulled some papers from his pockets and placed them onto the top shelf before closing the door.

"Hey there, Meghan and Ihan. How goes the recovery?"

At least one person around here didn't have the hots for her. She beamed with gratitude. "Hi, Stephan. Ihan is doing better and filling the empty hole with chow."

"That's good news. I'm sure this is the first kind of beating you have ever had, Ihan. I hope you're not disheartened thinking this happens all the time here."

Ihan swallowed. "I'm OK."

"Just know that we all have been through this kind of pain, so I understand what you're going through. I can assure you that something like that won't happen again while you're with us."

"Thanks."

Stephan smiled. Then his attention returned to Meghan. "What do you have planned in the near future?"

"I plan on taking Ihan over to Mona once he finishes eating."

"You may want to see your father before you do that."

"My father, why?"

"Just to get his permission and let him know the deal with Ihan."

Meghan crossed her arms. "I thought you already handled that earlier."

"I softened the blow with him, but it may be best that you make him feel better. You know as well as I that he will listen to you more than anyone else here."

Meghan smirked. "You sure about that?"

"Please just go see him before you take Ihan. I'll make sure a team member gets in here to watch Ihan while you're with Dusty."

Stephan turned and headed toward the door without waiting for her answer.

Chapter Twenty-Six

In his house, a few miles south of Lampasas, Texas, Herb McBride walked down the wooden stairs from the bedroom, luxuriating in the afterglow of spending the first night in months with his wife. He'd volunteered with UTC four months ago and was given a week of leave before his assignment to a team. As a cool breeze flowed through the open windows, Herb smelled the scent of jasmine. Angela had brought it from her mama's place and planted it under their bedroom window right after they were married, saying now their house would be a home full of love. He smiled, feeling home again.

Herb ambled toward the kitchen, past the family photos that hung along the walls in the living room—they all brought back powerful memories and made him appreciate what a lucky fellow he was to have the love of a sweet woman like his wife. The smell of cherry nut cake hit his nostrils and amplified his gratitude for making it back home, and for Angela's thoughtfulness in making his favorite cake. As he walked through the archway, Herb stopped and stared at her. She stood in front of the stove wearing her apron and mixing in a bowl. No woman could be as pretty as she was. He took a soft step toward her.

"That smells so good. I don't know if I will last, just thinking of the taste to come."

Angela slowly turned, holding the bowl in one hand and the spoon in the other. She smiled at Herb. Moisture and gratitude filled her eyes, and she lowered her head back down.

Herb closed the distance between them and gently removed the bowl and the spoon from her hands and set them on the back of the stove. He wrapped his arms around her waist and slowly pulled her closer to his body and locked his mouth upon hers. As he released gradually from her lips, he opened his eyes. Hers were still closed. He looked down and admired her body, then slid his hands down her hips, gently rocking them from side to side.

He groaned. "I've missed you so much, honey."

"Mmm." Angela smiled. "Same here. I don't know how much longer I could take, wondering how you were."

"I think about you all day. These past four months have been aged to the point where I don't know if hard." He nudged her with his hips. "One more day away from you would have killed me."

She captured his wrists in her slender hands, then pulled his arms up and slowly turned his hands around to examine his fingers. She counted them slowly. When she was done counting, she let his arms go and stepped back a little to count his toes.

Angela smirked. "OK. Twenty is the good number."

Herb raised an eyebrow. "Why, yes. Twenty is a good

number, but that makes me think you have some project in mind."

"You hit that nail on the head, Herb, but I won't put you to work till tomorrow. You have a week with me, and tonight is nothing but us." Angela winked. "As for what I need you to do…"

Herb quickly raised his hand. "How about you wait and explain that tomorrow like you just said."

"OK, Herb." Angela shook her head. "You go relax while I finish this dessert for you."

Herb saluted. "I can definitely follow those orders."

He started walking toward the living room.

"Oh, Herb! I forget to tell you we're out of milk. Come to think of it, Leila hasn't dropped by with any in about two weeks."

Herb stopped. "That's unusual. Have you walked over to see what the deal is?"

"You know I don't drink milk that often, so I guess I never really considered the need."

Herb's forehead tightened. "Not even to chat with her? Heck, Angela, it's just down the road. You two used to see each other every day."

"She has actually been strange for the past few weeks and we just don't see each other very often."

"Did you ever ask her why?"

"Not directly. Just threw in some other questions to see how she would answer but really didn't get any responses."

"Have you seen Dave recently?"

"The last time I walked over there, about two weeks

235

ago, I saw Dave sitting in their kitchen but he really didn't say much either. Maybe they're having a spat."

Herb crossed his arms. "Must be some spat. Dave never shuts his mouth. He just goes on and on and on about whatever's in his head."

"Well, soldier"—she winked at him—"maybe you could head that way and get some milk. They sure haven't seen you in some time and you know their dairy has always put out the tastiest milk." Angela winked again. "Besides, you always have milk with the cake and it's made with powdered milk." She frowned.

"Good point, doll. Plus, I need to catch up with Dave and see how things have been." Their neighbors' absence piqued his curiosity. And it made him more than a little worried. What could've kept Leila and Dave away for so long?

Herb slid his boots on then walked around the back of the house. The tramped pathway looked a little overgrown, but Herb didn't expect his wife to mow the lawn or cut the bushes around the tree lines. Once he passed the tree line, he noticed his neighbors' yard looked overgrown as well.

The sun reached the horizon. It would be getting dark in a few minutes. The light emanating from the neighbor's kitchen was low, but that meant someone was home.

Herb looked through a window and didn't see anyone. He headed to the front door and knocked a few times. He then noticed dust upon the chairs and weeds growing through the porch floor. He knocked again with no answer.

Herb shivered.

As he walked along the sidewalk toward the back of the house, he noticed a light shining from the barn door. It flickered off. *Dave must be here.* Herb felt his shoulders drop in relief. He'd go over and say hi and plan on it taking a while—Dave would have plenty of conversations to catch up on.

Once he reached the barn door, Herb grabbed the door handle, but it was locked. He knocked and listened for a few seconds but didn't hear anything. Dave usually used the side door, so Herb headed in that direction.

The door was ajar, and Herb cautiously walked into the expansive barn. He knew a light bulb hung a few feet in front of him. Raising his arm, he swung it back and forth until he hit the light bulb. He wrapped his hand around the chain and pulled. A bright light flickered and hummed. Herb looked around the barn. The equipment had been rearranged—a big job that might explain Dave and Leila's recent lack of visits to Angela. But why would Dave have moved his milking equipment?

Aligned in the middle of the barn were two rows of milking machine that went all the way to the back of the barn. To the sides were large plastic tarps that flowed to the back as well. Herb cocked his head, trying to figure out what Dave's purpose had been. Round objects were aligned under the tarps.

As he walked closer to the milking machines, Herb saw a gray substance coating them. He reached down and swiped the top of a machine and looked at his finger. Dust.

"What the hell."

He stepped back a few feet and remembered walking through the yard and not hearing any cattle noises or smelling manure. Curiosity overtook Herb. He took a few steps forward and grabbed the bottom of the tarp. He tugged it up slowly and studied the smooth metal object beneath it, one that looked familiar to him, but he couldn't identify it.

When lifting the tarp higher, he heard something move behind him. Herb quickly turned his head. Bright light burst into his eyes. He raised his hand over his eyes and saw one of the round metal objects above the light. It swayed toward him menacingly. Herb took a few steps backs. "Holy shit!"

The SecureCon raised its metal arm—the one Herb now remembered was its gun arm. Herb dropped to the floor and rolled to the left. Excruciatingly loud gunfire blasted across the barn. Herb crawled forward, raised the tarp, and crawled underneath it, seeking a place to hide. The gunfire halted, but Herb could hear metal feet banging along the wooden floor.

The light by the door flared brighter, then burned out with a whispered *puht*. As Herb crawled under the tarp in the inky darkness, he kept hitting solid metal objects. He immediately knew they were slumbering SecureCons— crawling hurt his knees but he knew he needed to find a better place to hide. When he guessed he was in the middle of the row of milking machines, he stopped. Herb reached into his cargo pocket and pulled out his communicator. He opened the lid and pushed the emergency call button.

"This is the Communications Center."

"This is team member six-point-five." Herb's voice tremored. "I'm being attacked by a SecureCon!"

A sharp pain dug into his ankle. He looked down and saw a metal arm reaching through the tarp. It snapped him backward and pulled him hard and fast toward a lighted opening inside a SecureCon.

Several other SecureCons came to life and swiftly circled him.

Herb screamed into the communicator. "There are way too many here…"

As he was dragged out of the tarp, Herb twisted around and looked up.

He saw the gun arm flash.

Chapter Twenty-Seven

Obeying Stephan's orders, Meghan arrived at her father's doorway. This visit would prolong her mission with Ihan, and having that ulterior motive gnawed at her conscience. She was Dusty's only family now, and she'd recently neglected him. Guilty, she hoped this visit would resolve that.

Meghan noticed the yellow light above her father's doorway that meant he was either asleep or didn't want to be disturbed. With her hand upon the sensor, the door opened and she tiptoed in. Meghan saw the bare concrete walls and the clean floor. She was astounded because her father normally didn't clean. But then again, protocol was normally served to leaders and that would explain the clean room.

"Hello, flower," Dusty said softly. "I'm happy to see you."

Her father rested on his bed with a wet cloth upon his forehead. Meghan cringed, knowing he didn't feel well. She grabbed a chair and sat at the edge of the bed with her hands folded in her lap.

Meghan smiled. "Howdy, Dad. I certainly never saw you look so comfortable."

"I guess you could call it comfort." Dusty coughed and wiped his mouth. He drew a rattly breath, blinking rapidly, and sweat dripped down his face, which had lost its normal ruddiness.

She kept her smile—her father needed it. "Are you OK, Dad?"

"I guess these past few days have kicked my butt."

Meghan winked. "The amount of work and lack of sleep are probably catching up to you."

"That could be." Dusty offered her a weak grin. "What brings you to my humble abode?"

Meghan took a deep breath. "You know that I don't normally hide anything, so here goes. Stephan asked me to come by and get your approval to let Ihan see his processor—Mona."

Dusty hesitated for a few seconds.

"I have always appreciated your openness. I'm proud to be your father for that trait." He winked. "Now for this Ihan linking up with that processor, well, that is questionable for many reasons."

Meghan leaned forward. "I understand your concerns, Dad. But how far have your technicians gotten with that processor? Last I heard, they're not even close to getting into it."

Dusty raised an eyebrow. "You're spot-on with that one."

She tilted her head. "Then doesn't it make sense to have Ihan get the information we need out of that advanced processor?"

"Kind of makes sense, but you must understand that our security takes priority over any of that."

Meghan widened her eyes. "You do trust me, right?"

"Of course I do."

"Then let me take Ihan in there. Nobody knows him like I do."

"Regardless of who Ihan is, my concern is more with that damn processor and what damage it can cause. Dallas has us beat hands down with their technologies. The last thing we can do is trust that processor."

"I understand how you feel about this, Dad. But if we don't utilize the potential weakness in Dallas, then we may never get another chance." Meghan lowered her eyelids. "For many years you have been reactive to Dallas and hesitant about attacking beforehand."

"Ouch." Dusty closed his eyes for a moment.

Meghan dropped her head. She knew her father needed to hear that. He just wasn't in the best shape to deal with it. Meghan lightly touched his leg and tried to show with her gaze how much she cared.

"I completely trust and respect you, Dad. I ask that you do the same for me."

Dusty stared at her, and uncertainty crawled through her, but then he nodded and gave her leg a pat.

"I have always trusted you, flower."

A wave of emotion hit Meghan faster than she could deal with it. She managed a smile and tapped his leg a few times before she stood and walked toward the door. She then turned around and placed her hand on the wall.

"I hope you feel better soon. Remember to drink water."

Meghan walked out of the room hoping her father didn't dilly-dally over his recovery. *I just don't have the time to nurse him through this, not when I have Ihan to worry about. Besides, he is the coalition leader and receives medical priority.*

After she closed the door and took a few steps, Meghan saw Stephan walking her way. He looked intrigued, more and more as he got closer.

"How did it go in there?" Stephan smirked as he turned and walked with her.

"We can bring Ihan in to see Mona," Meghan said solemnly.

"I guess you were the right one to send in to get permission."

Meghan widened her nostrils. "What's that supposed to mean?"

"I'm just pulling your leg, Meghan." Stephan winked. "He would have said no if I was the one in there." He winked again. "That's the truth."

Meghan kept silent as they continued to walk. *Stephan always has a negative comment about my father.* She knew Stephan disliked her father's leadership style and personality. That was status quo. However, his increased negative behavior and comments about her father was getting old.

He tapped her shoulder. "Have you heard about the latest incident?"

"Regarding what?"

"One of the Team Six recruits was killed not far from his house last night."

Meghan turned her head. "What happened?"

"He called back an emergency notice on his first leave night, said there were many SecureCons."

"Where was he?"

"Somewhere near Lampasas."

"Is that the reason these hallways are busy?"

"Yes. Four teams are heading out to man our defensive perimeter to the north.

Meghan wrinkled her forehead. "What's our status?"

"We are still undermanned and inert, but I was told we should be receiving a few more additions here shortly."

"Let's hope those new members are good additions."

"I got my fingers crossed. How's your father doing?"

"Not so hot right now. He's lying in his bed under the weather."

"Sorry to hear that."

He didn't sound too sorry, but she shrugged it off.

Once they entered the team room, Stephan went to his locker, which he opened, and placed something inside it. Seeing her bed empty, Meghan looked down the room and found Ihan sitting near a table where two team members were playing cards. She meandered closer. There were two aces, king, queen, and a diamond five being placed down.

"There it is, Labios, now show me what you got!" a team member said.

The other team member studied the cards and then threw his facedown onto the table. He then looked up and smiled at Meghan.

"Hey, cutie. What's the good word?"

Meghan clenched her fists. "You call me cutie again and I'll plant my boot in your jewels."

"Ow!" Both team members shouted and laughed.

Meghan placed her hand on Ihan's shoulder. He looked up and smiled before standing slowly, holding his arm around his ribs.

Poor guy. "How are you feeling?" she asked.

"I am starting to feel better, especially since I ate all that food you gave me earlier."

"That's good to hear. You ready to see Mona?"

Ihan smiled with his eyes. "Of course."

"Put on those shoes and let's go."

Meghan then looked over at the two team members playing cards.

"Hey, guys. I'm taking Ihan out of the room and was wondering if you both could go with us? I sure could use the added protection."

The men nodded and put their pistols into their cargo pockets. Meghan gently touched Ihan's shoulder and winked.

"Let's go see her."

The four of them headed down the hallway in single file due to the constant movements in the hallway. Meghan noticed Ihan staring at the soldiers who ran by. He started to look dizzy. She grabbed his hand.

When they reached the technical wing corridor, she stopped and looked around the corner. As she expected, there wasn't any traffic walking down that corridor. She turned the corner and quickly walked to the entrance door. She's never been into this room, but had learned about it in training. As they reached the entrance door, Meghan stopped and faced Ihan.

"Just so we get this straight, I promised you would see

Mona, and here we are." Meghan gave him a serious stare. "I need to remind you why you are here. I'm sure you noticed all the members running through the hallways?" Ihan nodded. "We have learned that Dallas is sending their army of SecureCons down here to attack us, and that means they will attack this complex and everyone in it. Including you and Mona. I don't know the exact time for this, but I can only guess it will be soon." As she emphasized the gravity of the situation, his eyes grew larger. "I ask that you please help us learn more about this. You know Mona better than anyone else, and I believe you can ask her to keep all of us safe."

A congenial look came upon Ihan's face. "I will do my best, Meghan."

She leaned forward and put her eye in front of darkened glass ball. Simultaneously, she pressed her finger against the print identifier. The light turned green, the door opened, and Meghan headed in with Ihan following. Along the length of the corridor was a floor-to-ceiling glass wall that allowed them to view the three rooms. All three were inundated with electronic devices strewn along tables and floors. Meghan stopped at the center door and pushed it open. Once they both entered, with two team members staying outside, the door closed and the lights illuminated the entire room. On the table in the center was a black box with many wires and lines crossing and attaching to it. Meghan looked at Ihan and then pointed to the box.

"There's Mona."

Ihan turned and stared at the box with a look of confusion. Meghan could see his emotions spark quickly—

this must be the first time he'd ever physically seen Mona. She watched him carefully as he worked out that Mona was not a true person but a processor. Ihan slumped and he raised his hands weakly, then let them drop to his sides. His skin paled. Meghan then noticed the veins in his temples swell and throb—memories would be overloading him right now. He backed away from the processor. His back hit the glass wall and he slid down until his butt hit the floor. His head lolled to one side.

"Ihan!"

Meghan ran over to him and dropped her knees. He was still staring at Mona in confusion. She snapped her fingers and waved her hand in front of his eyes.

"Are you OK?"

Ihan stared at Mona a moment longer, then smiled at Meghan. "I'm sorry I fell down."

Meghan slapped his knee gently, then stood up and put out her hand. As soon as he grabbed her hand, she pulled him to his feet. A bit of color gradually returned to his face

Meghan smiled. "You worried the shit out me."

He glanced at her pants in alarm, and then blushed as he understood the figure of speech. "I apologize for that."

"What was going through your head?"

"I guess the realization of Mona being a box and not a person flustered me, I lost the moment there."

"Flustered? You looked like a drunken clown." Meghan giggled. "I guess I could have done the same thing if I was brought up like you. You ready to chat with her?"

Ihan grinned. "Definitely!"

Meghan walked across the small room and pushed the start button upon the power strip. An energy flow throbbed, increasing in volume within a matter of seconds. A tiny red glow emanated from the top of Mona, glowing brighter as she powered up. Meghan pushed the speaker button and looked over at Ihan. She pointed her finger at him.

"Mona." Ihan hesitated a few seconds. "Mona." He then took a few steps forward. "Mona!"

A sudden deafening beep emanated—so loud Ihan closed his eyes and clapped his hands over his ears. Meghan grimaced. She quickly turned the volume down.

"Crap! I'm an idiot for not remembering that." Meghan shook her head. "We learned that Mona sends out this deafening noise to thwart us. I won't tell you all of it, but we're lucky that box isn't broken for how she pissed us off with that."

Ihan opened his eyes. "Hello, Mona. It's me, Ihan."

A few silent seconds went by.

"Hello, Ihan and it is great to hear from you."

Meghan smiled and raised her thumb at Ihan. He blasted out a huge smile and walked closer to the table.

"I have to ask you, Mona, if you are OK?"

"You have to ask, Ihan? You can hear me, right?"

"Of course I can hear you. I just need to know how you're feeling."

"I'm internally fine with only a few damaged external instruments."

Ihan shook his head sadly. "Me too."

"Who is the other person in this room, Ihan?"

Ihan raised his shoulders and sent Meghan a questioning look. She opened her hand in an inaugurate gesture. Ihan leaned forward.

"The other person is Meghan. She is our protector and friend."

Mona made a singsongy hum as she digested this. "How are you doing, Ihan?"

"Thanks for finally asking." Ihan smirked. "The past couple of days have been rough, but I'm happy knowing the both of us are alive and well."

"Same here, Ihan."

"Be lucky you can't feel the temperatures around here because it's chilly in this room. I have goose pimples and my hair is standing straight up as I speak."

"Do you have a thicker shirt?"

The voice modulation on this thing was really good. Meghan could almost swear Mona actually cared about Ihan.

"I don't have one with me right now and I truly don't know where to find one in this complex, which is—"

"One mile north of San Antonio, Ihan."

Meghan raised her head. She hurried closer to the table. "Mona, this is Meghan. How do you know that?"

"Hello, Meghan. I know the coordinates of our location because my global positioning system is active."

"And you can get an accurate position in here?" Through a hundred feet of dirt and rock.

"Yes, Meghan."

Putting both her hands upon the table, Meghan wondered whether she should turn Mona off right now. She couldn't imagine Mona being able to send data to Dallas, but if she really could receive satellite signal underground, who knew what her transmission capabilities might be? Meghan's hand hovered over the power button.

"How well are you receiving this data, Mona?"

"Wait one." A few seconds passed. "The data I'm receiving is eighty percent strong, so I may be off by a half mile in specific location. An antenna that was removed from me . . . one moment, please."

A loud beep emanated from the complex's speakers.

"Attention coalition! This is Operations." A male voice boomed through the speakers. "This is notification of the battle alert! All members report to battle stations immediately!"

Meghan took a few steps back from the table. Ihan gawked at the speaker. Meghan scrutinized Mona.

"Why did you hesitate before that alert, Mona?"

"My apologies for the pause, Meghan. I received data from home station that an unmanned aerial vehicle has arrived above our location."

"Whose location?"

"This complex, approximately one mile north of San Antonio."

Could a computer actually be smug?

"Meghan, what's going on?" Ihan's voice tremored.

Meghan shook her head. "Nothing but fun times ahead Ihan. I have to go to my team room."

She strode toward the glass door.

"What do I do?" Ihan said loudly.

"Stay here with Mona." She hesitated. Maybe she should shut Mona down—but if she left the processor on, Ihan would stay here with her, out of harm's way. Meghan reached into her cargo pocket and handed him a communicator. "Push the green button and ask for me or Dirk if you learn anything from Mona."

She trounced out the door in anticipation for an attack. Her steps faltered halfway down the hallway. She didn't want to leave Ihan alone, but her training was strong: One team, one fight. Meghan dashed to her team room.

CHAPTER TWENTY-EIGHT

Meghan ran into the organized chaos of her team room, where the other team members were placing their gear along their outfits and loading their weapons. She opened her locker and swiftly readied her own battle gear. Their faces were tense, but none as tense as Dirk's. He sat on the floor, methodically polishing his pistol before sliding it into his holster. To her right was Stephan's locker, still closed.

"Hey Dirk, where is Stephan?"

Dirk raised his shoulders. "You got me."

"Any word on where we're supposed to head to?"

"Once again, you got me."

Looking around the room, Meghan noticed everyone staring at her as though she'd voiced the question they were afraid to ask, and Dirk's answer troubled them. Once she finished her gear, Meghan reached back into the locker, pulled out her pistol, slapped the loaded clip into the handle, and walked over to Dirk.

"How about you and I head up to the Operations Center so we can see what's going on and where they're sending us."

Dirk took a step back. "Look at you, Meghan, putting on that leadership hat."

Meghan smirked before they both headed out of the team room. Along the corridor, many other team members hustled in the opposite direction, toward the supply and motor pool. As she and Dirk reached the Operations Center doorway, Meghan stopped in front of the guard and put her hand upon his shoulder.

"Is Stephan in there?"

"Of course, Meghan. He's been in there for quite a while."

"Thanks!" Of course their inquisitive team leader would spend most his time in an information area.

As the door opened, both Meghan and Dirk headed in, bombarded by the constant communication within the room and displays along the wall. They stopped and scanned the room. Meghan's attention instantly focused on the display screens. To the far left were live scenes and status displays of the current teams at their locations. The right screen was fuzzy, but the lower portion of the screen showed a number listing associated with an active surveillance device.

When Dirk tapped her side, Meghan turned her head. Across the room, Stephan was sitting next to an operational planning table and talking with several of the planners. He spent a lot of time in this room, and the planners often sought his insightful knowledge and opinions. Out of the corner of her eye, she noticed a man, whom she'd seen working here often, headed her way. He had his head down, focusing on a display sheet that likely showed current team numbers and deployments.

"Hey, Craig!"

He raised his head with a smile.

"What's happening, Meghan? Good to see you."

"Just here trying to figure out what's going on and what were supposed to do. By the way, what's the deal with that fuzzy screen?"

Craig glanced up at it. "Once our UAV over Lampasas started disseminating data, we noticed a missile alert. Seconds later, we lost signal."

Meghan crossed her arms. "So we have no clue where the CSD SecureCons are right now?"

Craig raised his finger. "That is somewhat true. We currently have six teams along route 46 defending our northern sector. Two other teams are to the west, and three to the east. We are also getting indicators and sightings from our Texas citizens."

The room silenced. Meghan viewed the screen and noticed a smoke-streaming missile striking the CSD UAV circling above their location. A loud "hooray" thundered across the room. Everyone slapped each other's hands in delight.

Dusty stood from a chair in the middle of the room. As he tapped a few officers' shoulders and headed toward the planning table, Meghan noticed he hadn't lost his pallor. She cringed, but had expected his leadership presence for such a vital incident.

Meghan and Dirk approached the table. Dusty sat at the head, and Meghan kept her eyes on him. His demeanor looked weak. He kept slanting forward and adjusting himself back. The bags under his eyes had grown darker since the last time she'd seen him. Dusty then loudly cleared his throat and coughed. Everyone surrounding the table stopped talking and focused on him.

"All right, gang. The defensive concept of operations will stay its course. The recent indicators we have experienced certainly show the signs of an attack. We must show the City-State of Dallas how tough we truly are." Dusty coughed and wiped his mouth with a cloth. "Whether this attack has any historical resemblance to the battles of Concepción or Alamo, that happened here in San Antonio, we will show CSD and the rest of our country just how patriotic Texas residents are—and how devoted we are to regaining democracy and freedom." Dusty took a deep breath. "Everyone stay attentive and focus on defeating these bastards."

Dusty's speech, as usual, ignited a palpable sense of determination in all the team members. They nodded to one another and stood a little taller as they dispersed back to their duty positions. Dusty rose with stiff movements out of his chair and headed toward his office. Meghan was surprised he hadn't noticed her.

"Dad!" She took a few steps closer. "You look like crap."

He gave her a weary smile. "Maybe I've always looked like this, and you're just noticing."

"Not funny, Dad." She raised her eyebrow. "Please get some rest."

"Looks like you need some chow to get your energy back," Stephan said as he reached them.

"I guess this stomach could use some, it has been a while," Dusty said, squaring his shoulders.

Meghan looked at Stephan askance, though she appreciated his unusually sympathetic words. She turned to observe her father's reaction. He looked awful, like he was getting as he stood there.

"Dad. How about you just go back to your residence and lie down for a while."

Dusty took a deep breath. "I promise to sit down at my desk and relax, Meghan." He took a few steps toward his office. "Like Stephan said, I could use some food."

"I will let that food server know you need some chow. She is pretty attentive, and you should be getting it soon," Stephan said loudly.

Dusty nodded as he continued toward his office. Meghan grinned at Stephan.

"Maybe you're right. Who knows the last time he ate. I just hope he feels better—right now is a bad time for one of our leaders to get sick."

"Let's hope, Meghan. I will contact that woman and get his food here."

As Stephan picked up a phone, Meghan wondered why he was being so supportive. Lately, all Stephan's moods and statements about her father were negative. Dirk came to her side and stood there watching Stephan on the phone.

"Is everything OK?"

Meghan raised her shoulders. "I guess."

"You don't look too sure."

She looked Dirk in the eyes. "Guess I'm just wondering why Stephan is being so kind to my father."

"You know as well as I that Stephan is a professional soldier and true leader. Even though he's been expressing discontent toward your father doesn't mean he won't do what needs to be done. Dusty is our commander and needs the support in these stressful times."

"I guess you're right, Dirk." She didn't feel any surer than she sounded.

He beckoned her. "Follow me."

Meghan followed Dirk toward Stephan, who put the phone down. Dirk put his hands upon his hips.

"Where do we stand, Stephan?"

"We are the last team here and will stay. This facility will need an internal team for last resorts. Besides, we're still short manned and won't receive any new bodies anytime soon. I will stay here to assist with planning." Stephan stared at Dirk. "Gather the team and manage the defensive perimeter around this facility." He then looked Meghan in the eyes. "You know the deal when it comes to Ihan. By the way, have you brought him down to see Mona yet?"

"I sure did. He finally got that processor to open up and speak."

Stephan raised his eyebrows. "Anything important?"

"You could say that. Mona said she's still connected to the Dallas network and knew the UAV was above our location about the same time we were alerted."

Stephan curled his lip. "That's actually a good thing. That processor is located in a safe room where it can't connect to any of our systems. At least let's hope. Where is Ihan?"

"He's with Mona."

"Go back over there and see what we can learn."

"Will do. Oh, and thanks for helping my father, Stephan." Meghan smiled. "I really appreciate that."

"Sure thing. Both of you go forth and get things done."

Meghan bowed her head and exited the Operations Center with Dirk. In the hallway, she gave him a thumbs-up. Dirk winked before he walked in the opposite direction. She watched him depart and prayed he stayed safe. *What am I thinking, Dirk is a soldier.* Meghan smiled ruefully and headed back to the room where she'd left Ihan. She hoped he'd gotten some useful information from Mona.

CHAPTER TWENTY-NINE

While Ihan waited in the technical room for Meghan, he realized how much he missed Mona. Several weeks had passed since their last real conversation, and he needed to share his experiences with her. Mona knew him best and he always shared his thoughts with her. Yes, there were many arguments and disagreements throughout his life, and yes, Mona was always right. Her crystal ball persona baffled Ihan, but he needed her.

He pulled a chair away from the wall and brought it closer to the center table. He hit the hard backing of the chair and grunted. Hunching forward, he wrapped his right arm around his battered ribs.

"Is everything OK, Ihan?" Mona said.

He viewed her black box then stared at the wall. "I really don't know, Mona. It seems as though things are going to be stressful around here."

"Why do you think that?"

"Because I was told this facility is going to be attacked by our"—Ihan shook his head—"I mean, Dallas's forces."

"Yes, Ihan. Those forces are currently heading this way to save us and bring us back home."

Ihan swayed his head back and frowned. "I wouldn't say save us, Mona."

"What do you mean?"

"I will make a long story short. The Dallas government told us that people interacting would mean contamination." Ihan took a deep breath. "Since I'm here interacting with many people, and not infected, that policy cannot be true. Why is Dallas isolating us from our friends at home?"

"I can't answer your question, Ihan. That data is not within me."

Ihan rolled his eyes, flaring a smirk. "You see what I'm saying? How can a person want to be rescued and brought back to a city of lies? I've been thinking about this for a little while and really just need more time to figure out my infected thoughts." He took a jerky breath. "You see, something got infected, Mona!"

"I don't know what to say, Ihan." Mona's voice pattern dawdled.

"Of course you don't, and that's my point. Neither you or I were told the truth."

Mona chose not to respond to that, and Ihan slumped in his chair and stared at the wall. Confusion circled in his thoughts. His perception of life and all he knew living in Dallas were beyond what he could visualize or solve. Several minutes went by.

"Do you trust me, Ihan?"

He detected a strange tone in Mona's voice. He moved his eyes slowly toward her.

"Why are you asking me that?"

"Do you?"

Ihan jutted his chin. "I always have. Now I'm beginning to feel you're hiding something." He sat forward in his chair and tilted his head forward. "If you are, I need to hear it now, because if I don't, Mona, I really won't know what to think."

Mona hummed. "To show you how much I'm committed to you, I'm going to tell you something that I was ordered not to."

Ihan shot straight up in the chair. "You mean to tell me you withheld information from me?"

"Yes." Mona continued to hum.

"I don't understand why you would keep something from me."

"I was ordered and..."

Ihan crossed his arms and hammered his fingers on his elbow. "Who ordered you to keep information from me?"

"Please calm down, Ihan, and let me tell you."

Flustered, Ihan braced his elbows upon his bruised knees and rubbed his temples. Thoughts flew through him as he contemplated the magnitude and ramifications of what Mona might be hiding from him. He took a deep breath. This was Mona. Any other person, he would have walked away.

"All right, Mona, I'm listening."

"Approximately two months ago I received classified data ordering my program to reduce your understanding and sidetrack your current thoughts upon your outer wall sensor decline. Once the sensors were compromised, that information posting was transmitted in the open. I was ordered to keep you focused upon your agriculture profession and not let you know of the situation."

Ihan lowered his head. "So the outer wall sensors broke down? Why wasn't Roger Bell alerted to this? He could have repaired those in no time." Or was his best friend withholding information from him too?

"Those sensors were not broken." Mona hesitated. "They were shut down."

"Shut down!" Ihan's face got hot. "Were they just being replaced, and you were told not to tell me so I would stay focused upon my harvesting?"

"The sensors were not replaced. They were shut down."

Her circuits must be fried.

"I'm confused, Mona. Please just tell me why they were shut down."

"My understanding is that the purpose of the sensor shutdown was to weaken that wall for an attack by the United Texas Coalition."

"What?"

Mona's humming silenced. "That is why we are here, Ihan."

Ihan's mind exploded with the incoherence of her rationale. He sat back in his chair and rubbed his temples hard. He was on track to becoming the best agricultural controller this year, and that made what Mona said even more irrational. Why wouldn't the City-State of Dallas not tell him of such an incident? All he had ever known were anxiety-driven events in which the City-State of Dallas government pressured him into increased production.

It occurred to him that many of the sensor alert incidents were recent.

"I can remember four or five sensor alerts, and my buddy Gerald Bacon investigated them for me. He was the neighborhood Security Controller, Mona. Did Gerald know about this?"

"I'm unaware of what he knows, Ihan."

Ihan smirked. "Of course he didn't know. He sounded confused when he told me of his move over to Security Headquarters near Highland Park. I could hear in his voice that he was clueless as to the rationale behind his move. We both thought it was a promotion."

"That makes sense, Ihan."

"What makes sense? This whole concept is stupid. Why would Dallas breach its own wall?"

"Dallas didn't break down that wall and capture both of us, Ihan."

Ihan rolled his eyes. "Good grief, Mona! You mean to tell me you back Dallas for what they did to us?"

"We were captured by a team from the United Texas Coalition."

"You just don't get it, do you? This is truly a first, I'm outthinking you."

Mona's humming started again. "I don't understand what you're asking."

"Of course you don't, Mona. You need to open your mind and understand the inequity behind all of this, because you and I are suffering the most, not Dallas or this Texas Coalition."

"We were ordered by Dallas to locate UTC headquarters."

Ihan impaled Mona's box with a glare. "Wake up, Mona!" *All of this awareness was most disturbing.* "I just don't understand why Dallas utilized me for such a devastating event. Why me?"

He stood and stormed toward the door. The thoughts spun in painful circles. He pulled the handle and the door wouldn't budge. He pushed, and felt no resistance.

"Ihan, where are you going?" Mona's volume increased.

Meghan hurried down the technical wing corridor. When she opened the door, she noticed Ihan's damp eyes and trembling lower lip as he aggressively pulled the glass door. She took a few steps and opened the door. Ihan brushed past her and kept his eyes straight as he headed for the outer door. He tugged the handle on the locked outer door. When it didn't open, he slapped his sides and glared back at Meghan. In shock, she released the glass door and heard it close swiftly as she trotted toward him.

"What's going on, Ihan?"

Ihan twisted his torso but kept his feet still. "I need to get out of this room."

"OK."

Meghan cautiously walked around Ihan and unlocked the outer door. He rushed out and stalked down the corridor. Behind him, Meghan imagined his thoughts spinning around in his head as he shook his head and his stature increasingly becoming solid. His frustration enticed her—maybe he was finally ready to believe her about CSD.

She followed Ihan at a distance. When he reached the end of the corridor, he stopped then looked left and right down the main hallway before shrugging his shoulders. As he averted his gaze from her, and it swung back up, Meghan smiled. She got closer to him, staring into his eyes and feeling a connection to him. *He truly is human.*

Ihan's nose twisted in sneer. "I don't know where I'm going."

"That's OK. Would you like a hot drink with some caffeine?"

He looked away and shrugged. "Sure."

Meghan stepped to his side and placed her arm under his. "Come on. To the dining hall we go." She smiled and guided him forward.

When they arrived at the dining facility, Meghan walked Ihan to a table and pulled out a chair. He slumped into it. A hundred emotions played across his face, and Meghan knew the first thing she had to do was comfort him.

She winked to him before she walked over to the drink counter. As she poured two mugs of hot coffee, she noticed a stale smell, so she added a flavored cream and sugar to freshen the taste. She carried the drinks back to the table and slid one toward Ihan. His face immediately softened as he looked down into his coffee mug. Meghan smiled as he took a sip.

"I can tell you drink coffee."

"Yes. Thanks, by the way."

"Just know that I'm here for you. So if you want to let it out, I will listen."

He took a deep breath. Finally, he nodded. "Where

do I begin with this? OK, first I must say that I always thought Mona was there for me. I mean, just for me and not the city-state. I've always trusted her. I assumed my whole life that her existence was for one person and obviously that person is me." Ihan sneered again.

"It's OK, Ihan, just spit it out."

"I guess you can see right through my frustrations. I'm going to ask you a question, Meghan, and I hope you will be honest with me."

Meghan slightly raised her eyebrows. "I will."

"Here it goes. I'm sure you heard an open transmission about two months ago that my wall sensors were turned off. I'm assuming you tested that wall about five times to verify that?"

"That's…good…I mean…" Meghan widened her eyes and sat back. "How the hell do you know that?"

"Now you can see why I'm frustrated. Mona was ordered by some jerk in the Dallas government to not tell me anything about the lapse in security. Even my neighborhood Security Controller wasn't told. He was sent away after you tested our security a few times."

"What are you saying?"

Ihan hunched forward. "I'm saying that both of us were ignorant when it came to Dallas turning off those wall sensors."

Meghan shook her head. "Why did Mona tell you?"

Ihan looked down into his coffee. "Dallas turned off the sensors so you would capture Mona and bring her here. They now know your position."

The corners of her mouth tugged down. "You have to be kidding me. We were set up?"

"Yes we were! Obviously I was not supposed to be captured by your team, because I would have known about this."

Meghan linked her hands behind her head and slid down a few inches in the chair.

"I understand how you feel and where you stand Ihan. I will support you through this."

"Thanks."

With his facial expression turning somber again, Meghan understood that there was some other issue floating around inside of him. She wondered what it was but didn't want to interfere with his figuring it out. Ihan grimaced.

"I really don't want you to take this the wrong way. I believe Mona will help us. I did question that, but she did tell me the truth. We can trust her."

"Even though what she told you was after the fact."

"Yes. For the past few months I did notice her acting differently. I wondered why, but couldn't figure it out. There were several times when I noticed Mona leaving some stuff around the house and forgetting to tell me things she normally did. I just thought she was overwhelmed with work because the Agricultural Commission was extensively examining me, or she just had some technical problems. I asked my best friend, Roger Bell, to technically check on her and he said she was fine. When I asked her status she always told me she was fine."

"So, what are you saying, Ihan?"

"Just before the latest harvesting work, Mona sounded strange. I told her she was getting more comical and bossy. She came back and told me that she was just an internal processor when she started and grew with me in many ways throughout the years. I said I was lucky to have her in my life. Then she asked me if I loved her! I didn't know what to say, Meghan. I didn't even know what love was, but I told her we were emotionally linked. She told me she loved me. I didn't know how to take that or why she said that to me. I just took it as motivation for the harvesting work I was about to perform."

"Do you still believe that was the reason she said it?"

Ihan raised his shoulders. "I'm not certain, but I do know she never said that before."

"I can see what you're saying, and it's a good thing you're telling me about this."

Ihan sat back. "Where do we go from here?"

"Well, we will leave her focused on you. Dallas already knows our location and is sending forces. Mona may be able to help us out."

"OK."

Meghan smiled. "How was that coffee?"

Ihan smiled back.

A loud beep startled them. She reached down into her cargo pocket and pulled her communicator up and clicked the button.

"This is Meghan."

"Meghan, this is Craig and you need to come to the infirmary ASAP."

She set down her cup hard, and coffee sloshed onto the table. "What's going on?"

"We just brought your father in here. He doesn't look well."

"I'll be right there." Jamming the communicator in her pocket, Meghan headed toward the door.

"Meghan!"

She turned back to Ihan, shuffling backward. Anxiety pinched his features. "Just go back to the team room and hang in there." She ran out the door.

Chapter Thirty

Meghan sprinted through the Infirmary main entrance door, searching for her father. She stopped in the middle of the corridor intersection and looked both ways. Down to the left she focused in and recognized Craig peering through a window into an emergency room. She dashed closer and slid into him.

"How is he?"

The room's bright lights sparkled against the white walls and the shiny white floors. In the middle of the pristine whiteness, her father convulsed on the hospital bed.

A doctor attached sensors along Dusty's arm. A nurse wiped his pale forehead with a towel.

Meghan felt numb. "What happened?"

Craig stepped back with a frown. "I'm glad you're here. He doesn't look good. All I remember is seeing Dusty collapse to the floor, twitching and sounding strange. I ran over to him. He looked . . . frail. Not truly there. I called the medics. They came and brought him here a few minutes ago."

Meghan shook her head. "Thanks for telling me about this, Craig."

Within the infirmary, the doctor inserted a needle

into Dusty's arm. He pulled the plastic backing off, and blood flowed into a container. To the rear of the bed, the heart rate monitor displayed steep stripes jetting up and down.

Meghan's lip started to tremble. "This isn't good!"

She pushed the door hard. It slammed against the wall. After she passed the nurse, Meghan stopped at the head of the bed and stared down. Her father's face looked pale and distant, and sweat flowed from his forehead. The doctor swung around and inserted a needle into an IV pump, then depressed the syringe's plunger. When the syringe emptied, the light on the machine turned red and emitted the clatter of a processor.

"What's going on with my father?" Meghan asked tersely.

"It's currently unknown. Mr. Rhodes just arrived and we are testing his blood. His symptoms look strange."

"Strange?" Meghan widened her eyes. "What does that mean?"

"I'm unsure, but can at least tell you he is not well."

She scowled. "Thanks for your professional opinion, Doc."

The nurse tossed a wet towel toward a hamper, and missed. It hit the wall. As she grabbed another, Meghan yanked it from her hands. "Thanks." Meghan wiped Dusty's forehead. The nurse raised an eyebrow and let out a snort before she turned around and headed to the cabinet.

Dusty's muscles continued to twitch. His breathing slowed. He grunted a few times, and his unfocused eyes shut fluttered.

Meghan looked up. "He's going out."

"No worries. I just gave him an injection to calm him."

Tears dribbled down her cheeks as Meghan stared at her father's closed eyes. Not knowing what he was experiencing, the pain, the feelings, and the weakness—things he always tried to hide—disturbed her. She dredged her mind for answers that might lie in his past medical problems; the twisting of his knee due to playing soccer with her, falling off a ladder and injuring his back, maybe the concussion he'd suffered protecting their property from thieves. Nothing that she remembered quite fit his current conditions and symptoms. She knew her father was aging, but he just hadn't reached that failing age of "over the hill." Back when she was younger, her father had violent coughing spells and never breathed well because his sinuses were perpetually clogged after a cold she'd passed to him and others in that neighborhood. No one else had suffered lasting effects, though. *I just don't understand what is causing this.*

When the blood test machine beeped, the doctor read the results. He pushed a few buttons on the keyboard and grumbled to himself. Meghan stood upright, staring at him in anticipation.

He flicked the paper. "Ah, shit!"

Meghan trembled. The doctor spun around and looked around the room.

"Nurse!"

As the nurse ran through the open doorway, the doctor ripped open Dusty's shirt.

"Grab that stomach tube and lubricate it now!"

The nurse opened the supply closet and pulled out a plastic package. As she headed back to the table, she tore open the package, unraveling a coil of clear tubing. She reached underneath a table to grab some lubrication, then pushed Meghan toward the foot of the bed.

"Please move out of the way."

Tears flooded Meghan's face. "What's going on?"

The doctor slid his arms under Dusty and elevated his torso. The nurse poured a vast amount of lubricant on the tube and rubbed it down with her latex gloved hands, then measured it against his chest. Tilting his head back, she jammed two fingers into his mouth, spread them to open it, and inserted the tube deep into his esophagus. She backed the tube out slightly a few times but kept pushing until it reached his stomach. The doctor stepped away and busied himself at the sink.

Reaching back under the table, the nurse lifted up a bedpan and placed it under Dusty's mouth before she pumped the tube.

Meghan watched with her hands pressed to her mouth as a yellow trickle flowed through the tube and dripped into the bedpan. The doctor came back from the sink, holding a beaker filled with clear liquid. "Saline," he explained to Meghan, and she nodded, understanding what he was going to do with it.

With the nurse raising the tube, the doctor poured the water down it. Dusty started refluxing and gagging.

"Begin pumping again," the doctor said.

Spurts of colored fluid and chunks of food flowed through the tube into the bedpan. The process slowed, then the doctor repeated it with another beaker of saline until they'd flushed the remaining contents from Dusty's stomach and Meghan half expected to see his innards come down the tube.

"OK, please go back there and get me some charcoal."

With one hand still over her mouth, Meghan watched the nurse run back into the closet.

"What is going on with my father?"

"Your father has been poisoned. The blood test results confirmed signs of a toxin in his system."

Meghan's mouth popped open. "Poisoned! With what?"

The doctor shook his head. "I don't know the specific kind, but I can confirm it's severe poisoning. His symptoms prove that. When he first arrived, I checked his skin for any needle penetrations. I then checked his lungs and both are fine."

"So what are you saying?"

"He ingested the poison."

"Someone poisoned his food? You got to be kidding me." Meghan's legs trembled. "Who would do that?"

"I don't know. Just know that we will take good care of him until he gets better. I will begin treatments right away."

Her trust in the personnel of UTF was tainted. Yet knowing the doctor was the best one in Texas meant some hope for her father. Not knowing who did this meant uncertainty about everyone she knew. Dirk came first into her thoughts, as well as her other teammates, and their trustworthiness.

Her new priority was making sure her father stayed

safe and secure. Finding the person who had harmed him was next. She grabbed her communicator, her jaw tightening.

"Dirk. Meet me in the team room ASAP."

"Is everything OK?"

Meghan turned off her communicator without answering, placed her palm on her father's shoulder for a second, then turned and headed out the door.

Chapter Thirty-One

Dirk sped toward the team room, absently waving at members he passed, his thoughts focused on the communication he'd received from Meghan. His feet ached from reconnoitering the facility, but the pain was secondary to reaching the team room and finding out what had her so upset.

He took a deep breath and squared his shoulders before he entered the team room, prepared for whatever she might throw at him. Meghan sat crying on her bed. Across the room, Ihan sat near a table and stared at her with a gloomy expression. If Ihan had caused Meghan's tears, Dirk would never, ever forgive him. He never should've agreed to keeping Ihan alone with Meghan.

Dirk charged toward the table and balanced his weapon on his hip. His chin jutted out as he stared at Ihan.

"All right, Ihan, what did you do to Meghan?"

"Hi, Dirk." Ihan gave a brief smile that quickly faded, and his lips closed. "I didn't do a thing to Meghan. She ran in here and started crying. She wouldn't answer me when I asked her if she was all right."

Dirk turned around and took a few steps toward Meghan. Ihan's chair squeaked. "Stay seated, Ihan."

As he arrived by her bed, Dirk looked at Meghan's slumped head, with tears gushing from her eyes and her elbows locked onto her knees. He hesitated. Something severe had happened to her; he'd never seen her this emotionally weakened. He looked up on to the ceiling and wondered if he were the best one to handle this conversation. He was more fit for combat, not for talking about feelings.

Dirk shook his head. This situation was new to him. His temples throbbed, and his throat went dry. He swallowed. He'd experienced many other emotional situations, but always alerted the appropriate professional for treatment. A professional soldier didn't handle medical or emotional problems.

But Meghan was more to him than just a soldier. Shit.

Dirk dropped down next to her and put his arm up behind her back. He lightly tapped her shoulder.

"What's going on, Meghan?"

She looked up. Her eyes were beet red, and nasal mucus had dribbled around her mouth. A look of despair and frustration contorted her face, and then she threw her arms around him. Her head slammed hard into his shoulder, soaking his sleeve. Dirk jerked a little but kept silent.

Meghan's body quivered for a few seconds, and he patted her back, hoping she would stop crying. After a minute, she peeled herself off his shoulder, sat straight, and swiped the snot off her face. She rubbed it on her pants—Dirk didn't look down.

Meghan cleared her throat. "Someone poisoned my father."

His eyebrows rose high. "Poisoned? What's his status?

"He's currently in the Infirmary and being taken care of by the doctor."

"Did you see him?"

"I got there a few minutes after he was brought in. After the doctor discovered he was poisoned, I about lost it." Meghan lowered her eyelids. "I just couldn't take it, Dirk. I had no clue what to do. You were the first one I called."

Dirk got excited. "You know I'm here for you."

Meghan shook her head. "Why would someone poison the Coalition leader?"

"It doesn't make sense. Especially since we're being attacked."

"Do you think someone loyal to Dallas did this?"

Dirk glanced at Ihan. "That's possible, but I highly doubt it. We were all psychologically checked for being UTC trustworthy before being allowed to work in here." He winked at her. "You know that."

Meghan squinted. "Then who would do this?"

"We'll figure it out. Did the doctor say how your father got poisoned?"

"He said he ingested it."

"There you go, someone covertly fed it to him."

Meghan's eyes were motionless. The blood vessels along her neck sprang out. She was thinking up a storm. Her body then violently shook.

"No! You got to be kidding me."

Dirk leaned forward. "What is it?"

"If that bitch did this, I'm going to strangle her."

He jerked back up. "Who?"

"Dottie. The new food server for my father."

"Why her?"

"Think about it. She's new to the Coalition, just got hired a few weeks ago, and was chosen by my father because he loves to look at those hot women. My damn father did this to himself." Meghan shook her head. "He's so weak when it comes to women! "

"If you're right, then someone close to your father hired her."

Meghan stared into Dirk's eyes. "Why do you say that?"

"Only a person close to him would know the extent of his weakness."

"Good point."

Dirk took a deep breath. "I must give you an order, Meghan, and that order is to stay focused on Ihan." He stood to his feet. "Dallas's forces are close but location unknown. Ihan and his processor might be our edge and give us some good poop."

"An order?" Meghan's mouth dropped wide open.

"Yes. A first isn't it?" Dirk winked. "You know I out-rank you. And I am being serious because it's one team, one fight, Meghan. A good buddy of mine is the chief of our internal police. He will get what we need out of Dottie."

She glared at him. "He'd better, because I know what I would do if I saw her right now."

Dirk tapped her knee. This incident with her father

was drastically swaying Meghan's thoughts, and she was too important for UTC's defense for him to let to her slip off task. His mission to strengthen the facility's defensive perimeter was important too. He needed to get back out there.

As he walked toward the door, Dirk looked back. Meghan was still staring down. Ihan was staring at Meghan, but why wasn't she looking back? Something wasn't sound here. Or had his feelings for Meghan softened his perspective? He took another deep breath.

"Meghan!"

As she raised her head, Dirk tossed a box of tissues her way.

"Stay focused on Ihan. I predict we'll need him later."

Chapter Thirty-Two

The sun rose over the horizon as Russ, Team leader Five, studied his designated northern defensive perimeter. His digital planner confirmed that his team members were in appropriate positions. He tracked positions of the other teams to his east and west. They were in place.

Ahead of him and as far as Russ could see along Highway 281 to the north and Canyon Lake to the northeast, the environment looked habitual. Increasing daylight glistened off the lake every minute that passed by. The night before, he'd heard distant gunfire that echoed from what was reported by the forward observers in the northern town of Spring Branch. A few reported faint movements along the plains while others claimed the town volunteers had battled a few SecureCons along their property lines. Russ listened to reports all night and read the data flowing through his operational channels. It meant long, exhausting hours on the job, but he refused to be taken by surprise.

For several days, his team had planted movement and identification sensors among their forward lines. He checked the sensors often, and they'd detected no movement. The airy feel to the clear sky, and the light breeze, kept him physically comfortable, but a temperate setting always meant some action was certain.

"Russ…I mean Team Leader Five. This is the Operations Center and I'm alerting you about five air blips heading…wait, one…three more just appeared ahead of those slower-moving blips heading south along Highway 281. Altitude is much lower for the five. The three that just appeared are currently at three thousand feet and heading south at a good pace."

"Roger that, Mac. Pass along the data and I will send to the other teams along the defensive line."

"Headed your way, Russ. Take care, buddy."

"Thanks, Mac."

"Roger, out."

As he viewed the data displayed on his screen, Russ noticed movements in the distance. Dallas widely used the unmanned aerial vehicles for first strikes. That formation made sense, but the five slow-moving objects behind the faster three didn't. He typed in the address listing and forwarded the data to the other teams before he switched screens and typed to his team members.

In front of Russ lay open plains. The long grass and overgrown weeds rippled briskly. Over the plain, in the distance, a flock of Canada geese flew above the tree line in perfect formation.

Russ stuck his finger in his mouth and raised it high above his head. The southerly wind was steady and flowed strong. As he looked back on to his screen, he noticed the three objects were close to Spring Branch. The blips then separated from each other. Russ knew that meant an offensive action.

He raised his head and squinted through his telescope. The digital view was good for the specific range because he trusted the GPS data. A glare trailed by a smoked line dropped into his field of vision, heading twenty degrees, as he zoomed in. He knew where it was heading. Another two smoked lines appeared. Russ raised his head and stared down range for a second before looking back into his telescope.

Seconds later, he saw flashes and smoke rise. His communicator beeped and displayed multiple verbal and data interactions flowing among the forward observer channels. A barrage of gunfire echoed in the distance, and smoke trails curled upward. An explosion slammed through the air.

CHAPTER THIRTY-THREE

Stephan noticed the fierce activity displayed in the Operations Center. The screens showed distant explosions, missiles flying in from above, and shaky displays of movement among the teams. Frantic conversations escalated to a deafening volume. Attack was inevitable; so was the staff disruption.

The executive officer, who should've taken charge, stood petrified in the middle aisle. Lack of leadership during such an intense action meant disaster. This group definitely needed a leader to bring the room back to focus.

He leaned back in his seat and stared at the executive officer. After a few seconds, Stephen shook his head. He uncrossed his legs, stomped his feet down, braced his hands on his knees, and stood tall. He then reached behind the chair and grabbed a metal pole normally used for pushing troops during tactical planning, and he slammed it down on a table. *Ping! Ping!* The earsplitting shriek silenced the room. Everyone stared at Stephan.

"You." Stephan pointed at the executive officer. "Get over here now."

The executive officer gulped before he walked up the

slanted row. He halted and stared at Stephan. His composure broke down, and he slumped in defeat.

Stephan raised his arm and pushed the officer away, and the whole room saw his shame.

Stephan took a few steps forward and assertively looked around the room.

"All of you listen up. There are teams getting shot at and all of them rely on this office to keep them focused and alive." He jutted his chin. "You hear me?"

Everyone in the room shook his head in unison, before they jumped back to their terminals. Along the communication row, all the specialists hacked away at their terminals, passing the information to the appropriate locations. The intelligence row analysts assessed the surveillance and reconnaissance data. Within the operations row, officers gathered the location data of the deployed teams and made sure those locations were correct.

Sudden red blips among the screen alerted several officers around the room. They all looked back to Stephan, who squinted and headed closer to the screen. The blips moved at a fast pace, then split into three directions. Stephan's lips pressed together.

"Tally that number."

An intelligence officer looked over at Stephan and pressed a button on his terminal. Next to the blips the number 30 appeared. Several in the room let out loud grunts.

As he turned around, Stephan pointed to the operations row.

"Y'all in the back two rows, get those birds flying now."

After the operations officers pressed several buttons, a scattered pattern of blue blips appeared on the southern side of the digital maps, and then aligned in a row heading north at a fast speed.

Stephan noticed bolt icons appearing upon the screens. "Zoom in," he yelled, pointing his finger at the screen. The screen then took over the other two screens. The larger screen showed the icons blipping over the towns of Boerne to the left and Bergheim to the right. Stephan had never seen those icons before. He knew the ground teams were currently at those locations. That meant an inevitable engagement. But what were their guys up against?

"What in the hell are those bolt icons?"

"Weapon and situational readiness icons," a guy from the operations desk yelled.

Several of the teams to the east of those locations didn't have those icons. *This damn map doesn't mean a thing when it comes to team status.* Stephan brushed the momentary stress aside. As a team leader, he too had often got sidetracked or busy due to other matters taking his time. Not reporting current status usually meant minor issues— technical problems, lack of coverage, or a team still getting its location established.

Knowing he was now running the Operations Center, Stephan let go of his doubts as he stood upright, pushed the shoulders back, and raised his chest higher. He remembered all those past operations where he'd wished he were the one calling the shots and managing the coalition's plans. Now he was.

Next to the lined blue blips upon the screen, the number 20 appeared. That provided the air elements' distance.

The coalition had engaged in unsuccessful air battles in the past. He considered what the best tactic could be to reduce the number of Dallas's aerial vehicles. As he stared at the displayed map, Stephan took a minute to survey the whole area. The planned defensive line was currently in the middle of the forces.

Dusty had told him about their latest acquisition. Those new missiles were dual orientated for both air and surface targets. Stephan smirked. Dusty didn't deserve credit for ordering those missiles. Besides, Stephan had told Dusty he believed India was now using the United Texas Coalition as a surrogate force against China. He shook his head and shoved this thought to the rear. Focus. Back to the battle. He looked over to the operations officers.

"Do our teams along the defensive line have the missiles?"

"Which ones?" the first officer in the row asked.

"The new ones we just got from India."

The officer raised a thumb. "They have plenty of those, Stephan."

These new missiles were small, light, and had a three-mile range. He considered how to time their usage to best benefit this battle. "I got it," Stephan said softly. He walked down the aisle to the front of the room and spun around facing the whole room. He raised his arms up and down.

"Everyone quiet down and hear me out."

Everyone in the room quieted and looked at Stephan. He dropped his arms and placed his hands on his hips.

"Here is our course of action on how this battle will

be fought. We are going to order the teams along the northern defensive line to get the new missiles loaded and target those Dallas UAVs." Stephan pointed to the screen. "Simultaneously, we need to slow our UAVs and keep them a mile south of the defensive line. As soon as those Dallas aerial vehicles get within three miles to our defensive line, fire away those new missiles. As soon as the missiles are fired, I want our aerial vehicles to move right in to the attack." He then pointed to the operations officers. "Synchronize this with the teams and make it happen!"

CHAPTER THIRTY-FOUR

Along the northern defensive border, Russ received new orders from the Operations Center. He raised his eyebrow at first; the Coalition forces had failed against CSD technology in the past, but this new plan made logical sense.

As he checked his operational display, Russ noticed the five low-flying red blips approaching. They passed over Spring Branch, heading south. He typed a message for his team:

Team Five. We have a new course of action. Load the new missiles and await my order to target and release at the enemy UAV in your lane. BTW, coalition leader Dusty Rhodes is ill and Team Leader 8 is taking charge. Not bad. Out.

Russ saw many read and reply dots fill into his team list. This made him smirk because his team was spread out farther than he liked. Russ raised his head and took a seat on the rock he stood on. That rock was large—in the middle of a prairie hill—and his legs were tired and wobbly.

A sudden *beep-beep* jolted Russ. He picked up his

terminal and noticed low-flying red blips only two miles to the north. As he put the terminal back down, Russ got back onto his feet, pulled his telescope out of his pocket, and focused on the flying objects. Their speed increased. Unease rippled through him.

Russ closed his eyes to clear the fuzziness exhaustion brought. He gazed back into his telescope and saw the flying objects had swirling tops. They were helicopters, but a type he couldn't recognize. The rotary top was small, while the body of the helicopter looked slim but long. Dangling from the main body of each chopper were two lines that hung from either side.

Russ zoomed in below one helicopter and noticed SecureCons dangled underneath. There were one, two, three…five on each side. He then pulled back the zoom and verified the five helicopters were loaded with Secure-Cons. Russ pursed his lips. There were fifty SecureCons heading his way—enough to threaten defense. He connected his telescope to his communicator and pressed the send button back to the Operations Center.

With violence inevitable, he leaned backward and opened the missile box. He pulled out the pieces and assembled the missile launcher, then placed the new, smaller missile into the load chamber. The light turned green on the active button.

The SecureCons would be landing and releasing soon—Dallas obviously knew where the Coalition's defensive line was. His team locations were composed of two members per site, and that meant both members could back each other and handle an additional option. Russ grabbed his terminal and tapped away:

Team Five. Set the mortars and load the jamming rounds. We have 50 SecureCons about to land with incoming helos. Once they land, launch rounds 2 miles forward in that direction. Repeat, 2 miles. Out.

In the distance, the helicopters hovered in a wider formation. He trailed the telescope downward. The bottom racks were empty. As he lowered his sights, he noticed fast movements within the fields. Russ grabbed his communicator.

"Launch the mortar rounds!"

Within seconds, bass-toned thumps sounded as the mortars were fired away. Russ kept his vision on the SecureCons. They were spread out and moved to the left and right of the paved roads. Russ dropped down on one knee. He waited in anticipation for the mortar rounds landing. He closed his eyes for a second and hoped all those rounds landed beyond the two-mile barrier, because if they didn't, their own rounds would jam all their communications equipment.

Russ focused his vision to the distance and saw a puff of dust. He jumped up and looked into his telescope. He zoomed in to the site, though the jammer wouldn't explode, it would just operate. Russ zoomed out and saw no movement, nor any SecureCons still upright. The speed those SecureCons moved would mean a tumble as they fell over. Russ squinted but didn't see any dust plumes. Those heavy metal robots should shoot up plenty of dust whether they were on the move or had fallen.

Russ raised his communicator. The connection bar was blank. He shook it, but still no signal.

"Damn!"

Russ lifted his missile launcher and noticed the technologically advanced weapon still seemed operational. He looked through the scope and switched on the thermal viewer and he saw five UAVs heading in his direction. He pressed the distance button that displayed back "1.3 Mile" data within the scope.

"Crap."

The UAVs were within a few minutes of his location. It was time to hurry and shoot as many missiles he could. Russ moved the launcher around in a tight circle. He centered the red target cross on one of the UAVs. The cross turned green and Russ pulled the trigger. The missile launch rammed him backward.

Russ' mouth dropped wide open. "Damn, that little thing is powerful."

His ears ached and buzzed as he grabbed another missile and placed it within the open door on the launcher. He aimed at another UAV and pushed the trigger. This round sent Russ farther back. He dropped down to one knee that slammed against a rock.

"Damn that hurt!"

Russ wondered how such a small missile could generate enough force to throw him back. He shook his head, reached down, grabbed another missile, and slid it into the open door. He looked up to see if his missiles were successful. As he raised his head, Russ followed the smoke path, and at the end a large smoke cloud billowed, with UAV parts falling to the ground. He saw the other smoke path, but noticed a third smoke path—this one was curving and getting closer.

Russ felt the blood drain from his face. "Oh shit!"

He realized the enemy had locked onto the launcher location. Russ dropped the missile launcher and sprinted down the side of the hill. All his gear and communication equipment were on the hill, but he needed to avoid the incoming mess. An explosion threw Russ forward. He tumbled down the hill, shielding his head with his arms as large rocks battered his body. Russ knew he grunted and screamed, but his ears were so numb he couldn't hear a thing. When he rolled to a stop, he looked up the small hill. Smoke and flames blew to the side from his launch site.

As he stood back on his feet, Russ was numb and weak. He stumbled forward and up the side of the hill. In the distance, he saw another smoke path, but this one was a distance away—it struck the ground and just a small dust cloud floated higher and dissipated fast. He got a little higher and noticed something moving, but couldn't identify it without the telescope.

Russ remembered he had his childhood binoculars in his cargo pocket. He pulled them out and extended the long barrels. When he focused the view, a metal pole appeared in the field. It grew taller. *What in the hell is that thing?* The pole stopped extending. Something moved in his peripheral vision, and he turned his head. The Secure-Cons were moving again, faster than normal. This mystified Russ; those jamming rounds lasted at least an hour.

He tied his thoughts back to the intelligence UTC received about Dallas obtaining anti-jamming devices from

China. He had just seen these new devices in operation. He had to pass this information back to the Operations Center.

Russ reached down into his cargo pocket and felt for his communicator. He must've left it behind when he ran from the missile. He tapped his sides for the reassurance of his pistol. That was gone too. He was incommunicado and defenseless.

As he reevaluated his tactical options, a SecureCon rose to its feet thirty yards in front of him. He froze. His confidence crumbled.

Russ clenched his hands. "Crap!"

The SecureCon raised its weapon arm and fired.

CHAPTER THIRTY-FIVE

Stephan observed the vast number of blinking icons on the screen in the operations center. He closed his irritated eyes to relieve them but opened them after a second—the display was too riveting to ignore for long. He heard footsteps behind him and turned to see an officer walk down the main row. Stephan snapped his fingers.

"Hey!"

The officer slightly raised his eyebrows. "Yes sir."

"Please grab me that chair."

Stephan pointed to the back of the room.

"Roger that."

The officer moved fast and grabbed a chair before he headed back and placed it behind Stephan, who stared back at the main screen. The officer tapped his back. Stephan jolted and spun around aggressively with a tight look on his face. The officer's facial expression didn't move a bit. He just stared at Stephan and smiled.

"You are doing a great job, Stephan."

The officer headed toward the room door.

Stephan was pent up with frustration but couldn't figure out why. This was the position and timing he'd focused on and worked toward for years to achieve. He knew all in the room well, and many of them stated he was the best man to take control now that Dusty was medically incapable. Stephan shook his head. He had to stay focused with hopes for winning this battle.

"Sir!" an operations officer yelled.

Stephan nodded to him. "Go ahead."

"The teams along the northern defensive line destroyed eight CSD UAVs. Many missiles were destroyed in flight due to what's got to be CSD advanced countermeasures. In addition, we're not communicating with Team Five and have no idea what their current status is."

"Team Five is protecting Highway 281. Right?"

"Yes sir."

Stephan pointed at the screen. "Well then, that explains why several of those red blips are now converging on that area."

"That is just happening now, sir."

"Go ahead and tell the reserve team to move into that area."

"Yes sir!" The operations officer sat back down, put his headphones on, and flicked a button. "Team Twelve. This is Operations Center. Over."

"Operations Center. This is Team Twelve. Over."

"Move immediately to highway 281 and 46 intersection. There are many SecureCons converging in that location. Do not pass 46 to the north due to jamming devices emitting. Over."

"Roger that. Why are SecureCons moving if that area is being jammed? Over."

"Just head there now. Over."

"Roger that. Out."

The officer stared at Stephan in confusion. Stephan looked back to the screen and saw the icons converge. He turned to the rear operation rows and pointed to them.

"Engage those UAVs!"

Operations officers in the last two rows grinned and shook their heads, getting back to their joysticks. On the main screen, the blue icons aligned themselves next to each other as they moved forward. The icons began to blink; that meant weapons engagement.

Stephan walked to the last row and stood behind a man who was controlling a UAV. His screen showed a visual perspective from the UAV. The sky looked clear but the smoke from the launched missile made the scene blurry.

An officer farther down the row grunted. Stephan walked down for a look at his screen. The image had rotated sideways, and the officer was bent to his side as a vivid red blip flashed. As the screen went back to level, the officer straightened in his chair, but another distant dot looped around in tight circles, heading directly at him. The officer bent to the other side as the screen tilted again. To the right of the screen, radar showed the missile blow past the UAV.

Stephan realized he was responding to the movements of the display the same way the officer was. As he straightened, he looked down the row and saw all the officers moving violently as they controlled their vehicles. He stood tall and looked forward as he walked down the row. Everyone watched the icons on the screens. He decided to return to his chair so he could observe the entire picture.

As he pulled back his perspective among the screens, Stephan gained a better view of the battlefield. The icons blinked, moved fast, and converged around each other. Stephan closed his eyes and cleared his thoughts. It allowed him to compile the current situation but with a different viewpoint. He knew he needed to counter the enemy tactics by adjusting his plan intermittently. He made sure to know his force's current strength and whereabouts.

Stephan wanted to make sure his battle staff was dutiful and coherent. He looked around the room and observed all their facial expressions and attitudes. Calmness flowed through Stephan as he reemphasized to himself that he was the right man for this situation, that no other person in the room could handle it as well as he could. Stephan leaned back in the chair and crossed his legs. His personal goal had been achieved.

CHAPTER THIRTY-SIX

Dirk watched through a one-way mirror as Dottie was brought into the brightly lit interrogation room. The tall and bulky Gary and the slim and fierce-looking Charlie escorted her in to the room. Gary pushed Dottie down onto a chair. Her mouth displayed a tight and pinched look Dirk had seen on many stubborn women before. Her eyes flicked from side to side.

Any time he'd seen her in the dining hall, she wore an unvarying look of cheer, but today her expression was one of pure guilt. Charlie dragged his chair back and sat down. Gary filled a glass of water and slammed it hard onto the table. Water splashed Dottie's arm. She didn't flinch.

Charlie stared down at his notes.

"Dorothy Marois, do you know why you are here?"

"I sure don't."

"Did you hear the latest on our coalition leader, Dusty Rhodes, and the fact that he was dreadfully poisoned?"

Dottie widened her eyes. "Oh my God. Is he OK?"

"Now do you wonder why you are here?" Charlie looked into her eyes. "Is it OK to call you Dottie?"

"I guess I do and yes, I prefer that name anyway."

"So you guess?"

Dottie pulled her eyebrows together. "Why are you asking me that?"

"For the past month you have been cooking and serving Mr. Rhodes?"

"The majority of the meals."

Charlie leaned back. "Why the majority and not all of them?"

"I sometimes get tasked to cook or clean for other people or projects."

"And who orders you to do that?"

Her forehead wrinkled. "Oh, come on. You know who heads the dining facility. I've seen you eating in there."

Charlie bulled forward and slammed his fist onto the table. "Who orders you to do that?"

Dottie raised her shoulders. "Daniel! Daniel Grincavitch is in charge of the dining facility!" She rubbed the back of her neck.

Charlie stopped for a few seconds and looked back down into his notebook. He raised his head and winked to Gary, who screeched his chair closer to Dottie. She kept her head still. Charlie stared back at Dottie and took a deep breath.

"Did Daniel order you to poison Mr. Rhodes?"

"No! And why would I poison Mr. Rhodes?"

"You tell me, Dottie."

"Why would I poison the leader, the person I was assigned to?"

Charlie looked back down into his notebook and printed many words with a black pen. A low screech filled the room as his elbow drifted back and forth against the steel table. He tapped the pen into the notebook, reached over, and opened a folder. He pulled out a sheet of paper and tossed it in front of Dottie.

"Those are your fingerprints?"

Dottie hesitated but then looked down. "I guess they are."

"You do remember signing it, right?"

Dirk squinted and bent forward behind the glass window. He couldn't see what was printed on the paper. Dottie raised the paper, and Dirk instantly recognized the in-processing report.

"That is my signature, but I really don't remember signing it."

Charlie's head tilted forward. "But this was only a month ago. Can you explain why you can't remember?"

"I guess I was overloaded with work that first day."

"So is that a denial?"

Dottie tilted up her chin. "Excuse me?"

"How can you forget signing something so important?"

"I don't know. I guess I was busy."

"Can you remember how you got this job?"

"Yes, I was asked—" she hesitated—"and agreed right away."

Dirk sprang backward and raised his eyes as he stared through the window. *Dottie just opened the interrogation success door.* He then noticed Charlie raise one eyebrow.

"Who asked you?"

"A childhood friend of mine."

"What's the name?"

Dottie's face turned pale. "Why are you asking me?"

Gary reached around and slapped his open hand into the back of Dottie's head. She bent forward and grunted loudly.

"Ouch!" Dottie turned her head. "What was that for?"

Gary flared his nostrils. "What's the name?"

"Why did you hit me?" Dottie's face turned red as sweat gleamed upon her forehead.

Gary jumped to his feet and pushed the metal chair back against the wall. He opened his hand and slapped her face. Dottie's head flung to the side. Charlie slammed his hands down on the table and jolted from his chair.

"Who is this person?"

"Stephan! Stephan Grabowski!" Tears flowed down her face.

Charlie sat back down with a smirk. "Very good, Dottie."

Dirk shook his head as he stood in the back room. He wondered how this woman could be guilty if Stephan hired her. *Stephan is the most professional and devoted member of the coalition.* Meghan *had* mentioned Stephan getting close with Dottie. *He could be knocking those boots.* Dirk smirked.

But then, frustration or anger colored Stephan's every mention of Dusty. "This can't be," Dirk whispered. His thoughts spun around as he placed his arm on the table and slowly sat down. Just the fact that Stephan knew this woman didn't mean he was connected with this tragedy. Or did it?

Dirk remembered training with Stephan on a pistol range a year ago. All the team members sat on bleachers, after shooting all day, and listened to Stephan telling jokes. He kept picking on this one member who was a virgin. During that conversation, Stephan mentioned his girlfriend, who was the daughter of his father's best friend, and his face turned hard as stone when he told them about his father's death and how he was left behind to die by the team's leader. *Dusty was his father's team leader.*

Dirk raised his head and closed his eyes as he attempted to put all this together. The thought of Stephan bottling up his anger for so many years didn't make sense. Stephan was always professional and calm, especially during the worst firefights and missions Team Eight experienced.

Other team members had mentioned Stephan taking care of his best friend after her mother died. *Could that be Dottie?* Stephan taking care of Dottie was one thing. Dottie's being the daughter of the man Stephan's father died with was another.

Dirk stood up and paced across the little room. He spun around and walked back and forth, not wanting to believe the picture that was forming in his head. But any other conclusion was impossible. He grunted and reached down for his communicator. He tapped a few buttons and put it to his ear.

"Hey, Dirk." Meghan sounded dreary. "Where are you?"

"Hi, Meghan. I wanted to..." Dirk closed his eyes and clenched his teeth. Why had he called Meghan? Her father was the victim!

"What? What is it?" Her voice sounded anxious.

"Nothing, Meghan. I just wanted to ask how you're doing."

"I'm fine…" She hesitated. "Where are you?"

"Nowhere special." Dirk needed to divert this issue. "You with Ihan?"

"He's here. You need him for something? Hell. You need me?"

"Just checking on both of you. I will be up there shortly."

"OK, but…"

Dirk clicked the button—double-checked the screen to make sure he turned it off—and shook the communicator as he walked in circles. *What in the hell was I thinking?* This information would push her off the sane path.

Dirk clenched his fists. "I knew better than that!"

His flustered feelings shifted gears and focused in on Meghan. He loved to see her smile and hear her laugh. His feelings for her were getting stronger by the day, and it made him feel strange. He'd never allowed himself to have these feelings of desire before and didn't know how to express them to Meghan. There was definitely something about Meghan that attracted him. He couldn't figure what it was. It wasn't as simple as her being good-looking. He'd met plenty of pretty women throughout the years. He just never had a desire for any of them. Megan was different. Her intelligence, openness, and humor guided him closer to her.

Dirk just wondered if his attraction should be expressed to Meghan. She was under tremendous stress; impending CSD attack, a mission to utilize Mona though Ihan, and her father's poisoning. Dirk took a deep breath and headed out the door. His needs would have to wait. Meghan could use his support.

CHAPTER THIRTY-SEVEN

In the Operations Center, two operators Stephan had respected—until now—yelled at each other. They pointed their fingers at each other, screaming about the undetected mortar strike that moments ago hit the ground above their facility. Morons. He needed to take charge and voice himself to clear things up. He stood out of his chair and headed over to their row.

"That's enough, you idiots! Back to work."

The officer sitting closer to Stephan rolled his eyes to the other officer. He reached over and lightly punched the other's arm before swinging toward Stephan.

"Sir. Both of us detected an evacuating helicopter leaving our area just minutes before that mortar strike. That obviously was the chopper that dropped off those SecureCons."

"No shit!" Stephan jammed his hands on his hips. "Why didn't you detect that helicopter infiltrating our area?"

"It had to be below our radar detection level."

"That's not what I asked, knucklehead!" Stephan shook his head. "Why didn't our surrogate forces within

San Antonio, our patriots, verbally inform us of that helicopter?"

"We already thought of that, sir, and as you can tell on the map screen"—the officer pointed to the display—"that helicopter took the river route in and followed it out."

Stephan squinted. "Where are you going from here?"

"Sir. Plan B is now in effect, and I just told Team Eight's Leader—I mean sub leader, Dirk Young—to set that plan in motion."

"Good timing because our deployed teams are all busy fighting the other SecureCons to our north and east. I do know those Dallas imbeciles are not aware of how tied together this coalition is with the rest of the Texas citizens—ones who learned how evil Dallas has become."

The officer smiled. "Yes sir."

"Where is Dirk located now?"

"He is on level six and heading up to the surface."

Stephan sneered. "Level six! Where the hell was he when you last talked with him, taking a nap?"

"Level two, sir."

Stephan lowered his head. Why had Dirk been on level two? Dirk was always the hard charger and one who never left his post. He was ordered to protect the defensive perimeter. *Why is he inside the facility?*

Stephan spun around, charged up the middle aisle and into the commander's office, and slammed the door. He sat on Dusty's desk and touched his computer screen, pressing buttons and pulling up the current status report for action on level two—the Interrogation Center. The display screen showed current staff biographies and picture listings. Stephan pointed down to the bottom of the screen and pulled the "current reports" icon to the top. He clicked the Interrogation tab. Dottie's picture blinked on the screen, and a sudden surge of blood flowed through his veins.

"Why the hell is she in there?" And why hadn't he been informed about it?

He pressed her picture on the screen:

Security Investigation Incident #105: As of 0535 hours, Dottie Marois chosen for security-related questions due to Dusty Rhodes's poison being medically assessed as stomach ingested. Interview is ongoing...

Stephan's frustration grew by the second. He understood why Dottie was being interrogated, but he had to do something quickly before the questioning got out of hand. The fact that he was now in charge of the coalition, albeit temporarily, was now simply a goal he'd achieved. He couldn't let Dottie suffer for this. He couldn't live with himself if something happened to her. She was his best friend, the only person he respected. She'd been there with him his whole life.

A much larger and more important goal loomed in his mind. More important than his leading the coalition, a goal that had created the coalition, was to take down the City-State of Dallas so Texas could get back to normal. But was that nationalistic perspective more important than his personal feelings? Stephan gripped his head with both hands as he continued to dissect his situation.

His goal was falling apart. It either wasn't meant to happen or he hadn't planned it well enough. All that really didn't matter anymore, because Dottie was suffering for this. Stephan closed his eyes for a second and shook his head.

He had to fix this. He stood up and looked around the room. Dusty's glass gun case stood against the wall. Stephan picked up a colored brick from the side table and took aim, then hurled the brick. The glass shattered. He reached into the case and grabbed the old Uzi submachine gun. It was small enough to hide and could spray plenty of bullets in a small area.

Stephan searched through the drawers and found a box of 9x19mm rounds. He loaded two clips fast and inserted one into the Uzi. The other clip he tossed into his cargo pocket. He reached down and attached the thin straps over his shoulders before he attached the Uzi to the end point. His vest was thin and worn, but he flung the Uzi behind his back and placed the vest over it to hide the weapon.

As soon as he walked out of the room, Stephan stopped and looked up at the display screens. All the icons blinked. The officers were busy either communicating or working actions through their joysticks. Stephan took a deep breath as he sucked all this action and situation in. He would greatly miss this office, but Dottie was now his focus.

Dusty once told him, "Our future is bound to appear as a video-game battle since both sides are fighting from their terminals. However, Dallas has much greater technology than we do, so this unfortunately won't last long unless we become Roger's Rangers and fight unconventional." Stephan's distrust and hatred toward Dusty boiled inside him. What he'd done to Dusty ensured the coalition's success. Dusty was nothing more than a theoretical leader, albeit the one who'd brought the coalition into existence. He just didn't have the tactical whereabouts and timing needed to bring the state of Texas back. And Stephan did.

Stephan strode toward the back door, the weight of the Uzi between his shoulder blades coldly comforting. There was an additional elevator that he had the entrance code for.

Chapter Thirty-Eight

Several minutes dragged by before Meghan found Dirk in the hallway leading to the Operations Center. Minutes of searching, wondering, of allowing herself to fear the worst about him even though that was absolutely the wrong thing to be doing. Dirk had always been an ideal soldier, and she had no reason to believe he was in trouble. He looked startled when he noticed her.

"Hey, Meghan! What are you doing here?"

"Looking for you."

He rubbed the side of his neck. "*Why* are you looking for me?"

"To be honest Dirk, you sounded strange on that last call. I wondered if you got yourself into a bind. I knew you were on the beat level."

Dirk grinned. "Beat level? That about sums up level two." He hesitated. "By the way, did you feel that blast a few minutes ago?"

Blast? "I felt something in the elevator, but I didn't think much about it."

"I just talked to the Operations Center and they calculated a mortar strike from the west. Guess that means we have SecureCons to deal with aboveground."

"Yeah, a mortar strike does mean they're close. Hey, that doesn't answer my question, Dirk. Why were you down on the beat level?"

Dirk rapidly blinked. "I'll tell you later."

They both walked through the main corridor and came close to the Operations Center door. Dirk maintained his pace, passing the door, and Meghan grabbed his arm.

"Aren't you going in there?"

He stopped. "No. I'm heading to the motor pool and taking a vehicle up to the surface."

Meghan stood still for a few seconds and wondered if she would ever see Dirk again—an uncomfortable feeling of clairvoyance made her sense the worst. She reached her arms around Dirk and pulled him in tight against her. She felt him tighten up, but knew he wasn't used to her acting like a girl.

"Please take care of yourself," she whispered in his ear.

He gave her a brief, awkward squeeze. "I promise."

Then he let her go, and he jogged away in the direction of the motor pool.

In the Operations Center, Meghan heard the chatter and saw that everyone was behind his terminal and concentrating on his mission. It should make her feel confident, but instead she couldn't shake the feeling that things were about to go badly wrong. She hurried to the center of the room, looking for Stephan.

She didn't see him anywhere, but over to her left, sitting at the table, was Craig. Meghan flinched. He always asked her out, but he always knew personnel status. She got closer to the table and put her hand on his shoulder.

He whipped his head around. "Damn! You scared the shit out of me."

"Where's Stephan?"

"He was in here a few minutes ago." Craig squinted and looked around the room. He then turned and looked through the window into Dusty's office. He pointed forward. "He was in there."

"Thanks." Meghan looked over Craig's shoulder and saw the base plan schematic laid out with yellow highlighted lines drawn all over it. "What are you doing?"

"That last mortar attack was either lucky or planned by Dallas, because it hit our covered primary radar device dead-on. That radar is currently down and we're utilizing the weaker secondary radar device. I know there's another power line but I can't find it."

"Well—" Meghan blinked. "Good luck with that, Craig."

She patted his shoulder and looked into her father's office. The computer screen was lighted. *Stephan was in there a few minutes ago.* She wondered if he was just hitting the bathroom or getting something to eat. Intrigued by what he was doing on Dusty's computer, Meghan moved closer to the office. Stepping through the door, she heard crackling and felt lumps under her feet. She looked down and saw glass particles strewn across the floor. She looked up. Her father's treasured gun rack, one that had been in their family for many generations, was smashed, and the bottom drawer was open.

Meghan moved closer and looked in the drawer. Her

father's Uzi and ammunition rounds—his most precious possessions, the ones he showed to visiting dignitaries who supported their cause—were missing. "What the hell!"

Meghan curtly shook her head and crossed her arms. She'd always wondered why her father loved antique weapons. Some form of manhood validation she just couldn't understand.

She headed over to the computer terminal and sat down at Dusty's desk. Her heart instantly became bitter when she saw Dottie's picture and biographical report flashing on the screen. To the left of that picture was a tab for the Interrogation Center—the tab Dottie's file was under. Meghan clicked the file and read the Security Investigation Incident # 105 Report. Comprehending the information, she became utterly sick to her stomach. "Dottie, you bitch."

Part of her enjoyed knowing that the sinful woman would bear the consequences if she'd really poisoned Dusty. But then, a bunch of recent memories flashed in her head. Conversations that Stephan shared with her in reference to Dottie. Times when she'd seen Stephan talking with Dottie and touching her.

It then dawned on Meghan. The man who was talking with Dottie in the supply closet was Stephan! A violent red flush heated Meghan's cheeks. Her pulse thumped in her neck.

As Meghan sat stiff in her father's chair, she clenched her teeth Just the fact that Stephan would be involved in such a thing was unthinkable, but everything pointed not just to his taking part in it, but to his actually planning it.

He was greatly respected by her father. Hell, he was the team leader she'd highly admired until a minute ago.

Meghan slammed her fist down on the desk. Papers flew off the desk and floated to the floor. "I am going to kill him!" Meghan stood upright and paced around the room in circles. Her fists clenched by her sides, and she shook uncontrollably.

"Craig!"

Seconds after she called him, he ran into the office. Once through the door, his feet sounded off some crackling glass. He looked confused but didn't speak.

Meghan headed toward the broken gun rack and pulled out a Colt .45 automatic pistol, model 1911. She opened the top drawer and loaded the rounds into the clip.

"What are you doing, Meghan?" Craig said loudly.

Meghan reached into the gun rack and tossed a pistol to Craig. "Take this." She then threw him a box of ammunition.

Craig gawked at his pistol. "Can you please tell me why I have this pistol?"

"We are going to get Stephan."

Worry creased his face. "Is something wrong with him? Has he been taken?"

Meghan jutted her chin. "There is definitely something wrong with him."

After she finished loading the second clip, Meghan grabbed Craig's shoulder and lugged him out of the office. As she hauled him through the corridor, Meghan looked back at Craig fumbling with his clip and stumbling over his feet. When they reached the elevator, Meghan walked in and punched the button for level two. Craig walked in, still loading his clip, and the door closed, hit his hip, and reopened. Meghan rolled her eyes, grabbed his shirt, and pulled him in before the door closed on him again.

Once the elevator door opened, Meghan pulled the pistol's slide back and flicked the safety off before heading out in a combat stance. She looked up to the ceiling several times due to the red lights flashing and the low beeping from the speakers.

As she opened Interrogation Center's door, Meghan strode in crouched low, with her pistol held straight out and steady. The guard desk was empty. She looked ahead but saw something out of the corner of her eye. She stopped and looked over while keeping her pistol straight. On the floor was the guard she knew; he lay motionless with multiple bloody gunshot wounds upon his chest. Meghan blinked and continued forward. Craig's heavy footsteps sounded behind her.

"Holy shit."

When she reached the doorway, Meghan saw the lock had been shot out. Whoever had done it must've really wanted in there—there was nothing left but a hole where the lock had been. She kicked the door. It slammed open and banged into the wall.

With her shoulder down and pistol raised to her side, Meghan lunged forward and opened the inner door. The metal table and chair were overturned. Half underneath the table a man lay in a pool of blood. Craig lurched around Meghan and pulled the table to the side. He crouched and stuck his fingers on the man's neck. Meghan recognized the guy. Charlie. Craig looked up to Meghan and shook his head.

Across the room, a large man slumped against the wall. Blood spots spread over his chest. His eyes slowly opened.

"You're not going to hit me again, are you?" Gary said. His face remained expressionless.

Meghan smiled lightly as she walked toward Gary. She maintained an eye lock with him. As she lowered to her knees, she put her hand on his shoulder. Guilt trickled through her, though she didn't know why.

"No. No more hits from me." Meghan gave the dying man a wider smile.

Craig walked over and took his communicator out of his pocket. He dialed in a number.

"We have an emergency in room 211 and need immediate medical recovery."

An affirmative response came fast.

"Who did this?" Meghan asked Gary.

"Your team leader. Stephan. Busted in here and spoke with bullets. Guess he's a true warrior." Gary winked. Then he coughed.

"He took Dottie out of here?"

"Yes. Can't blame him for taking . . . that easy woman." Gary coughed again. "She talked fast when we got her in here."

"Do you know where he went?"

Gary pointed a red security light that was blinking. "Back door."

Meghan pulled his arm back down and placed it gently on his leg.

"Stay with it and please don't move. The medics are on their way."

Meghan stood tall and headed for the door.

"Where are you going now, Meghan?" Craig looked confused again.

"Stay with this man until the medics arrive." Having an order to follow would make the poor klutz feel useful, and staying put would keep him from hurting himself. Meghan walked out the door.

Down at the end of the hallway, the back door was open. She stepped closer with her pistol held straight out. She carefully opened the door and looked into the dark hallway. It smelled cruddy and stale. The elevator door's illuminated digital sign blinked. Meghan stepped closer. She pressed the screen and saw its last movement was to the surface and not level six—where the motor pool was located.

She wondered why Stephan would take Dottie to the surface without a vehicle to head out quickly in. Who was he trying to mislead, and why? She thought he might still be in the complex and that definitely sounded like a Stephan tactic.

Chapter Thirty-Nine

Ihan awoke in the team room. He was alone. He softly whistled as he gazed around the empty room and wondered where Meghan was. He whistled louder. Got no reaction. This felt strange.

A feeling of having been annulled grew within him. The absolute solitude made him smirk, then frown. Mona had been continuously there for him his entire life. This constant interaction ignited a dichotomy of emotion for him. He felt cared for by Mona but also annoyed. He had no privacy knowing he was constantly observed. However, being held in this room alone felt strange as well. That strange feeling was one he never felt before, but he thought he could name it: loneliness.

Where is Meghan? Ihan grew worried as he speculated why he hadn't heard from her in quiet some time. Sure, the coalition members didn't know him well, but they also mistrusted him. *So why am I alone?*

Ihan's thoughts spun in circles. He'd been physically introduced to humans, albeit with violence surrounding them, and it made him wonder why he was now left alone. *Is this their idea of turning me back to who I was? Are they sending me back to Dallas?* He stared at the ceiling. After

318

being physically near Meghan and the team members, he wasn't sure he would cope too well with isolation again.

As the door beeped, Ihan was startled, but felt relieved once Meghan walked into the room. She looked straight ahead and nowhere else but the lockers. She stopped in front of Stephan's locker and tugged the door. She then ran her hands up, down, and around the locker. She looked for ways to get in, but that locker was secure.

"Good to see you, Meghan." Ihan said as he wondered why she seemed so focused on that locker.

Meghan kept her eyes forward. "Hey, Ihan."

"Is everything OK?"

"Not now, Ihan. Please cover your ears."

He obeyed.

Meghan took a few steps back from the locker and pulled out her pistol. She cocked it and held it out straight. After she squinted her eye and squared the digital lock into the aiming piece, Meghan pulled the trigger twice. The lock exploded. She stepped forward and pulled the door open.

She pulled a small stack of papers out and carried it over to the table.

A somber look upon Meghan's face scared Ihan. He sat up in the bed and stridently cleared his throat. Meghan kept her head straight but poked her eyes over at him.

"Just please sit there quietly for a few minutes."

Meghan thumped down onto a chair at the table and reflected upon all the times she remembered Stephan walking into the team room, opening his locker, and placing some paper in before he slammed it shut and headed out without saying a word. This annoyed Meghan all the time and piqued her curiosity. Now that she had the stack of papers, she immediately started going through them.

The first couple of sheets were standard critiques and professional development reports. The next few were team member evaluation reports that Stephan had to write and submit to the Human Resources Section.

One report had her name on top. She grunted, rolled it up quickly, and threw it down to the floor. She then kept sorting papers, tossing some to the side. A few smaller pieces of paper were handwritten notes. She stopped rummaging and read a couple.

After a couple of notes, she recognized Dottie's handwriting. She remembered seeing the same feminine script on the dining facility signs, and Dottie was the only female who worked in there.

The wording content was illusory, but Meghan could see through the double meanings and discerned a pattern, one that led to the poisoning. An emotional pattern emerged, too. The older notes, especially the first couple, revealed that Dottie was nervous and really didn't feel what they were doing was right. A few notes later, Dottie mentioned her understanding that their undertaking was for their fathers. Meghan bared her teeth and snarled.

The last couple of notes didn't make sense. Dottie kept mentioning her sister and how she wasn't doing well at their hometown. Would a hometown problem have sped up their malicious task? *Why else would Stephan rush an action? This is not who he is. Nothing ever sidetracked him.*

Meghan pieced together Stephan's latest actions and

comments, ones that had made her think twice and wonder what his problems were. She just hadn't put it together, until now.

"Damn!"

Meghan crumpled the notes together and threw them across the room. She started to shake. Her emotions were beyond composure as she stood up and staggered in circles. Numb, she realized the Stephan she knew was bogus. He'd lied to her the whole time she knew him.

Ihan watched as Meghan steamed around in circles. She was angrier than anyone he'd ever seen. He couldn't help but remember back to when he had the same type of stressful moments, but it was only when he couldn't handle the CSD agricultural department's constant pressure for harvesting his crops while they conducted inspections.

He knew Meghan was going through a more severe problem—greater than any he had ever experienced. Her emotional body language left no doubt. He wasn't certain, but felt it best to show her someone cared for her even though it may not solve anything.

Ihan jumped out of the bed, with a congenial face, and hopped in front of Meghan. He wrapped his arms around her as her tight body shook and her breath rushed out of her nose and mouth. Startled by his boldness, he held her tighter. Meghan sniffled, and her body softened as she raised her arms around his ribs and squeezed. The loud weeping and sniffles made Ihan's ears ring, and his battered ribs ached, but he kept his stance and held her tightly.

After a few seconds, Ihan felt Meghan become more serene, and her crying tapered down to a few tears. He tapped her back and let go of her gently. Ihan grabbed her hand and guided her over to the bed, where both of them sat down and looked at each other. Meghan wiped her nose on her sleeve.

"Thanks, Ihan. That was very brave of you."

"You can say that again." Ihan grinned. "I was terrified about how you were going to react to me."

They both chuckled. Ihan knew it wasn't the right time to ask her what her problem was. He felt she was exhausted and didn't need to waste any more energy discussing it.

A few minutes went by in silence as both stared at the floor. Meghan then tapped Ihan's knee as she stood up and took a few steps forward. She turned around and looked right into his eyes.

"I am going to see my father, and I want you to go with me."

Ihan stood to his feet. "Lead the way, Meghan."

Chapter Forty

Several hours after the escape, Stephan viewed the Texas hill country as he drove Dottie closer to their home in Odessa. The landscape along the roadway subdued to a scant agricultural environment, still a vast frontier area. The horizon was nearly flat, with a few distant mountain ranges that made Stephan and Dottie feel safer knowing they were closer to home.

After Stephan had forcefully freed Dottie, and they escaped the underground facility north of San Antonio, they ran through the open fields into the city. Exhaustion quickly slowed them down to a stagger. Stephan knew the City-State of Dallas's threat overwhelmed the coalition, that meant temporary safety, but they'd pressed on until they reached the vehicle Stephan had hidden. He knew they would be hunted soon.

However, none of that mattered to Stephan. His focus was now Dottie; his best friend and the woman he had always loved.

As they drove a little further, Stephan noticed the fuel gauge was on empty. Dottie continued to stare out the window as the vehicle sputtered then slowed down, and he pulled it to the side of the road. When the car stopped and the dust had swept forward along the sides of the vehicle, Stephan turned his head and smirked over to Dottie. She looked over and winked. Not many words had been exchanged since they left the coalition, but Stephan knew they were on the right path.

He opened his door and walked to the rear of the vehicle, where he opened the trunk, pulled out two gas containers, and dragged them to the side of the vehicle. He filled the gas tank and saw Dottie reach into the backseat and rummage through the heavy bag he'd brought with them. A surprised look came over her face as she pulled a bottle of water into the front seat. Stephan smirked and knew he needed to answer.

As Stephan sat back in the car, turned the key, and fired up the engine again, Dottie took a few sips out of the bottle but held her closed hand tight.

"What do you have in your hand?"

Dottie placed the bottle along her leg. She looked over and raised her eyebrows slightly as she opened her hand, revealing a gold coin. Stephan kept his face composed, but stared down with a grin.

Dottie tilted her head. "Can you please tell me why you have these gold coins? I by no means want to know how you got them, just what they're for," she said. He heard a subtle longing in her voice.

"Your sister is all that matters right now, and we need to make sure we get her cared for by the doctor."

Dottie looked back down at the coin, and Stephan could tell from the bowing of her shoulders that she was burdened by her sister's pain. Taking her to the doctor in Odessa—the only one in town—never went well because he cared only for residents with money.

Dottie looked down at the coin. "What about you, Stephan, what is your goal?"

"That's not important right now."

Dottie glanced back to Stephan. "Sure it is."

Stephan leaned over and kissed her lightly on the cheek. "Like I said, your sister takes priority."

"I really do appreciate that. But we both know my sister isn't going to—" Her voice broke, and she looked out the window again. "I just want her to be comfortable . . . until it's time."

What she said wakened Stephan. He'd never known she thought that way, seeing how all he heard her talk about was her sister. It didn't matter though, Dottie was right, her sister needed pain medicine to make her peaceful as she passed.

"We'll make sure she gets everything she needs." He rubbed her shoulder until he felt her relax. "And then I plan on meeting with that posse in West Texas. They're doing wonderful things, bringing west Texas back to a society. And they're affiliated with Mexico. They're both against this foreign power presence within Texas."

Dottie looked back into Stephan's eyes. "So what do you have in mind? What is your focus?"

"After your sister, our focus is to bring back freedom to Texas. Our government must return. We'll work with the posse and form a territorial army in west Texas. The coalition can work with us or oppose us, but I won't let it get in my way again." Stephan gently placed his hand on Dottie's leg. "I promise to not go beyond focus this time. Texas is that focus."

Chapter Forty-One

Dirk drove at a measured speed along a winding road outside the facility. He glanced down often at the ground motion sensors that surrounded the complex's perimeter. The setting sun painted a line of red and gold along the horizon, and he slowed the vehicle to a stop along the road. He stared through the window, soaking in the beauty of Texas that never failed to empower his internal motivation.

As he rolled down the passenger-side window, Dirk closed his eyes and gasped the chill breeze. It made him smile. He captured those fresh smells every chance he had; they made him feel alive.

The control panel beeped. He opened his eyes and checked the status of the exterior systems. One of the Vulcan guns emanated a minor maintenance alert. Dirk pushed the display screen and saw the M61 location was only a mile south of his current location. He slammed down on the pedal, spun the tires, and got the vehicle moving out at high speed. The threat was current and present, and Dirk needed to ensure all the defensive measures were working.

Nearing a camouflaged rock, Dirk slowed the vehicle

down and did a visual search around the area. He didn't notice any unusual movements or objects. He parked and stepped out of the vehicle. As he walked around the large fake rock, Dirk looked up and down to see if there were any leaks. Nothing out of the ordinary. He heard a strange, muffled yap, and he stopped and cocked his head, listening. It sounded like it came from inside the rock.

Dirk took a few steps back and heard the sound again. He crouched to look lower. There was a small, rough opening along the bottom of the rock. That confused him; an alert notification should have sounded if the rock device had been violated.

He heard the muffled yap again. Dirk stuck his ear closer to the opening and listened, then he smiled. An animal had burrowed under the Vulcan, but unfortunately it needed to vacate its new home. He stood back up and walked around the rock to the control panel. He pushed the button and the outer camouflaged screen parted and shuffled back to the rear. The Vulcan rose and locked into position.

Dirk cautiously climbed to the top of the rock. He took his mini flashlight out of his pocket and pointed it into the opening. Nestled between the lubrication lines, a nest of cradled three tiny squirrels—so young—were nearly bald and kept their eyes closed. He noticed a puddle below the nest and could smell lubricant. He directed the flashlight along the lines and detected a tear, one that looked like a bite.

"Those damned squirrels."

The parents were around somewhere, probably gathering chow. Another beep emitted. Dirk reached into his cargo pocket, pulled his communicator out, and pressed the button.

"Go ahead, Ops Center."

"We are receiving a distant motion detection about a mile to your west."

Dirk raised his head and squinted into the distance. He panned the horizon but couldn't notice any movement. All of a sudden, two thumps sounded, then their echoes rolled across the field. Two smoke patterns close together, quite a ways in the distance. He then heard two incoming rounds moving at a rapid rate.

"Ah, shit!"

Dirk rolled off the rock and hit the ground hard. He rolled a few times and crawled in front of the rock, tucking into a tight ball. The whistling got louder and slammed the hillside across the road, dislodging tons of rock debris. Dust billowed from the impact site, obscuring everything around him. Dirk stayed in his fetal position until the explosion fragments settled. He then leaped to his feet and ran over to the vehicle. As he jumped in, the motion detector blinked. He pressed the button and saw numerous displayed icons moving at a fast pace—right in front of him.

Dirk cringed. *This is a crappy location*. He pressed the activation button for the weapons. The Vulcans to the north and south rose from their camouflaged rocks and moved back and forth, seeking their targets.

As he looked down to his control panel, the gun icons turned green and began flashing. He covered his ears. The loud pattering from the Vulcan cannons made Dirk grin. Even the encroaching darkness, he could see the tree line get torn to pieces. Plenty of sparks flew off the tree trunks and rocks.

Once one Vulcan stopped firing, another started flinging numerous rounds down range. The deluge of action and sound engrossed Dirk as he continued to look into the tree line.

As both guns halted fire, Dirk could hear the spinning barrels slow and stop as he surveyed the shattered tree line. The falling limbs and dust began to settle. Silence fell, and this made Dirk nervous. Stillness usually meant trouble was abounding.

A sudden flash and loud shriek came from the tree line and slammed into the southern gun. The explosion was blinding and debris flew all over. Another loud shriek zoomed in, and Dirk turned around and saw the northern gun explode.

He jammed his foot down on the pedal and spun the tires, knowing the gun he was near would be next. Out of his peripheral vision, Dirk saw a missile heading directly at him. He slammed on the brakes, and the missile passed right in front of him. It hit the hillside hard and the explosion rocked the ground. Dirk slammed the pedal down again as another missile slammed into the back of his vehicle. The vehicle was thrown into the air and spun sideways as Dirk grunted and flung down onto the seat. The side of the vehicle smashed into the dirt road.

Dirk moaned and sank into blackness.

The Vulcan cannon opened fire as another two missiles headed its way. One missile was hit and exploded in midair, but the other slammed into the gun as it exploded and toppled over.

Five SecureCons advanced out of the tree line and headed through the grass opening toward the road. All had their arms raised and were searching for targets back and forth. Once they reached the road, the smoke and dust settled as they stopped in a line and looked north and south.

One of the SecureCons quickly twisted and zoomed in to the ground, homing in on a squirrel hastily digging a hole near a tree stump. The SecureCon paused, then it twisted back.

All of a sudden, three tiny metal balls rolled down the hillside and halted underneath the SecureCons. Simultaneously, the three balls exploded, tearing three of the SecureCons to pieces and sending the other two into the air and pounding hard to the ground.

With their guns pointed forward as they rappelled forward down the hillside, four team members opened fire and tore the two SecureCons to bits and pieces. Once they reached the road, all four stood alert, with their weapons raised. "Clear!" They removed their rappel cords and ran to Dirk's vehicle that still had flames flashing in the rear. Two of the team members went to the front of the vehicle and positioned their guns forward while the other two jumped on top of the vehicle and wrenched open the side door.

As the two members reached down into the vehicle, they grabbed Dirk carefully and pulled him out. He was unconscious and covered with dirt. Both of the team members then jumped on to the ground, grabbed Dirk gently, and carried him to the side of the road, where they lowered him to the ground.

"Dirk!" A team member lightly tapped his face. "Dirk!"

"Please don't hit me again." Dirk said before he opened his eyes and coughed.

"How are you, buddy?"

"A little jingled but can feel all the stumps."

The team member chuckled as he stood to his feet and extended his arm down to Dirk. Dirk raised his hand and accepted the pull. He stomped his feet and shook a dust cloud off his head. He then looked around and observed all the damage surrounding him. The sudden feeling of gratefulness engulfed his thoughts as it sank in that he'd made it through another unfriendly encounter.

A few explosions and gunfire thudded in the distance. Dirk listened closely and presumed it was coming from the south.

"You guys hear that?"

A team member nodded. "Yes. That started a few minutes ago."

"That's sounds like downtown San Antonio." Dirk rapidly blinked.

"It sure does. Those Dallas idiots don't know about downtown."

Dirk smirked. "You got that right."

"I'm assuming you alerted those surrogates, Dirk?"

"They were informed of this potential attack yesterday and obviously have their ducks in a row."

"Where do we head next?"

"Wait one!"

Dirk grabbed his communicator, tapped it a few times, and blew the dust off the screen. It was intact. He smiled when he realized this device could survive what he went through, especially considering the pain in his leg where the device was held. Dirk rubbed his leg with his free hand.

"Ops Center. This is Team Eight. Over."

"Go ahead, Team Eight. Over."

"What's the current status of the enemy? Over."

"We're still analyzing and corroborating the status but want to let you know that their main attack force has been destroyed. There are minor attack locations still active, but we are noticing many retreating and no incoming movements. Over."

"Good news. We are going to stay active and explore the surroundings. Over."

"Roger that and good luck. Out."

Dirk put his communicator back in his pocket and continued to slap the dust off his pants. He then walked back to his burnt vehicle and jumped on top of the dented side. He looked inside, reached down, and grabbed his weapon. As he brushed the dust off his gun, the team members stared at him with incredulity.

"All right, gents. It's time for us to patrol the perimeter and make sure all is clear."

CHAPTER FORTY-TWO

Meghan sat by her father's bedside in the infirmary and stared at his motionless face. He was pale, but with a tinge of vigor and hopefulness. She knew her father well and wondered how long he would let this sickness hold before he got bored and started fighting to recover.

The nurse walked through the door and wrapped the black Velcro of a sphygmomanometer around his arm. She pumped up the device and let it exhale. She then stuck the needle into his arm and drew some blood. After she put the vial into her breast pocket, she tapped the IV pump to make sure it was still dripping the way it should. She glanced at Meghan with a sorrowful expression.

"Your father is getting better. I'll let you know his blood results when I get them."

"Thanks."

The nurse then stared behind Meghan. "Who is that man sitting behind you?"

"That's Ihan." Meghan turned around and blinked at Ihan. "Please say hello to this nurse, Ihan."

Ihan smiled and waved. "Hello and nice to meet you."

"Nice to meet you as well, Ihan." The nurse smiled,

and her cheeks colored a rose red before she walked into the other room. Meghan contemplated that compassionate tone and appearance the nurse had directed toward Ihan. *Ihan sure hooked a visual crush.*

Meghan rubbed her forehead, realizing with despair that this woman's finding Ihan attractive, something she would normally find fascinating, didn't excite her at all. She swallowed as she realized she was crying. She couldn't count the number of events that had been happening recently, ones that depressed her greatly. Deep in her heart, Meghan knew that her father had a special power to lift her spirits in her worst times.

As she lowered her head down and prayed for her father, Meghan felt his arm quiver. She laid her hand on it; his skin felt warmer. She stared into his face, and his head moved slightly while his cheeks gradually rose up and down.

"Dad!" Meghan sat tall and caressed his arm. "Dad, it's your flower."

Dusty's eyes opened and got wider as he turned his head toward Meghan. His eyes were bloodshot, but a smile emerged.

"Hey there, flower." He coughed.

Meghan leaned forward. "Just be still and don't say a word."

"Where are we?" Dusty moved his eyes around the room.

"You're in the infirmary, Dad."

"Why are we in here and why do I feel like shit?"

Dusty raised his arm, and Meghan gently pushed it down.

334

"Stay still, you grouchy old fart. You were poisoned recently. Lucky for you, we got you treated in time."

"Poisoned? Who would do that to me?"

Resentment turned to fire in her stomach. "It was Stephan. And your cook, Dottie."

Dusty stared up at the ceiling, blinking his eyes. His expression turned to one of uncertainty.

"I don't believe it. Why would those two do such a thing?"

"Who knows, Daddy? Maybe Stephan just wanted power."

"Power!" Dusty chuckled, but then halted, grunting. He rubbed his stomach. "There is no such thing as power here. If there was, we would all be in a pile of shit."

"Just rest, Dad."

"Where is Stephan?"

"I don't know. He grabbed Dottie and left the facility."

"Nobody chased him, right?"

She shook her head. "We're under attack. We don't have enough personnel to send anyone after him."

"Who's in charge right now?"

"That's a good question." Meghan felt her eyes soften, and she worked to guard her expression. "You can feel safe knowing Dirk Young is out there defending this facility."

"Dirk sure is a respected soldier. Who is that behind you?"

"That's Ihan." Meghan kept her head straight.

"Why is he in here with you?"

"You know my job is to watch out for him."

"Then why are both of you in here and not down with that processor?" Dusty lifted his eyebrow. "You're obviously beyond focus."

Meghan felt numb. She leaned back against the chair. Just the thought that her dad was right and her focus was tainted made her cringe. Especially since kudos was to him and not her.

This chaotic internal state battle against the City-State of Dallas meant her focus should be for the coalition and not specifically her father. She then considered why she was in here and why she mistimed her location. Her feelings for her father were powerful and had guided her to where she currently was. She also knew her father's point, and perspective, trumped those feelings; her personal needs had gotten in the way of the greater goal.

Meghan looked down at her father and saw him smile. That instantly fueled her focus. She needed to finish her mission with Ihan. Meghan grinned. She knew where she was headed was also right for her father.

"I hate to admit it, Dad, but you're right. I promise to get back down there shortly. Do me favor—your nurse said she would get me your blood results. Please remind her for me."

"I sure will, flower."

Meghan bent down and kissed his cheek. Dusty winked and nodded his head. She tapped his arm and stood tall before she walked toward the door.

"Follow me, Ihan, we have some work to do." Meghan said with an imperative tone while waving him to get up and come with her.

"It was great to see you, Mr. Rhodes, and I hope you get better." Ihan waved as he followed Meghan.

As the door closed, Ihan stopped and just stood in the hallway staring at the wall. She turned around and moved closer to him before grabbing his shoulder and looking into his eyes—which appeared vacant.

"Is everything all right, Ihan?"

"Everything's fine with me." Ihan turned his head and smiled.

"What are you thinking about?"

He shrugged. "Seeing you and your father together just made me feel strange. Not that I'm saying anything bad. I just never saw any kind of personal interaction like that between anyone. You made me feel happy and sad at the same time. I don't know if this is making any sense, but I just never experienced anything like that. I'm sort of jealous of you Meghan, for what you have in your life."

Meghan frowned at first, but then smiled as she grabbed his shoulder tighter.

"I can understand what you're saying Ihan, and yes, I'm grateful I have my father in my life. I know you've been by yourself your whole life and you just never experienced anything like this. However, now that you are free and with all of us you have many open personal roads ahead. Hell, you need to know that I will definitely watch your back."

He whipped his head around and strained to view his back. "What's on my back?"

Meghan laughed while Ihan attempted to look behind himself.

"I'm here for you, Ihan. That's your back."

"Oh." He straightened and rubbed his head as though

it hurt from the new terminology. "Where are we going now, Meghan?"

"We're going to talk with Mona and see if she knows of anything that can help the coalition."

"Mona! I'm not sure that is a good place to go, Meghan."

Meghan raised her eyebrows. "What do you mean?"

"I just don't know if we can trust her. Look at what she hid from me for the longest time, and I only found that out being here with her."

"So what you're saying is, you never want to see her again?"

"I wouldn't say that. I just don't know what to think right now." Ihan frowned. "Look at how you and your father are together. I bet you always can trust him?"

"Good question. I can understand how close you and Mona are together. She has been with you for several years, right?"

"As long as I can remember."

"Well, think of it this way, Ihan. Mona was there for you all the time and never left you. The only reason she is not with you at this moment is because we took both of you away from each other, but not for long. I want you to know that's why we're heading down to see her. You need to. Besides, you know I'm watching your back."

He gave her a slow grin. "I understand, Meghan, and will clear my head on all of this."

Meghan patted his shoulder. "There you go, Ihan. Now let's get down there and see her."

Trusting a processor might be a big mistake, but she hoped Mona would have Ihan's back too.

Chapter Forty-Three

Dirk drove into the facility's motor pool, and when he saw the carnage, he let the vehicle roll to a stop. Shredded vehicles and bleeding teammates were strewn around the large facility. As he slowly stepped out of his vehicle, he noticed a burned team member being pulled out of the back of a vehicle that was missing its entire left-side paneling.

A medic jabbed a needle into a screaming team member as his other teammates held him down. Along one wall, personnel lined up with covered bodies on the ground and ID tagged them. Two vehicles, to the front of the facility, were being hosed with a powerful stream of cleanser, and blood and mess flowed to the ground.

Dirk stood still, with clenched fists, as he pictured residents in Dallas sitting comfortably back into their chairs after their SecureCons were destroyed. This made Dirk grow angrier, and more frustrated, with this whole mess. He knew why all his friends and teammates were there for each other. Their esprit de corps was all he knew and believed in.

Dirk couldn't grasp how Dallas citizens survived without camaraderie. However, their isolation meant weakness, and this flaw motivated his desire to stay focused.

After he gathered his equipment and slung it over his shoulder, Dirk looked around and counted the team members. He wondered who was still out there and whether this battle was truly over. He then headed through the door and up the stairs, dodging other members and equipment scattered along the base of the stairs. One by one, the other team members aligned on the stairs, passing equipment to each other and tossing it into the hallway.

When he reached the top of the stairs, Dirk looked both ways and saw nothing but more injured members being treated by medics and their buddies. Most were unconscious, while precious few were smiling and laughing. They probably had the appropriate amount of shots and alcohol relief. Dirk shook his head with a grin. Taking care of the injured was informally ritualized. All team members knew what to do to help and treat others.

A few minutes later, Dirk stepped into the Operations Center and set his gear on the floor. A few officers stared at him with a peculiar gaze before they returned their attention to the displays.

Countless blue and red icons filled the wall screen with frenetic motion. Operations officers viewed the screen as they talked with several teams that were still deployed. To the far left of the screen, colored statistical numbers illustrated team strength: One held wounded in action, the other killed in action, and the last was missing in action. The discouraging vastness of the numbers in each category made him feel ill.

Dirk then saw an old buddy sitting behind one of the

operation terminals, his head so close to the screen, someone would have to pull his boots out of that screen soon. John always focused deeply on his assignment. Sometimes too deep. Dirk stepped closer and tapped his shoulder.

The man jerked backward and looked up. "Dirk. How are you, man?"

"Hey, John."

"You look like crap. Are you OK?"

"Thanks. You too." Dirk grinned. "What's on TV?"

"Looks like this battle is close to being a victory. Y'all sure did kick those robot butts!"

Dirk looked up at the screen. "What's the status?"

"The Dallas forces took a whooping and are now retreating back to the city."

Dirk pointed to the screen. "Why are those blue icons so far away?"

"A couple of teams got entirely too eager and kept hunting those SecureCons. Just before you came in, I ordered all of them to head back to the facility."

"Those team strength numbers sure don't look good."

John's shoulders drop. "We took a beating but held our ground. I wish I could get back out there."

Dirk reached down and tapped John's leg a couple of times. A hollow pinging rang out. "You did your ground service, John. Where you sit now is just as important."

"I guess." John turned his head and looked around the room. He gave Dirk a confused look. "Do you know where Stephan Grabowski is? We're missing his leadership in here."

"I don't know his current location. I can only assume he's either hiding or running away."

"What the hell did he do?"

"He poisoned Dusty Rhodes."

John's jaw dropped open. "That's unbelievable. Why would he do that and especially when we're under attack?"

"Guess his personal focus overtook our coalition purpose."

"You got that right." John nodded. "Who's going to take the lead now?"

Dirk sneered. "Don't ask me."

"OK. Don't need to ask you anyway." John winked.

John swiveled the chair around, grabbed his cane, and stood up. The other officers sitting in his row continued communicating and controlling the data flow within their databases. Dirk followed John as he walked down the row. Out of the corner of his eye, Dirk saw an officer moving quickly down the row and trying to make eye contact with him.

"Sir. Can you come with me and talk with the military advisor from India?"

Dirk stopped. Beside the officer, the military advisor from India stood in a well-pressed professional uniform holding a handcuffed briefcase in his left arm. That gentleman looked directly at him and saluted. Dirk rolled his eyes.

"Why me?"

"I thought you are in charge, sir?"

"Who the hell told you that?"

John turned around and tapped Dirk's chest.

"It doesn't matter, Dirk. Just get your butt over there and talk with our friendly nation partner. Somebody has to do it, and why not the best one?"

Dirk raised his eyebrows then sarcastically pointed at John with a grin. He glanced ahead at the Indian soldier, whose uniform and professional composure were foreign to him. The man's gray uniform was well pressed, with brightly colored medals stacked in three rows along the left side of his chest. A red and yellow cord draped over his shoulder, and he wore a bright red rank insignia on his collar. Over his head was a black Sikh turban decorated with a red ribbon along the sides, leading to a gold medal on top. The Indian soldier's black beard was perfectly trimmed along his neck. He clicked his boots together.

"Sir. I'm Major Dayanand Beti, and it's a pleasure to meet you."

The major extended his hand. Dirk reach out before he got there, grabbed the major's hand hard, and shook it. The major's forehead rumpled, and Dirk knew he was being a little aggressive. He softened his grip, and that smoothed the major's forehead.

"Hello, Major. I'm Dirk Young."

"Mr. Young, I—"

"Please just call me Dirk."

"Yes, sir." The major tilted his head down. "I shall call you Dirk from here on out. I have some sensitive intelligence to share with you."

Dirk stood there staring at the major for few seconds, waiting to hear what he had to share. A few seconds of silence and the anticipation upon the major's face made

Dirk realize he was being coaxed into doing, or saying, something specific.

"Did you need something from me, major?"

"Yes, Dirk. A more secure location to talk with you."

"Roger that."

Dirk looked all around the room and realized there were only Dusty's room and a supply closet that were accessible from this room. He then wondered why another secure room was needed since they were standing in the most secure room he knew of. The Operations Center held and ran all the United Texas Coalition information. Dirk looked past the major and saw that Dusty's office was empty. He pointed in that direction.

"Let's go in there, Major."

As both of them walked into the room, Dirk closed the door. The chairs were either stacked with paper or had trash dangling around them. He grabbed a chair and let the paper fall along the floor as he dragged it over to the desk. Dirk wiped his hand quickly over the seat. He then tapped it loudly a couple of times while looking at the major.

Dirk then put his arm straight out over Dusty's desk and swept it hard and fast to push off all the paper and other items. They clattered to the floor. As Dirk sat down on Dusty's chair, the Major placed his briefcase upon the desk. He typed a few numbers into the digital lock. The briefcase opened, and the major spun it around in front of Dirk.

Dirk focused in on the sharply colored imagery depiction. He had seen many imagery reports, but this one far exceeded any others when it came to clarity and quality. A smaller inset digital map on the top right side of the image, one that showed specific location for the image, showed an area in-between Dallas and Grapevine lakes.

Dirk perused the image and first noticed a large steel building that looked like a hangar. He then glanced at the surrounding terrain and noticed no airfield of any kind, just a winding road that couldn't land airplanes. Evenly placed, several hundred yards away from the building entrance were three circular concrete pads that had steel-fenced structures placed in the middle. It dawned on him that all three of these structures were missile launchers.

Dirk judged the size of the missile launchers based on some of the bushes and trees that were several feet away. He knew these launchers were designated for short-range ballistic missiles, not surface-to-air missiles.

"You got to be kidding me!" Dirk looked up at the Major and shook his head. "How did they get these missile launchers, and who did they get them from?"

"We noticed this site several months ago and figured some nefarious off-site was being created. Approximately five weeks ago, we noticed these modern missile launchers were placed on the site but knew Dallas still had no missiles. Two days ago, we received multiple-sourced intelligence reports that Dallas acquired three CSS-25 missiles from China. I'm sure you are aware of these missile specifications, but I just wanted to let you know that the three specific missiles they recently received are armed with the most technological, deep-penetrating warheads."

"Of course, Major. They want to destroy us in one

quick attack. This intelligence tells me that China just pushed a little too far into our matters."

"Our government agrees with you, Dirk."

"So let me get this straight. We've been told that the Chinese and Indian advisors are here in Texas for political support and assistance. China has stepped up a notch with weapons of greater destruction. I'm assuming your cold war is going to be located here."

"I'm not saying that, Dirk. We feel your internal state conflict is for your citizens to handle. However, now that China provided an unfair advantage, we feel compelled to advance your support."

Dirk blinked. "I can understand your territory and land grab. Hell, the United States and Soviet Union did the same throughout the twentieth century. What can you do for us, Major?"

"I was ordered to get the United Texas Coalition's approval before we send you the most advanced defensive materials. The most modern anti-missile system will be the first, along with many other defensive materials, to greatly enhance your defense here."

Dirk swallowed hard. "How much is that going to cost, and how fast will it get here?"

"There is no expense, Dirk. This is our contribution to the coalition." The Major then delicately smiled. "You can receive these upgrades within a week."

"A week!" Dirk widened his eyes. "Come on, Major, you know the current battle status and can see that Dallas is retreating from their latest failed attack. They are not going to waste any time. If they have those missiles, we will be hit sooner than a week."

"I understand. I just want to reiterate to you that India supports your side."

"Thanks, Major."

They stood up and shook hands before the major reached down and closed his briefcase. He lifted it and headed out of the room. Dirk followed him out of the office and stood at the back of the Operations Center. He stared at the screen and drifted away into thoughts about how the coalition could alleviate this inevitable potential missile strike. He knew the coalition force had been severely damaged in the latest ground attack. They didn't have enough strength to launch an offensive at Dallas. There were many loyal and dedicated surrogate forces strewn throughout Texas, but getting them together would take time.

Dirk then assessed all the weapons and technology they currently had in their inventory. There wasn't any system that would counter ballistic missiles. He remembered visiting the old U.S. Army posts at Fort Hood and Fort Bliss. Both those posts had Patriot missiles, the ones that were an air-defense system used during the Persian Gulf War. Both posts were several hundred miles away, and those missiles were probably either inoperative or too rusted to defend against these new ballistic missiles.

Within his thoughts, Dirk kept flashing back to Ihan's face. He initially pushed those thoughts aside, but then realized Ihan's processor, Mona, had identified the UAV above their facility about the same time the Ops Center did. If Mona did have access to the Dallas mainframe, and Ihan was able to get her to infiltrate the missile sector, then that may be a hope, at least one that may curb this latest predicament.

Dirk pulled out his communicator and pressed the Meghan button. She was down a level—the level where Mona was located. Dirk pushed the button. As the communicator clicked, Dirk couldn't stop wondering how Meghan was doing lately. Her emotions were flying all over the place. Especially with her father being poisoned by Stephan. That horrific event must have her thoughts off center. Nevertheless, he trusted Meghan and knew she was strong. Besides, she was the only person who knew Ihan well enough to get any of this done.

"Hey, Dirk."

"Meghan. It's good to hear your voice. Where are you now?"

"A few feet from our Tech Center. What's up?"

"I have something to ask you about Ihan."

"What about him, Dirk?"

"Can he still work with Mona and get her to do us a favor?"

"I assume he can. What are you talking about?"

"Out combat advisor from India just informed me Dallas has three Chinese ballistic missiles and intends to launch them shortly."

"They have what?" Meghan shrieked.

"Ballistic missiles attached with underground penetrating warheads. They can destroy our facility."

"So—" Meghan hesitated. "What are we doing about this?"

Dirk bit back a chuckle, realizing he was talking to a strong woman, a woman who didn't appreciate roundabout speeches. She was a woman who preferred the bot-tom-line truth. He respected that about her.

"You know I'm an honest guy, so here it is. We don't have any technology or defensive weapons that can coun-ter those missiles. The only defense we have is Mona. I know this is pressure on you, but you are truly the only one who knows Ihan well enough to get him to help us. Bottom line, our survival is now placed on you and Ihan."

"You got to be kidding me."

"Good luck with him, and I will be here for you if you need me. Out."

Meghan heard the phone connection click off. "Shit!"

There was a moment of silence before Meghan noticed Ihan's facial expression indicated confusion and worry. The last thing he needed was more of that. She took a deep breath and cleared her uncertainties. She then focused on Ihan, because their mission was Mona.

Meghan knew Ihan felt remorse about Mona, and that meant he needed to be refocused. She reached over and straightened his shirt. She swept her hands along his shoulders and pulled his sleeves down farther. She then lightly tapped his chest and grinned at him.

"You look good, Ihan. Now let's go in there and see how Mona is doing."

Ihan widened his eyes. "You know she has no vision, don't you?"

"Of course, Ihan. I just wanted to let you know how much better you look these past few days."

Meghan smiled with her teeth together. She reached over and opened the door. As Ihan walked in, Meghan looked up at the ceiling, crossed her fingers, and shook her head before following him in.

Her emotions and stress levels were far beyond any others she'd ever experienced. Just knowing what significance these next few minutes with Mona entailed made Meghan giggle hysterically inside.

Chapter Forty-Four

Jerry Adams woke up not feeling particularly refreshed. He still felt drained, both emotionally and physically, after his External Security Unit's ground attack failure against UTC.

He stared out the window at the City-State of Dallas's peaceful skyline. The lights within Jerry's residence suddenly got brighter as he sat with extended legs and feet crossed on top of the desk. He glanced through the large window, where a thin arc of the sun threw its brilliance across the city.

As he looked back into to the monitor that displayed economic numbers, Jerry yawned. Numbers, though necessary, were boring.

"So as you can see sir, the numbers reflect the city's macroeconomic statistics compiled and analyzed by the Internal Control Division and the Agricultural Control Division," CSD Economic Director said.

Jerry gazed at his fingernails. "Good, good."

"When it comes to predicted economic and agricultural forecasting, I would say the numbers should increase due to many technologically upgraded machinery and control mechanisms." The director squinted at Jerry. "Are you OK, sir?"

"Yeah!" Jerry leaned forward, and coughed, before looking at the director.

"Would you like me to call a MedCon, sir?"

"Of course not. I just didn't sleep well last night."

The director gave him a knowing look. "I can understand, sir. We got word last night about the External Security Unit's retreat near San Antonio. I do believe early withdrawal decision makes sense. The last thing we need to do is deplete our reduced budget by purchasing additional robotic devices before the next fiscal year."

Jerry tried to keep his face composed, but he suspected he was sneering. Knowing the director was accurate and forthright was one thing. Hearing it twice in twenty-four hours was another. But then, Jerry had slept only a few hours last night, and anything less than his normal ten hours meant crankiness. In addition, the current battle status irked him beyond any other crisis.

Jerry respected the director's openness, had for many years, but just couldn't stand his personality anymore. Recent city-state troubles were now switching from local matters to United Texas Coalition matters, and they'd somehow spurred distrust of Jerry throughout the city. All these harmful matters compiled and greatly overwhelmed Jerry's thoughts.

Jerry slammed his fist down on the control panel. The connection with the director turned off. His recent days had been dominated by stress. Jerry shook his head and contemplated how best to relieve his anxiety.

All of a sudden, his assistant, Roger Buss, came into

Jerry's thoughts. He wondered what the special project status was, because according to Roger this project was the quickest and easiest way to erode the United Texas Coalition. This project had been worked behind the scenes for many months. Jerry utterly believed that demolishing UTC forever ensured CSD success.

He let out a loud yawn and attempted to push his tiresome feelings to the side. He sat up straight and lightly tapped his face. This exhaustion was definitely his greatest weakness.

"Liz. Get Roger Buss on the line."

"Can I suggest you get some sleep before I connect you?"

"No you can't, Liz." Jerry shook his head. "I need to talk with him now."

"Do you remember those several occasions when you kept ordering me to inform you of your fatigue?"

"I need to deal with something before I sleep."

"Yes, sir. I will turn on your coffeemaker."

Jerry let out a deep breath. Liz tended to annoy him during tumultuous times. He respected her processing personality more than that of many previous processors he'd tossed away. Liz was the Jekyll for his Hyde personality. She handled him far better than any others. His communication light glowed bright red.

"Good morning, sir. Are you feeling OK? I heard you stayed up most of the night."

"Feeling just ducky this morning, Roger."

"I can understand how you feel about our failed ground assault yesterday. Most city-state residents do too, and didn't sleep much either."

"OK—enough of that. I need to know what the current status is with that special project."

"No problem, sir. The missile assembly and arming considerations are complete. It took many overtime duties, but everything is geared up and ready for action."

"How long will it take to get this ball rolling?"

"With the movement to the launchers, flight pattern verification within their internal databases, supporting personnel's control elements—"

Jerry shook his head. "Get on with it!"

"Should take a couple of hours, sir!"

"Make it happen, Roger."

"Yes, sir."

Jerry looked out the window again. He didn't want to think about this event. All he could imagine dealing with was the political repercussions among the city-state residents and those stubborn voted representatives who constantly had been questioning his past actions. The last thing Jerry wanted to worry about was this exterior problem. The faster it went away the better. He could then focus on getting his interior troubles resolved.

Roger gulped. "Can I ask you a personal question, sir?"

Jerry's focus swerved to Roger. The solemn tone of his voice was one Jerry had never heard from him before. Jerry looked into the screen and directly at Roger's eyes. They were relaxed and down-to-earth. *Is this another Dallas resident who is thinking twice of me? Or, even worse, be another who tries to manipulate my actions?* The many hostile incidents in the past few years, especially ones that Jerry had to deal with personally, bugged him beyond belief. The most persistent weakness his city-state's government was knowledge. Total ignorance was pushed hard and residents were kept within their control levels to know their specialties and nothing more. If this was ever thought as being incorrect, then that was individual belief and not this city-state's belief, which was based on survival and success.

But this was Roger, and he had done nothing but bend over backward for Jerry and support him for the past two years. Jerry pushed his annoyance to the side and wondered what Roger was getting at.

"Of course you can, Roger. Is there something you need from me?"

"No. I don't need anything from you, sir. I just wanted to make sure you knew that the Dallas resident who was captured last week, Ihan Duncan, is genetically similar to you? That normally is not something people care about any more, and the genetically pooled database is not even viewed much anymore, but . . ."

"Roger, I know that. Why are you asking me?"

"I'm just making sure you know what could happen once we accomplish this event. I know Ihan's genetic similarity to you is classified and not many others are aware. I'm just double checking with you to make sure you won't regret this."

Jerry turned his head and looked back outside the window at his city.

"Thanks for asking, Roger. What we're about to do is for the greater good and will benefit our city-state. I by no means will regret this."

"Yes, sir. I will make this happen."

Once the red light went dark, Jerry sat still for a few moments. He then got up and walked across the room, where he picked up a crystal glass and filled it to the brim with Armadale vodka. He gulped down the entire glass. As he licked the last drop from the rim, he smelled coffee and heard a beep in the kitchen.

"Liz. Please turn that coffee off. I'm going to bed and don't want to be disturbed for several hours."

"Yes, sir. Have a good sleep."

He intended to, and the fact that an individual with a genetic similarity would soon cease to exist wouldn't get in the way of his sleep in the least.

Jerry headed down the hallway. He held the glass over the table and let it go. The glass clattered on the table, rolled off, and smashed on to the floor. Jerry marched resolutely toward his bedroom.

CHAPTER FORTY-FIVE

As Meghan expected, Ihan halted in front of the glass door leading into Mona's room. He stood there motionless and stared at the processor. Meghan moved closer and gently placed her arm upon his shoulder. As he gave her a glance, Meghan smiled and winked. She knew Ihan needed to squelch his frustrations with Mona so he could gain the confidence he needed to get her to help the Coalition.

The red light on the wall meant Mona was operative. Meghan felt confident knowing this event had started well. She reached down and opened the door.

Ihan didn't hesitate. He headed directly to the far wall, grabbed a chair, and sat down. The power light against the wall grew brighter, and the small light upon Mona started to blink. Mona knew Ihan was in the room.

Ihan sat tall and cleared his throat.

"Mona. It's Ihan and I'm back to apologize for walking out on you."

"Hello, Ihan. I understand why you did what you did."

A series of increasingly confident expressions transformed Ihan's face. He took a deep breath and beamed

357

a glance her way. Meghan hoped he'd pushed his heart-rending doubts aside.

"Mona, I need to ask you—"

"Ihan."

Ihan's eyes widened. "Yes, Mona."

"Do you remember when I said I love you?"

His jaw went slack. His eyes glistened as though lit from within by a sacred fire; he blushed crimson, though whether from rage or delight it was impossible to tell. After a few seconds, though, the battle between his emotions looked as though it had ended.

"I remember when you said that, but I thought you were just energizing me to finish the harvesting?"

"That was part of it, Ihan. I also wanted to make sure you knew how I felt about you. I didn't know when we would be attacked, but I knew it would be soon."

"So, you felt guilty for hiding that attack information?"

"I don't understand, Ihan."

"Of course you do, Mona. Motivating me to harvest is one thing. Telling me that you loved me because we were going to be attacked meant you felt guilty. You would have told me that sooner, but felt you had to say something. That attack could have separated or destroyed both of us forever."

"I didn't view it that way."

"Of course you didn't, and that's why you need to listen to Meghan. Please help her, because what she's about to ask will help all of us stay alive."

"I will, Ihan."

"Hello Mona, this is Meghan," Meghan said while looking at Ihan.

"Hello, Meghan. What can I help you with?"

"What Ihan said is true. Our lives are in danger. We just learned that Dallas has three ballistic missiles that will be launched soon to destroy this facility. We know you are still connected to the Dallas system, and we want you to help us stop those missiles from being launched."

"Yes, Meghan. I will attempt to discover what you're talking about. Please give me a few minutes."

"Thanks, Mona, and we'll be right here."

Mona fathomed deep into herself and processed a way to enter the Dallas supersystem unnoticed. She then sent out a concealed data packet through the highly advanced switching network—one that could find the direct path to where the missile information was held. In a matter of seconds, Mona produced her path and sent it over the open network. She instantly received a return signal that entered the network.

A few seconds later, Mona received a collaborative response through ten different avenues. She instantly analyzed all ten and found one that was the weakest. She then sent a new data packet through that avenue and waited for a response.

Mona speculated why a response was not sent quickly. She contemplated what the troubles could be and the best way to reenter the system. A signal then came through. She discovered that a path was available, but it was blocked by a code she didn't recognize.

Meghan tapped her fingers on her thigh as Mona did her thing. After a few seconds, the red light glowed bright again.

"Ihan. I have a question for you."

Ihan raised his eyebrows. "Go ahead, Mona."

"I have found the information, but my access code is out of date."

He glanced at Meghan, and she nodded for him to continue.

"Is there something you need from me?"

"Yes, Ihan. I need your permission because what I'm about to do will lead to detection of your name for what I'm about to enter."

Ihan smirked. "I'm OK with that, Mona. Hell, I'm not in Dallas anymore and don't really plan on being there any time soon. Please let me know how you're going to do this."

"Gerald Bacon's processor, Jean-Marie, owes me a favor."

"Gerald Bacon!" Ihan shook his head. "You mean to tell me he's in the middle of this missile action?"

"Yes, Ihan. Gerald is now working this special project, and Jean-Marie has the access code."

Ihan raised both hands to the sides of his face and stared at Meghan. "I cannot believe the irony of all this, and how small this world really is."

Meghan nodded discreetly, wanting him to believe she understood and agreed with everything he'd said. "It is, isn't it?"

"Not only is Gerald a good friend of mine, but he was

also the one who controlled the SecureCon we encountered in that roadside bathroom."

"That SecureCon?" Meghan felt a flutter of trepidation. "You mean he was controlling that robot that almost killed us?"

"That's him, and we're lucky that SecureCon was his."

"I would say so." Was there any way this *couldn't* go wrong? "If he's now working with those missiles, and his processor owes Mona a favor then—" Meghan looked directly at Mona. "Mona. I'm so impressed by you and will cross my fingers."

"Why are you crossing your fingers, Meghan?" Mona's tone sounded confused.

"It just means good luck, Mona!" Meghan said cheerfully and looked at Ihan. The way he'd been raised, he shouldn't know anything about faith or loyalty, but those qualities blazed from his face, and God help her, she believed in Mona because he did.

"Thank you, Meghan. I shall proceed."

Mona sent a signal through the network to Jean-Marie and instantly received a code from Jean-Marie. That code had an additional message attached:

It is great to communicate with you, Mona, and I'm glad to know you're still active. It's been ten point five days, three hours, and thirty-six minutes since the last time we corresponded. I have no way to stop your identification number from going higher. I wish you the best and look forward to communicating with you again.

Mona then utilized the code and accessed the domain.

She then retrieved all the information, but quickly learned that all of it would fill her memory card and exceed her data capacity. She kept the channel open, analyzing the data and observing the most current reporting and orders that were sent.

Meghan had waited long enough. "Mona, did you get the code yet?"

Mona hummed. It sounded a lot like she'd be smirking, if she had a face. "I'm into the missile code domain and have just learned that the missiles will be launched in fifteen minutes."

"Fifteen minutes! Holy shit, Mona! What can you do to stop them from launching?"

"Wait one, Meghan."

Mona went back into the domain and searched for a way to control the missiles. All avenues leading to the launch codes were now frozen, and that meant a separate timer had control. Mona then analyzed different methods and techniques of rupturing the timer.

"Meghan." She twitched at the sound of the processor saying her name. Even though she wanted to keep positive, Mona's announcements had been bad news followed by worse news. "I just learned that I currently cannot stop the launch."

She remembered how Ihan handled Mona a few minutes ago. "What are you needing from me?"

"Connection to not only your facility signal hub but also more power."

"Ah, crap!"

Meghan looked around the room. Was it connected to the facility's signal hub? She then saw the power cord and circuit that it was attached into. That circuit was top of the line and one that was attached to the entire facility.

She thought of a way to get Mona the power, just didn't know how to do it herself. She reached down into her cargo pants and pulled out her communicator. She tapped Dirk's button. The communicator clicked.

"Hey, Meghan. How are things going down there?"

"Dirk. It's great to hear your voice, and I need your help. Mona is going to need a lot more electrical and signal strength to keep those missiles from launching."

"Damn. That processor can do that?"

"Only if she gets more strength. Is this room connected to the facilities signal hub?"

"Wait one, Meghan." Dirk's next words were muffled. He'd be running the request past someone in the Operations Center. "A communications officer gave me a thumbs-up. It sure is connected."

"How long will it take?"

"We have two guys working their magic as fast as they can. I will let you know when they're finished."

"Less than fifteen minutes would be good."

Dirk cursed, and the connection ended.

Meghan informed Mona she'd have what she needed soon and walked around the central table, staring at her watch every few seconds. After a few laps around, eight minutes remained until the predicted launch. Agonizing worry swelled within her. She needed to know what the status was and why she hadn't heard anything from Dirk yet.

Meghan tapped the redial communicator button hard. "Come on, Dirk, answer the damn thing!" She continued to tap her communicator. "Where the hell are you?"

"I'm here, Meghan. Just got word from the electrician that he made a connection. He's headed your way to install it into the circuit."

"How much longer, Dirk?" Meghan's shoulders tensed. She then heard a sudden loud knock on the hallway door. She threw the glass door open and hurried to grab the outer door. As she opened it, the electrician, with his tool belt wrapped around his shoulder, breathed heavy. He had to have run down four hallways. Meghan waved him in.

The electrician pointed at the middle room "Is that the room?"

"Yes. Now get in there!"

He flicked the door open and walked directly to the outlet where Mona was connected. He took a hammer out of his tool belt and knocked holes into the wall. He then looked over and waved while grabbing another hammer out of his belt. He tossed it to Meghan.

She caught it and slammed several holes into the wall. After a few strikes, she paused.

"Where am I hitting?" Meghan asked, staring at the wall.

The electrician reached in front of her, his finger tracing to where his holes were already hammered. Meghan rushed to the far left side and whacked away as fast as she could. She made it to the electrician's side in record time.

The electrician tossed his hammer to the floor and reached into the line that showed a favorable impression. He found what he was looking for. He then reached down around his waist and unraveled a thick plastic cord. He shoved it into the wall while peeling off the end, exposing wire, and wrapped it together with the existing wire in the wall. He attached an outlet to the other end of the wire and pulled it over to the existing outlet. He then yanked Mona's wire out of the outlet and inserted it into the new one. Mona's blinking light got dramatically brighter.

The electrician raised his thumb with a smile.

Meghan looked down at her watch. Two minutes remained.

Within the missile facility, approximately twelve miles northwest of Dallas, a large hangar door closed while many SecureCons continued to span out around the missile launchers to provide security. All three of the missile launcher railings rose slowly before popping off the security tags. A gust of wind stirred the tags around the complex.

When the launcher railings came to a ninety-degree angle, all locked in unison. A metal clicking echoed around the complex. As the sun arched incrementally higher, the bright reflection shone off all three of the missile heads. Colored leaves and tiny sticks blew across the dirt roads, and the wind caught them up in dust devils that headed in strange directions before disappearing, only to spring up in a different location.

The digital clock, visible at the bottom of the launcher, flicked brightly and hit the one-minute mark. Immediately, the safety rings at the top and bottom of the launcher released and were mechanically moved to the bottom. The missiles stood tall among the base pegs of the launchers, their slight sideward movements echoing the wind. Underneath the missiles, the long, but thin, launcher pegs compensated for the wind by moving in several directions and degrees to keep each missile upright and stable.

A loud and thunderous beep echoed throughout the missile facility. All the SecureCons stepped farther away from the launchers. A sudden dramatic rumble. Flames synchronized at the base of all three missiles.

Within seconds, the flames intensified and shot out of the missiles, forcing debris and massive smoke clouds against the ground. The missiles elevated slowly for one hundred feet before an even more powerful flame shot from the bottom of each device and propelled the missiles into extreme speed.

The surrounding SecureCons raised their heads—as though in adoration—as the missiles crackled and rumbled higher.

CHAPTER FORTY-SIX

In the Operations Center, Dirk sat back in his chair holding his handgun in one hand and releasing the magazine into the other. He slid it in and released it, slid it in and released it, faster each time. A sudden beep emanated in the room, and everyone fell silent. Dirk looked up onto the screen. Three red icons were blinking northwest of Dallas.

Textual reporting streams, too small to read, appeared on the sides of the icons. "Zoom in on that!" Dirk yelled as he pointed to the screen. The streams indicated altitude and speed, which increased rapidly. "I can't believe this!"

An Operations Officer calculated the speed and distance of the missiles to their location. He then brought it up onto the screen for the room to view. Below that calculation popped up a clock. The clock blinked: 18:49.

Dirk slammed the magazine back into the gun. What the hell was happening with Meghan, and why hadn't that processor stopped the missiles from launching?

Meghan stood next to Mona and looked down at her watch. Their time was up. She bit her lip and looked up at Ihan, wondering if Mona could still stop the launch. He blinked back at her, his eyes wide.

"Mona," Meghan said. "What's the status?"

"I'm sorry, Meghan. The missiles launched."

"You got to be kidding me!"

"No, Meghan. I'm not kidding you."

Hearing her communicator beep, Meghan looked down and saw that Dirk was calling her. She instantly knew what he was going to say, just didn't know how to respond. She took a few steps back and sat down, took a deep breath, then pressed the button.

"Meghan. Those missiles just launched!"

"Mona just told us, Dirk."

"Were you able to get her power attached?"

"Yes, but it was just connected a couple seconds ago."

A few moments went by in silence.

"OK. I'm going to get this facility evacuated because we only have about seventeen minutes until those missiles hit. I will personally make sure your father gets out of here safely."

"OK."

"I order you to take Ihan out of there and go to the designated meeting site. We have four team vehicles, that's plenty enough for you to get one."

"Roger that, Dirk."

As soon as Meghan turned off her communicator, a loud announcement beep blared through the speakers, followed by Dirk telling the whole facility to evacuate as soon as possible and leave all behind. He emphasized an order to leave the facility and not waste any time bringing anything—lives are more important.

When the announcement was finished, Meghan felt tears flow down her cheeks. She raised her sleeve and wiped them off.

Ihan stepped a little closer to Meghan and felt like hugging her. He thought about it for a few seconds, but knew there just wasn't enough time to console her. He then looked at Mona and realized that if they evacuated she would be destroyed and never heard from again. The thought of a personality he'd known his whole life coming to a quick end just didn't make sense to him.

"Mona. Is there anything else you could do to stop those missiles from hitting?"

Meghan stood to her feet and trounced closer to him. She grabbed his arm.

"We have to leave now, Ihan. There is nothing Mona can do now!"

She turned and strode toward the door. Ihan kept his arm solid and stationary. Meghan's hand flung off his arm. Coming to a sudden halt, Meghan turned around and widened her eyes at him. Ihan felt calm. He somehow knew there was still a possibility that Mona could stop the missiles.

Meghan raised her arms. "What are you doing, Ihan?" For the first time since he met her, she looked scared.

"We haven't heard back from Mona yet," he voiced in a surreal tone.

A click sounded, and then a low buzzing that quickly got louder. Ihan instantly knew where it was coming from. He looked down at Mona and put his hand on top of her, feeling the vibration and heat increase.

Meghan squinted. "What is she doing, destroying herself?"

"No, Meghan." A wave of pride spread through him. "She is working for us."

Instantly, the buzzing and vibrations lessened.

"Ihan. I was able to penetrate the navigational control system," Mona said calmly.

Ihan raised his head with a smile. "That's wonderful to hear, Mona."

Meghan cleared her throat. "So what you're saying, Mona, is that you can control all three of those missiles?"

"Yes, Meghan. Where would you like them to go?"

"Oh my god!" Meghan pulled her communicator off the table and pressed a few buttons to view a map. "Mona, where are those missiles currently located?"

"They are approximately ninety-three miles south of Dallas."

"Oh, good grief, Mona. What city or town are they currently over?"

"Waco."

Meghan viewed many open areas on her map—ones she knew were desolate and lacked housing. She then zoomed the map and looked at other areas. She just couldn't stop wondering if any of those areas had people in them. Even a few. Even one. She shook her head, staring at the map while her hands started to shake. The map got blurry.

"What the hell am I thinking? Send them back to Dallas, Mona!"

"Will do, Meghan."

The missiles flew at a fast pace through the clear sky. They were aligned and spitting out a ton of smoke as they thrust forward. Continuous movements in their tail fins kept the missiles on their flight bearing correcting for the wind gusts that grew stronger as their altitude peaked. In unison, their signal processors blinked as an order was received. In a matter of seconds, all the missiles swerved 180 degrees, the trailing smoke lines behind them curving and angling down.

Chapter Forty-Seven

Before Dirk exited the Operations Center door, he stopped and double-checked the room to make sure it was clear. A commotion erupted in the hallway. He stuck his head out and saw a bunch of members running behind each other with rucksacks, equipment, personal bags, and books. Most of the members didn't listen to his orders to calm down and evacuate in an orderly manner. They grabbed as much as they could carry. However, Dirk would probably do the same.

A loud beep emanated in the room. Dirk didn't move his head, but his eyes turned to left as the beep got louder. He knew the alert's likelihood of importance was next to nothing, but his curiosity and responsibility wouldn't let him leave the facility without checking it out, regardless of the danger in lagging behind the rest of the team members.

He turned around and looked up at the screen, where a single icon blinked red. Uncertain, Dirk turned and glanced outside the door to the rapidly emptying hallway, but his curiosity about that red icon took over his focus.

He walked back into the room and got closer to the screen. He then reached down to a terminal, pressed a few buttons, to section off the location and zoom in. He noticed the three red icons were now heading north. *Why are those missiles heading back to Dallas? This makes no sense.* Dirk kept his gaze scrupulously on the screen, but tapped the update button. The screen blinked for less than a second and the picture remained the same.

Dirk tapped the icon and saw the statistical information appear. Reading it twice, Dirk blinked his eyes in amazement. He couldn't believe this was accurate.

Dirk picked up his communicator quickly and wondered if Meghan made it out of the facility yet. He pressed her location button and frowned. *She's still in that room!* He pressed her connection button and heard the ring.

"Hey, Dirk."

"Meghan. What in world are you doing? You should be out of here by now."

"Guess Ihan's belief and focus on Mona kept us in here. Mona is quiet the processor, Dirk. She got into the missile's navigational control system and turned them around."

Dirk leaned back and took a seat. "That is . . . great to hear! The operational screen shows those missiles heading back to Dallas. I thought I was going crazy."

Dirk heard Meghan scream in delight, followed by Ihan, then Mona. As he pulled the communicator away from his ear, Dirk smiled and wondered what was happening. The irony of the two individuals they stole from Dallas saving their lives overwhelmed Dirk. He shook his head, listening to their joyful laughter.

Deep within her biochips, Mona felt an internal problem when the reactionary signal hit the circuit with a power spike. She quickly checked her signal card specifics and learned that she was being sent a malicious signal from Dallas. This was a standard reaction signal, one she was aware of for entering into a classified realm. Mona worked around within her internal systems to try and compensate or block. A number of options shut down and overwhelmed her controls. Mona's logic circuit indicated it was the appropriate time to inform Ihan and Meghan.

Meghan and Ihan held hands and danced for another few minutes, twisting two or three more times with laughter. They let go of each other and started to calm down by catching their breaths.

Mona started to vibrate and hum again. Her sounds increased by the second. Ihan leaned closer as her clicking grew noticeably louder. He stepped back, watching her nervously.

"Mona! What's happening?"

"I'm going to ask that you and Meghan quickly leave this room."

Ihan's eyebrows rose high. "What are you talking about, Mona?"

"I'm receiving a protective reactionary signal from Dallas. That signal is corrupting my internal programs, and I don't know how much longer I can hold it."

"You're getting what? No!" Ihan spun to look at Meghan. "Please help me take her antenna away. We need to get her separated."

Meghan and Ihan reached down and looked for Mona's antenna. They traced their hands all over Mona's rectangular surface, felt a few curves and jagged corners, but couldn't tell where her antenna was located.

"Ihan, if you love me, please take Meghan and both of you leave this room." Mona said as Meghan and Ihan continued searching.

"Pull her power cord!" Meghan yelled, and Ihan grabbed the cord and yanked it from the power outlet. "Where the hell is the antenna?"

"I don't know!" Ihan raised his hands.

With their hands on Mona again, Meghan and Ihan frantically felt for anything that might be an antenna. A massive jolt of electricity flung them backward. Meghan got up and shook her hands, feeling nothing but numb fingers.

Ihan rubbed his sides. "What the hell was that?"

"I don't know, but it sure was a message." Meghan said noticing smoke flowing out of Mona's air vent. She reached over and grabbed Ihan from behind by swinging her arms around his waist. She then heaved him toward the door. Ihan resisted, bucking and pushing forward.

"What are you doing, Meghan? Let me go!"

Meghan rammed her backside against the glass door. It hurt like hell, but the door crashed open. She dragged Ihan as fast as she could, but the door swung back and hit her hard. The sudden pain loosened her grip, and Ihan flung forward.

An explosion ignited and flung shards of plastic and metal everywhere. Meghan hit the floor. A second later, she looked up and saw Ihan motionless on the floor, pieces of shrapnel sticking out of his clothes.

Meghan reached out, grabbed his ankles, and pulled

him back. She knew the oxygen would be sucked out of the room quickly. She kept pulling him on his stomach until the door closed and locked shut.

A red light flashed above the room, and the smoke sucked through the ventilation system at a faster rate every second. Once the smoke cleared the room, Meghan saw the table and pieces of Mona scattered everywhere.

Ihan rolled over to his back and held his arm over his face. Meghan reached down and tapped his shoulder. He lowered his arm slowly down to his side. Meghan looked into his eyes, saw the sorrow he was trying to hide beneath his anger, and realized just how important her answer was going to be.

"Are you OK Ihan?"

"Why did she do that?"

"I don't think she had a choice either way." Meghan let out a breath. "She saved our lives, Ihan."

Ihan blinked. "I guess she really did love me."

"She sure did, Ihan. She sure did." Meghan nodded and pressed her lips together so they wouldn't tremble.

As Meghan extended her arm to Ihan and opened her hand, he gently grabbed it and sprang up to his feet. Meghan stared at Ihan sadly, realizing he'd just lost his lifetime friend. She wondered how he was going to handle this and move on with his life.

Meghan stepped forward and wrapped her arms around Ihan. She swallowed, feeling too emotional to speak. She didn't know what to say to Ihan to make him feel better. As she leaned back and looked into his blood-shot eyes, Meghan thought of how lucky she she was to know him. She then thought back to when she first saw

Ihan. Just the thought of leaving him in his Dallas residence, unconscious under his mattress, was unconscionable. He'd earned her respect ten times over—and she considered herself blessed to know him.

And she'd accomplished her mission with Ihan. That put the wind back in her sails, and all Meghan wanted was to see her father and Dirk. She reached down and gently grabbed Ihan's hand, leading him out the door.

Within the missile facility, SecureCons chained the launchers and manuevered them back to the hangar in unison. A sudden crackling sound increased. Every SecureCon dropped its chains and looked up to the sky to see the incoming missiles.

The missiles slammed the facility with a colossal explosion, followed by hot, greedy flames that engulfed the surrounding area.

Within the Operations Center, the officers headed back in and put their bags next to their desks. They laughed and joked with each other as they took their seats.

As he stood in the middle of the doorway to Dusty's office, Dirk listened to everyone in the room and took in their happy emotions. But something was missing inside of him. He could no longer deny that something was Meghan. He wondered where she was and hoped she was OK. He respected the hell out of her for achieving her mission, but this new emotion was so much more than respect.

The depth of his attraction to her felt strange to Dirk.

Because this was Meghan, a woman with a strapping personality, he needed to grab a pair, search deep inside of himself, and see where his feelings went. Very few women in UTC commanded profound esteem like Meghan did. Dirk knew he was a relationship rookie and that made him chuckle. Operationally, he was the most experienced. He put his internal foot down and decided to emotionally focus on Meghan and take that relationship path. He knew she'd make sure it was a wild ride.

A doctor and nurse pushed Dusty on a squeaky wheelchair into the room. Dirk looked over and noticed Dusty's face had some color and liveliness. He'd recovered faster than expected.

As Dusty's wheelchair stopped in front of Dirk, each of them smiled. Dirk reached over and shook his hand, and Dusty's wink told him the older man understood the esteem Dirk felt for him. The rest of the room noticed Dusty and congregated around him to congratulate him on his recovery.

When the main door opened, Dirk looked over and noticed Meghan and Ihan walk in and look around the room. A flood of gratitude washed over him as he stared at Meghan.

The crowd surrounding Dusty settled down as they noticed Dirk gaze over their heads. Everyone turned, in utter silence, and glanced at Meghan.

Meghan suddenly stopped and widened her eyes. She then looked over at Ihan, who winked at her with a grin. Dirk started to softly clap his hands. A proud smile lit up his face. The rest of the room followed suit and applauded her.

The crowd of officers surrounding Dusty then split apart, creating an open lane. Meghan lowered her eyes as Dusty held out his arms. She slowly blinked her eyes before tears flowed. She released Ihan's hand and ran to her father. She slid to her knees and firmly hugged him. Dusty grunted, still beaming. Meghan loosened her grip and leaned backward, putting her hands upon his face.

"I love you, Dad."

"I love you, flower."

Meghan twisted her head to look back and waved Ihan over. Ihan looked into Dusty's eyes as he got closer. Acceptance shone on Dusty's face, and Ihan's elation made him bounce as he walked. Ihan stood by Meghan's side and shook Dusty's hand.

Dusty winked. "You are truly a Texan now, Ihan."

"Thank you, sir." Ihan said with a mile-long grin.

When Meghan rose back to her feet, she looked directly into Dirk's eyes. For the next few moments, everyone else in the room seemed to disappear. She took a few steps and wrapped her arms around him before standing on her toes and softly kissing his lips. She then turned to his left side, keeping her arm around his waist. The kiss was far too short for Dirk's liking, but he trusted there would be many more to come. Now was a time for celebration.

Ihan walked closer and shook his hand. Dirk shot a respecting blink his way.

"We owe you big, Ihan."

"No, Dirk. I owe you for my freedom."

A murmured phrase started somewhere nearby, and it spread through the crowd like wildfire. Moments later, the entire room screamed at the top of their lungs, "REMEMBER THE ALAMO!"